DOPPLEGANGER

When they brought him in, he didn't look at me. I think he knew if he raised them, the eyes he would be looking into would be his own. Or *my* own. Ours.

He had my face, my hair color, even my little thinning patch on top. There were small differences—he was maybe six or eight pounds lighter than I, and what he was wearing was no garment I had ever owned. It was a one-piece coverall made out of some shiny forest-green fabric, with pockets all over the chest.

I made myself say: "Dominic. Look at me."

Silence. The other Dominic didn't answer.

I tried again. "Dominic!" For God's sake, tell me what's happening."

Then he looked up, but not at me. He gazed at the clock on the wall, making some sort of calculation. Then he turned to me and spoke: "Dominic," he said, "for God's sake, I can't."

And then he disappeared.

THE COMING OF THE QUANTUM CATS

Frederik Pohl

BANTAM BOOKS

TORONTO · NEW YORK · LONDON · SYDNEY · AUCKLAND

THE COMING OF THE QUANTUM CATS

A Bantam Spectra Book / May 1986

ISBN 0-553-25786-2

Published simultaneously in the United States and Canada

Bantam Books are published by Bantam Books, Inc. Its trade-
mark, consisting of the words "Bantam Books" and the por-
trayal of a rooster, is Registered in U.S. Patent and Trademark
Office and in other countries. Marca Registrada. Bantam
Books, Inc., 666 Fifth Avenue, New York, New York 10103.

PRINTED IN THE UNITED STATES OF AMERICA

H   0 9 8 7 6 5 4 3 2 1

It is customary to print a disclaimer in novels, saying that the characters are fictitious and that no resemblance to any real person, living or dead, is intended. This is, in the case of this book, wholly true, in spite of the fact that some of the characters have names made famous by position and deeds. The reason is that, in each case, the characters portrayed are what the real-life characters would have been . . . if they had been someone other than the persons they were.

16 August 1983
8:20 P.M. Nicky DeSota

When my beeper sounded I had one hand on the gearshift, ready to jump into second, and the other sticking out the window to signal a left turn. My attention was on the traffic cop, who was taking an annoyingly long time to let the Meacham Road traffic through. My head was full of adjustable rate mortgages, points, GI loan eligibilities, and whether or not I could still get in a swim with my girl friend after dinner. It was a Tuesday. Therefore a good time to swim, because sometimes on a weekday night, after it gets dark, the lifeguard looks the other way if somebody goes topless.

The beeper shattered all of that.

I hate to let a phone go on ringing. I took a chance. I took my hand off the gearshift to pick up the phone. "Dominic DeSota speaking, yes?" I said, just as the cop remembered that there was traffic waiting on Meacham, and waved peremptorily to me to make the turn.

So then everything happened at once.

The motorman on the interurban trolley saw that I was hesitating, so he started across the intersection at the same moment I stepped on the gas. The operator on the other end of the phone said something that sounded like Chinese, or maybe Choctaw. It wasn't either of those, it was just that she wasn't tuned in right. You know how they get when it's near the end of a shift and they're getting tired and a little sloppy and they just make a stab at your frequency

1

without worrying about getting it exact? I didn't understand a word of what she said. I didn't care just then, either, because all of a sudden there was a twenty-ton lump of tandem trolley right in front of me, a lot too close for me to stop. The trolley couldn't turn away. I had to. And there was only one way I could go to miss the collision, and unfortunately the traffic cop was standing right in the middle of that way.

I didn't hit him.

That was more to his credit than to mine, though. He jumped out of the way. *Barely* out of the way. Enough so that I took the polish off his boots but didn't mangle his toes.

I don't blame him for giving me a ticket. I would have done the same thing. I would have done a lot worse; I wouldn't have blamed him if he'd run me in then and there, but he didn't. He just kept me hanging for three-quarters of an hour, parked on the shoulder of the road in front of the forest preserve, with all the other motorists rubbernecking at the poor simp who was getting a ticket as they went by. He spaced it out. He'd come over and ask for my license and study it for a while. Then he'd go back to untangle the traffic snarls while he thought it over. Then he'd come back and ask for some other I.D., or for my employment history, or about how long I'd lived around Chicago or how come I didn't know a car was supposed to yield the right-of-way to a trolley.

In between times I kept trying to raise my beeper call. In my business you live by the telephone; somebody calls up and needs a mortgage, and if you don't service them right away they'll just call somebody else. Besides, this particular call had sounded a little worrying. It was hopeless. You never get the same car-phone operator twice, of course. The ones I did get were highly amused at my quaint notion that they had nothing better to do than check out calls that had already been passed along to the subscribers.

Then, when I insisted, they were scandalized. "Do you have any *idea*, Mr. Dominic," demanded one, "how many call slips I'd have to *look* through to find yours?"

I said, "I guess about a million, as long as you're looking under the wrong name. It's not Mr. Dominic. It's Mr. DeSota. Dominic DeSota."

To that thrust, no counter. Instead, "You're not even sure she had the right frequency," she said, as indignant as though I'd betrayed her trust by switching the frequencies on her myself. "The call could have been for somebody else's number completely."

"Not, I think, with my name," I offered, but by then the traffic cop was on his way back, to ask me if my parents had been citizens of a foreign power or whether I had any communicable diseases. He looked quite annoyed to see that I was talking on the phone instead of devoting my complete attention to the repenting of my sins. "Forget it," I told the operator. Took my ticket. Licked the officer's boots (metaphorically). Swore I'd never do it again (fervently). Drove at a prim thirty-two miles an hour to my bachelor home, and wished that the day had gone better. It hadn't. It didn't show any signs of getting that way. Greta didn't answer her phone. That meant she'd gone out shopping or something. By the time she got back the pool in the Mekhtab ibn Bawzi Forest Preserve would be closed for the night. And I hadn't clinched the mortgage deal. And I hadn't even called the prospects back to keep them on the stick.

And I wondered, I truly wondered, if through the squeaky, squawky static on that abortive beeper call I had really heard, as I almost thought I had heard, the words "to the FBI."

What I started out to be was a real-estate dealer . . . well, no, tell the truth and shame the Devil, what I *really* started out to be was a scientist of some kind.

But there's no living in that, so by the time I got to college I was studying real estate.

Then I got sidetracked into mortgages.

If I tell somebody that the reason for the switch was that mortgage brokers have a more interesting life than realtors, they just stare at me. It's true, though. There's a lot of excitement to mortgages. You're making people's dreams come true, you see, and there are no more interesting people to be around than dreamers. Sometimes the dreams worry me a little, because some of the dreamers are pathetically young couples, just married; I don't know if they know what they're getting into, with interest rates all the way up to five and a half, sometimes five and five-eighths percent. But they pay the rates. They borrow thousands of dollars, sometimes two or three years' pay, to get the vine-covered cottage of their dreams. And I was the one who helped them make those dreams come true.

It would have been even more satisfying, I guess, to be a loan officer at a big bank somewhere. Around Chicago that doesn't happen unless you're a relative of somebody powerful, and somebody powerful isn't Italian, of course. In banking, it's Arab. Not that that's so unusual—how many banks are there in America that aren't Arab-backed? Certainly not very many of the big and prosperous ones. So there wasn't much future for me in a bank job, but the Arabs didn't bother about some of the service jobs, such as mortgage broker.

Maybe the reason for that was that they didn't know what a mortgage broker was. Most people don't. I was the one who interviewed the clients, helped them choose the product they could afford— or could almost afford—checked out their credit ratings, guided them through the preparation of the application forms and the securing of the waivers and variances and permits everyone needs if he wants to own a house.

It's a living. It's also interesting—I know I keep on saying that, perhaps to convince myself. My girl Greta says it to me when I don't say it to myself; she is a big believer in a solid job and savings in the bank before you get married, and we're going to get married one of these days. The job will make that possible.

One of these days.

Meanwhile, it's still interesting, I say for at least the third time, and it also gives me time to myself when I want it. The time when I want time to myself is usually when I can spend it with Greta. The company has a rule that every one of us salesmen must put in five hours a week "floor time"—that's being there, on the floor of the agency, for drop-in or phone-in customers. Outside of that I make my own hours. So when Greta is on a run—she's a stewardess—I put in long days. When she's between assignments I try to make time to be with her. I'm really pleased she has the job she has. . . . No, that's a lie. I'm not. I worry about all the guys she meets, back and forth between Chicago and New York, and where she stays when she overnights in New York. Of course all the stews are chaperoned by the Little Fatimas, but chaperons can be evaded. We know all about that, Greta and I. I really hate the idea that I'm teaching her how to do that in Chicago, and she's using those skills with somebody else in New York. I hate to think that.

So I try not to think it.

And I did get to go swimming with her that night, after all. As soon as I got home I skinned down to my underwear, pulled down the shades, locked the doors, and took a bottle of beer out of the secret under-the-stairs cupboard. While it was chilling in the freezer compartment I tried again to check out my mysterious phone call. By then it was hopeless, of course. My call slip was well buried under hours of accumulation of others. But then I sat down with that luscious cold bottle, sweat glistening along its sides. The phone rang. Greta. "Nicky, honey? You in the mood for a late swim?"

I was, of course. I swallowed the beer so fast it made my teeth crackle as it went past, put on my suit, was already in the water by the time she got there and dove in beside me.

There weren't many people in the pool at that hour, but all the male eyes were aimed at her as she came off the diving board. Greta is a pretty sight. She is five feet eight, blonde, green-eyed, very slim-waisted. Men look at her a lot. In a bathing suit, even in the skirted, thigh-length kind of suit our pool guards made mandatory, men sometimes drooled. I know. I did it myself.

I swam her down to the dark end of the pool to kiss her. They'd put the lights out to save electricity, and only the bathing pavilion was still bright. We stood in water about shoulder high on me, chin high on Greta, sort of bouncing on the tips of our toes the way you do in the water, and I kissed her thoroughly, and then pulled her close to kiss her again.

She kissed me back. For quite a long time. Then she pulled away and let some of the cold water get between us, sort of giggling. When I reached out again she said, "Uh-uh, honey. You're getting me real steamed up."

I said, "I wish—" and she stopped me.

"I know what you wish. Maybe I do, too, but we can't."

"There's nobody around this part of the pool. . . ."

"Oh, Nicky, you know that's not it. What if I, you know, got, well, *caught*?"

"That's not very likely." No response to that. "Anyway, there are things that can be done."

"No, they can't, Nicky dear. Not if you mean the 'A' word. I could never destroy my child's life.

Anyway, those places aren't easy to find, and then who knows if they'll kill you or spoil you for life?"

The trouble was that she was right and we both knew it. There wasn't a day that went by without some police raid on a back-door abortionist, with the criminal dragged away by the police and all the patients trying to hide their faces from the news cameras. We certainly didn't want that.

There was hardly anyone left in the pool now. No one seemed to notice that we weren't swimming. Greta eased back closer to me, did not resist when I kissed her again.

"Nicky?" she whispered in my ear.

"What, honey?"

Faint giggle, then a whisper so low I could hardly hear the words: "What about going topless now?"

I looked around. Apart from a couple of elderly men in bathing suits and robes, finishing out a checker game, the only person left in the pool area was the lifeguard. He was reading a newspaper under the exit light.

"Why not?" I said.

And I reached down between us and slowly, slowly unzipped the top part of my bathing suit.

Now, you have to remember that going topless is not really some big crime. In the city code it's called a Class 3 misdemeanor—that means they never arrest you for it, just give you a ticket, as for parking in the wrong place. The fine is never more than five or ten dollars and the judges hardly ever give a jail sentence. Often when a man goes topless they'll let him off with just a warning, if it's a first offense.

So I did not expect what happened.

I did not expect that all the pool lights would come on at once. The checker players yawped in surprise as someone came running right through them, sending the board flying. That was only one someone, and there were others coming from all directions—through the men's dressing room, through the ladies', even over the fence; and they all converged on me. Two large men jumped right in the pool, clothes and all, to grab me and drag me out.

Greta stood staring; chin-deep in the water—terrified and bewildered, and no more so than I.

The world whirled, and didn't stop whirling until they had me bent over the hood of a car, just outside the pool fence. The metal was hot; the car had just got here, and it felt as though it had been driven hard. They made me spread my feet wide apart, while a nastily unfriendly cop's hand ran over the wet seat of my bathing suit—searching for weapons, for God's sake? There were two other cars, headlights on and pointed straight at me, at least half a dozen men—and they were pointed straight at me too; I was the center of it all.

And the only thing I could think of to say was, "Listen! All I did was take my damn top off!"

The queerness that developed—the questions that were unanswered!

Why should the residents of Los Angeles suddenly complain that their sweet, orange-scented air was being invaded by gusts of poison gas?

What made twenty thousand peaceable subjects of the czar suddenly march through downtown Kiev chanting revolutionary slogans?

Why were so many persons being admitted to mental institutions with a diagnosis of paranoid schizophrenia, characterized by a terrified conviction that they were being watched by unseen eyes?

Why were things suddenly so strange?

17 August 1983
1:18 A.M. Nicky DeSota

I've taken the Daley Expressway down into the city a thousand times. Never like this before. Never with sirens going and overhead lights flashing off the hood ornament of the big Cadillac. At that hour of the morning there were not that many other cars on the road, but the ones that were scooted out of our way as soon as they saw the flashers of the Chicago Police Department cruiser that ran interference for us. We made it in twenty-one minutes. Faster than the train; but it was the longest twenty-one minutes of my life.

No one would tell me a thing. "What are you pulling me in for?" "Shut up, Dominic." "What did I do?" "You'll find out." "Can't you tell me anything?" "Listen, son, for the last time, shut up. Chief Agent Christophe will tell you all you want to know—a lot more, even!"

"Son" he called me. That was the gorilla on my right—dripping wet from coming into the pool after me, at least two years younger than I. But there was a big difference between us. I was the prisoner, and he was the one who knew the answers he wouldn't tell.

There wasn't any sign on the office building on Wabash, but the night watchman let us in at once. There was no name on the door of the suite on the twentieth floor. There was no one in the anteroom of the suite. No one would tell me anything still; but at least one question got answered. I saw the portrait on the wall over the receptionist's desk. I recognized that hallowed old face at once—anybody would—stern as a snapping turtle, determined as an avalanche.

J. Edgar Hoover.

The phone message hadn't been that garbled after all. I was in the hands of the FBI.

I don't know if you truly see all your life flashing before you when you're drowning. I do know that over the next few minutes I reviewed every punish-able thing I'd ever done. Not just going topless or nearly demolishing a Chicago traffic cop. I went way back. I started with the time I peed against the back wall of Olivet Presbyterian Church in Arlington Heights, when I was nine years old and caught short on my way to Sunday School. I covered cheating on my college entrance examination, and the false claim I'd filed for fire losses when my dormitory burned—the bed and innerspring mattress I'd claimed hadn't really belonged to me at all, but to my buddy in Alpha Kappa Nu. I even remembered what I had censored clear out of my waking consciousness, the one time I'd really got close to serious trouble with the Arabs. It wasn't a prideful memory. My high-school buddy Tim Karasueritis and I had put away three bottles of illegal beer, practicing to be macho. It wasn't bad enough that I threw up. What made it really bad was that I did it right on the corner of Randolph and Wacker, in front of the biggest, richest mosque in all Chicagoland. And when I had poured it all out on the sidewalk Tim took his turn. While I was holding his head over the curb, I looked up. There was a hajji, white beard and green turban, looking at us with furious and accusing eyes. Bad scene! I thought we'd had it for sure, but I guess even Arab hajjis have teenaged kids. He didn't say a word. He just stared at us for a long, long moment, then turned and went into the mosque. Maybe he came out again with the Arab equivalent of the cops, but before then we were long gone, running when we could manage it and somehow staggering away anyway when we couldn't.

Oh, I plumbed my depths. I searched every indictable or reprehensible or merely obnoxious memory I had, without finding one that would justify the FBI coming after me in the middle of the night.

After ten minutes, I got brave enough to decide to tell somebody this fact. There wasn't anybody to tell. They had sat me down in a small room with little furniture. Bear in mind that all I was wearing was a bathing suit. It had long since dried out, sure, but they had the windows open somewhere in the offices, and cold Lake Michigan breezes were coming in under the door—the, as I discovered when my courage reached the point of trying it, *locked* door.

Funnily, even though I wore so little, they had insisted on searching me. They were taking no chance that I might be carrying a weapon, I supposed—either to attack one of them, or (maybe in a fit of contrition at the enormity of my crimes, whatever those crimes might turn out to be) to kill myself and spoil their plans for me.

Unfortunately I couldn't think of anything in my past worth killing for. It was embarrassing not to know what I was arrested for, but I couldn't do anything about that. I couldn't do anything much at all. Not only was the door locked, but there was very little in this tiny room to do anything with. There was a loudspeaker up high, behind a grille, that was playing music—violins, mostly; longhair stuff. There was a desk. It was absolutely bare on top, and what it might have inside its drawers I could not know. When I got up the nerve to just accidentally happen to tug at one of them it was as locked as the door. There was an upholstered swivel chair behind the desk, and a straight-backed wooden one before it. No one was present to tell me which one I might sit in, but I took the wooden one anyway.

I sat, my arms wrapped around me against the cold, and thought.

And then, without warning, the door opened, and Chief Agent Christophe came in.

Chief Agent Christophe was a woman.

Chief Agent Nyla Christophe was not the only one who came through the door, but there was no doubt who was who. She was the boss. The others with her, two men and a plump, middle-aged woman, demonstrated that fact by body language.

It took me a while to get over my surprise. Of course, everybody knew that the FBI had begun recruiting woman agents a while earlier. No one would expect to *see* one. They were like woman taxi drivers or woman doctors; you knew they existed because when one did show up anywhere it got onto the newsreels and you saw it the next time you went to the movies. That wouldn't happen with FBI agents, of course. No personality story about an FBI agent was ever going to turn up as a human-interest brightener in the weekly newsreel. Any cameraman who tried to do one would be in the soup—charged, probably, with something like reckless endangerment, for exposing a government operative to possible criminal retribution. Then he would turn up in an interrogation room in fear of his life. . . .

Very much like me.

Anyway, in she came. First there was a big guy to open the door for her, then Chief Agent Christophe, then the fat lady, then another big guy to close it. She glanced at me as she came in, abstractedly: Oh, yes, there's the piece of furniture that belongs in this room. I looked back at her, with, I am sure, a lot more concentration. Nyla Christophe was a good-looking woman of a certain type. The type was big-boned and athletic. She had her hair tied behind in a ponytail, and pale blue eyes. She kept her hands folded behind her as she walked, in the style of a British admiral from the age of sail. She gave commands like an admiral. To the two huskies: "Tie him." To the plump lady who panted to the desk and pulled out a shorthand pad: "Write: August seventeenth, 1983, Chief Agent N. Christophe conducting interview of Dominic DeSota." To me:

"Make it easy on yourself, DeSota. Just give us the truth, answer all the questions, and we'll be through here in twenty minutes. First take the oath."

That wasn't good. To be put on oath right away meant that they were pretty serious. What I was going to tell them wasn't just going to be information received in an investigation. It was going to be evidence. The woman-stenographer stood up and held out the books to me, wheezing the words for me to repeat after her. I stretched my hand from Bible to Koran, little finger on one, thumb touching the binding of the other, and swore to tell the truth, the whole truth, and nothing but the truth, so help me God the Merciful, the All-Seeing, and the Avenging. "Fine, Dominic," said Christophe as the huskies retied my right hand. She glanced at her watch as though she really thought we might get out of there in twenty minutes. "Now, just tell me why you were trying to break into Daleylab."

I goggled. "Do what?"

"Break into Daleylab," she said patiently. "What were you looking for?"

"I don't know what you're talking about," I said.

It was not the answer Agent Christophe wanted to hear. "Oh, shit, Dominic," she said crossly, "I hoped you were going to be sensible about this. Are you pretending you never heard of Daleylab?"

"Of course not." Everybody knew what Daleylab was—or, anyway, knew that it was some kind of hush-hush military research place, way southwest of Chicago. I'd driven near it dozens of times. "But, Miss Christophe—"

"*Agent* Christophe."

"Agent Christophe, I really don't know what you

mean. I've never been in Daleylab. I certainly didn't try to break in."

"Oh, sweet Fatima," she said with a groan, bringing her hands together for the first time. There was a surprise. Chief Agent Christophe would have had a little trouble taking the oath herself if anyone had asked her to. She didn't have any thumbs.

It was not that unusual to see thumbless people, of course. It was a standard sentence for, like, second-offense thieves, or pickpockets, or sometimes an adulteress or a death-by-auto killer. But it was quite unusual, I thought, to come across a thumbless FBI agent.

It took an effort to get my mind off Christophe's missing thumbs, but the ropes were cutting into my arms. "Agent Christophe," I said, getting almost indignant, "I don't know where you got this notion, but it simply isn't even arguable. There is no chance I was anywhere near Daleylab in the last month or more."

She looked at the two bullies, then back at me. "No chance," she repeated thoughtfully.

"No chance at all," I said firmly.

"No chance at all," she echoed. Then she held out a hand.

One of the bullies filled it with a file folder. The top item inside the folder was a photograph. She glanced at it to make sure it was right way up, then held it before me so that I could see it clearly. It was a man at the door of a building.

The man was me.

He was me but wearing a suit I had never owned, a sort of one-piece coverall of the sort Winston Churchill made famous in World War II. But he was me, all right. "This was taken," Christophe said colorlessly, "by the surveillance cameras at Daleylab night before last. So were these others." She flipped through them quickly. They were not all taken with the same camera, because the background was different from the first one. But it was the same familiar face, in the same unfamiliar clothes. "And these," she said, taking a cardboard form out of the folder, "are your fingerprints as filed with your college I.D. at Northwestern. The ones under them were found at the lab."

There were only four prints below the full line of ten on the sample—all they'd recovered from the scene, I supposed. But even an amateur could see that the spirals and grooves on the thumb and middle finger of the right hand, and the index fingers of both, looked a lot like my reference prints above.

"But it's not true!" I wailed.

"Are you going to stick to your story?" Christophe asked incredulously.

"I have to! I wasn't there! I didn't do it!"

"Oh, hell, Dominic," she said, sighing, "I thought you had better sense." And she locked her thumbless hands together and gazed down at the ground. She didn't signal to her helpers. She didn't have to. They knew what came next and, as they moved toward me, so did I.

They didn't beat me very much. You know the gossip about how they treat suspects. By those standards they barely laid a finger on me. It isn't all gossip, either, I think, because I wrote a mortgage for a bartender once, and then he got arrested on suspicion of selling hard liquor to a person under the age of thirty-five. He didn't need any mortgage after that. What his widow whispered to me about the condition of the body when they gave it back to her for burial would pretty nearly turn your stomach.

I got nothing like that.

I got slapped around. It hurt, sure. It hurts twice as much when you're tied up because you can't hit back—well, you wouldn't do that anyway, not if you knew what was good for you—or even try to catch some of the blows on an arm instead of the side of the head. My head was ringing long before they were through, but it was all open-hand stuff, no bruises, no breaking the skin, and they stopped every few minutes so Agent Christophe could pick up the questioning:

"That's you in the pictures, isn't it, Dominic?"

"How do I know? It—ouch!—*looks* like me, a little."

"And the fingerprints?"

"I don't know anything about fingerprints."

"Oh, hell, go on, boys."

After a while they got tired of the side of my head. Or maybe they noticed that I was beginning to have trouble hearing Christophe; anyway, they began punching me in the belly or whacking me across the back. Since I was still wearing only the bathing suit, there was no protection. It hurt. But hitting me on the back must have hurt their hands some, too, because they weren't nearly as enthusiastic. They paused more frequently.

"Want to change your mind, Dominic?"

"There's nothing to change, damn it!"

And then they'd switch to the belly again. That did hurt. It took the wind out of me. I doubled over and could hardly hear what Agent Christophe was saying.

And so I almost missed it when she said, "Jerk, are you still denying you were in Daleylab on Saturday, August thirteenth?"

I gasped. "Wait a minute." Naturally they didn't wait, just kept trying to get a good punch in at my doubled-over belly. "No, please," I begged, and Christophe stopped them. I took a couple of deep breaths and managed to say, "Did you mean last Saturday? The thirteenth?"

"Right, Dominic. When you were caught at Daleylab."

I sat up straighter. "But I couldn't have been, Agent Christophe," I said, "because last Saturday I was weekending in New York City. My fiancée was there. She'll testify. Honest, Agent Christophe! I don't know who it was but it couldn't have been me!"

Well, it wasn't as easy as that. I took a couple of good shots after that before they were convinced—or not convinced, exactly, but at least confused. They got Greta out of bed to confirm my story, and she told them her whole crew would remember me, and they got all of them on the phone too. They all did. I didn't often go with Greta on her New York runs, and they were in no doubt about the date.

They untied me and let me stand up. One of them even lent me a trenchcoat to put on over my bathing suit to go home in the bright dawn. They weren't graceful about it, though. Agent Christophe didn't speak to me again, just put her head down over the file folder, gnawing at her lips furiously. One of the beaters-up was the one who told me I could go. "But not far, DeSota. No New York trips, understand? Just stay where we can find you when we want you."

"But I've proved I was innocent."

"DeSota," he snarled, "you've proved nothing. We've got all the *proof* we need. Surveillance photos, fingerprints. We could put you away for a hundred years with just that."

"Except that I wasn't there," I said, and then said no more, because Nyla Christophe had looked up from her folder and was looking straight at me.

It would have been only decent of them to give me a ride back home, but I didn't think it was worthwhile lingering long enough to ask. I found a cabby who took me, and waited outside while I went in to get my wallet and pay him off. Twelve dollars. A day's pay. But I never paid a bill more gladly.

Deputy Chief Inspector William Brzolyak, walking into his local precinct house with a .45 automatic in his hand, explained that he had shot and killed his wife and five children because they were staring at him behind his back. "They should've left me alone," he told reporters.

Bathers along the South Side beaches complained that the presence of dark-brown, greasy balls of matter floating in the lake waters made swimming unattractive and constituted a possible health hazard.

The summer storm that dropped as much as 3.4 inches of rain on New York City suburbs within a four-hour period was described by U.S. Weather Bureau spokespersons as "a meteorological freak." It was not associated with any identified frontal system or low-pressure area. Property damage in Queens and Richmond counties alone was estimated in the millions of dollars.

18 August 1983
11:15 A.M. Nicky DeSota

A day later none of it seemed so bad. "Just mistaken identity," I assured Greta when she called to say good-bye—she was on another New York run.

"Even the fingerprints?"

"Come on, Greta," I said, looking at my boss, who was looking thoughtfully at me, and at the clock behind him, which was telling me I only had two hours before I was due in traffic court. "*You* know where I was that night!"

"Of course I do," she said with a sigh in a tone of voice as though she weren't really sure any more. I guessed that was what being questioned by the FBI did. I could hear her yawning. "Goodness sake," she apologized, "I hope I'm not like this on my run. It was all that noise last night."

"What noise?" I hadn't heard anything, but then once I'm asleep I seldom do.

"That kind of roaring, didn't you hear? Sort of like thunder? Only there wasn't any thunder?—'Scuse me," she added, and I could hear her saying something with her hand over the mouthpiece. Then, "Sorry, honey, but they're loading up. I've got to go. See you in a couple of days—"

"I love you," I said, but I was talking to a dead phone. What's more, Mr. Ruppert was coming toward me, so I added swiftly, to the dead microphone, "I only wish I had a dozen more clients like you! Take care, and I'll get back to you with the quotations."

I hung up, gazing blandly at him, and bent quickly to the paper on my desk. I always keep a lot of it there for floor-time days. This time, though, it was actual work, quotations I had to prepare for clients in six different municipalities. Since each municipality had its own fire and safety codes—and thus its own insurance premiums—and since every client was different anyway in terms of credit standing and down payment, I had a good two hours of work with the adding machine. I had hoped for a nice lunch on the way over to Barrington, but I was lucky to get a hot dog and a root beer along the highway. I got there two minutes before the 1:30 P.M. on my ticket, which meant I was late. Not *late* late. The judge hadn't even shown up yet, and probably wouldn't for at least another quarter of an hour—that was what you got to be a judge for. But everybody else had been there long enough to hand in his ticket, announce his plea, and get a number. I got a number. There were forty-two people summoned for that session. I was number forty-two.

I sat down in the back, calculating as best I could. Number forty-two. Say, at the most optimistic, an average of a minute and a half a case. That meant the judge would get to me in a little over an hour. Still, that wasn't so bad, I reassured myself, because I had a briefcase full of credit reports to check over. I could be sitting right there in the back row and catching up on my paperwork.

I opened the case, pulled out the first half-dozen folders, and glanced around, reasonably well content. It was interesting to somebody who'd never been in traffic court before. The judge's bench was in a little playpen sort of a thing, flanked by two flags. On the left was the old Stars and Stripes, the forty-eight stars bright on the blue background; on the right, the white of Illinois. Between them—

Between them was a sign on the wall. It said:

NO SMOKING
NO EATING
NO DRINKING
NO READING
NO WRITING
NO SLEEPING

So the afternoon would not be as productive as I had hoped.

I tested it out by opening my briefcase in my lap, but the test came out negative. A fat, elderly guy in Barrington Police Department uniform came strolling down the aisle to watch what I did. There was no rule against having reading or writing materials out on your lap, it seemed; he didn't tell me to put them away. But you could see that he was waiting to pounce—one little stroke of the pen, one word scanned out of the corner of my eye, and pow!

I gave him a patronizing smile and turned to the citizen two seats away from me. "Hot in here, isn't it?" I asked. "You'd think they'd turn the fans on."

"Fans don't work," he said. That was all he said. There wasn't any rule against talking, but he wasn't taking any chances. A voice from behind me explained:

"They work all right, it's just that this court's electric bills are getting too high." I looked around. Dapper young man grinning at me; he wore a white jacket, white pants, and next to him on a vacant chair was a white panama hat. A very flashy dresser, I thought. "It's hard to stay awake, though, isn't it?" he added. "Especially when that noise keeps you awake all night."

That noise again. Again I said that I hadn't heard a thing, and both he and the guy in my row were glad to supply details. Like from the sky, see? No, not like an airplane—with an airplane you can hear the motors going; this wasn't a motor, it was more like something roaring—although, yeah, come to think of it, it did seem to come from around the airport. Midway? No, not Midway—that little private field off to the northwest, Old Orchard, they called it, though some people wanted to change the name to O'Hare. And, boy! that noise was *something*. On this all parties agreed—all but me, who had little to contribute but ears—and we probably would have gone on concurring for another half hour if the court attendant hadn't called out: "His Honor Timothy P. Magrahan, all rise!"

And we rose. His Honor came in, sweating in his dollar-ninety-eight black judicial robes, gazing out at us like an actor counting a sparse house, without much pleasure. When we were allowed to sit down again he sighed and gave us a little speech:

"Ladies and gentlemen, most of you here today have been accused of traffic offenses. Now, I don't know how you people feel, but to me this has to be taken seriously. A traffic offense isn't some little thing that doesn't matter much one way or another. Not at all. A traffic offense is an offense against driving. An offense against driving is an offense against the good people who make our driving possible—our friends from the Middle East, including Mekhtab ibn Bawzi himself. An offense against our friends from the Middle East is an offense against the principles of religious toleration and democratic friendship among peoples. . . ."

It was not a surprise to me when the snappy customer in the white suit whispered in my ear that Judge Magrahan was coming up for reelection that November. By the time the judge got around to telling us that an offense against the Koran was an offense against religion generally, including our own Judeo-Christian denominations, I began to see that this traffic ticket could be serious. My only hope for getting off scot-free would have been if the summonsing officer hadn't shown up in court. That wasn't happening. There was a bench along the side of the room, and among the five or six men sitting there—a couple in state police uniforms, the others from various municipalities—there was my good friend from Meacham Road. He knew I was there too. He didn't smile at me, or nod, but I could feel his eyes on me from time to time.

The first case came up for decision, scared-looking young woman with a baby in a stroller, sixty-eight miles an hour in a sixty-mile-an-hour zone. A twenty-five-dollar fine and six months' probation. The second case was worse, driving under the influence of alcohol, third offense, along with reckless endangerment and failure to observe posted stop signs. That was a man of no more than twenty, and he did not leave the courtroom under his own power. One of the officers took him away in handcuffs, to be held awaiting sentencing, and as he left I could see him looking at his thumbs wistfully, as though he didn't expect to have them much longer.

I sat up straighter and put my briefcase away. Most of the people in the courtroom were doing the same thing. It seemed that Judge Magrahan's political strategy had been set: losing votes among the people he sentenced would cost him less than those he would gain by working up a reputation as a fearless crusader for traffic safety.

There was also the consideration, I realized, that most of the persons awaiting hearing came from other municipalities, like myself, and therefore were of no interest to the judge's vote counters.

So I watched for half an hour as the justice meted out justice to his subjects, one by one. I decided that it wasn't my month. Chief Agent Nyla Christophe was bad enough, but at least I'd been able to clear myself with her. With this judge, I had no hope. I watched my acquaintance in the white suit wander around the courtroom like a friend of the family at a picnic, stopping to chat with this one and that. When he leaned over to whisper in the ear of the cop who'd summonsed me, I began to pay closer attention. When the cop glanced at me, shaking his head, I sat up straight. When, a couple of minutes later, the two of them walked out of the courtroom together, still talking, I almost got up to follow; but the courtroom attendant who had so faithfully monitored what I was doing with my briefcase stood at the end of my row, watching me assessingly. I stayed put. For a while. When a few minutes later curiosity overcame caution it was too late. "Men's room?" I whispered to the attendant; he nodded. I went where he pointed; neither cop nor man in white were in sight anywhere around.

And when, half an hour later, the clerk at last called my name, the judge conferred in whispers with another court attendant, then scowled at me. "Mr. DeSota," he said, "your summonsing officer has been called away on urgent police business and cannot testify against you. Therefore, under the law, I have no option but to dismiss the charges. You're a free man, Mr. DeSota, and, I may add, a very lucky one."

I did not disagree at all.

I was so pleased to be out of it that I was halfway home before I realized my beeper was beeping. I stopped at a filling station and while the high-test was running into my tank I called the message center. This time they had tuned me in exactly and the operator had every word of the message. So, this time, it was the message itself that left me bewildered. Pronounced syllable by syllable with care, it said:

"You don't need to know my name and you don't need to know why I care what happens to you or how I know who you are or anything like that. But if you want help with the thumbless lady, have a tunafish-salad sandwich at the Carson, Pirie, Scott coffee shop this evening at six P.M."

"That's it?" I asked.

"Yes, sir," said the operator, very sweet, very

competent. "Would you like me to repeat the message? No? Then just let me say, sir, that it's the occasional message like yours that makes this job such a fun thing to do! Thank you, Mr. DeSota, thank you very much."

"You're welcome," I said, and sat there staring out the windshield until the gas jockey rapped on my window. "Sorry," I said, and fished out the money to pay him—sixty-nine cents a gallon! If I'd looked at the prices I never would have stopped there.

But I didn't have room in my head to think about that; I was too busy thinking about the message. *And* the mistaken-identity thing with the FBI. *And* getting off so lightly in traffic court. *And* all the other weirdnesses that were infesting my life and the world. Under normal circumstances I would have ignored the message. It was exactly the kind of cloak-and-dagger thing that a sensible person would stay far away from. Taking time off to go there would, as a minimum, mean taking off more time from my main business in life, namely the arranging of mortgages for needy home buyers. The boss would not be pleased. And the whole thing was fishy. Going there might easily get me in trouble I couldn't get out of.

Naturally I went.

There was a novel that Greta and I were reading once where one of the characters said something like, "She went into a department store, one of the places where women gladly go but few men are willing to follow." Greta said she thought that was sort of derogatory toward women. "Women don't *like* to shop," she said. "It's just that they *have* to. They're the ones that buy the groceries and the household furnishings and all the other things people have to buy for a family."

"They don't buy the cars," I pointed out.

"No, of course. They don't buy the major capital-expense items, naturally," she agreed. "But that sort of thing you only do once every few years. Day in, day out, there's all the consumable stuff that has to be bought. If a woman spends a lot of time buying it, that's because it's her job. To compare prices and values. It's how she conserves her family's spending money. Whether she likes it or not doesn't matter. She has to do it anyway."

"Right, honey," I said, grinning.

She didn't like the grin. "No, Nick, I'm serious! You shouldn't say women *like* to shop. You should just say it's their *job* to shop."

"Now, Greta," I said reasonably, "just think this thing through, will you? How can you say it's derogatory to somebody to say she likes to do her job? I like my job too."

"That's not at all the same thing," she said, but she didn't say it angrily, and then she changed the subject. She was good about that. Greta was not one of your suffragettes. She told me a hundred times that if she got the vote she wouldn't know what to do with it. But the thing about Greta was that she had a good job as a stewardess, and it made her a little— well—I don't want to say mannish or anything like that. Not independent, exactly. And it was all conversation, of course; if I ever popped the question I knew what she would say, and once we were married there'd be no more of those funny ideas.

I did worry about her a little now and then, though.

Right then my worries were a lot more immediate. What made me think about all this was that, looking around the Carson coffee shop, I felt that line from the novel was right on target. There were a hundred customers scattered around the big room— green porch furniture for tables and chairs, hanging plants everywhere—and ninety-five of them were women. There were no single men, or pairs of men. Here and there a couple, maybe, the man generally elderly, and always with that hangdog "Oh-my-God-I've-blundered-into-the-ladies'-toilet" look.

I guess that was why I assumed that my Mystery Caller would be female. That shows how reliable my assumptions are.

After twenty minutes, and the third time the elderly waitresses came by to inquire if I was ready to order, I was. After another twenty minutes my tuna-salad sandwich arrived.

And twenty minutes after that—after I had eaten half the sandwich and was trying to make myself leave the other half on the plate as a recognition signal—I felt someone pass rapidly behind me. When I looked up there was a man already seated across the table.

I knew him. He wasn't wearing a white suit, but he had been not too many hours earlier.

"Well, hello," I said. "I might have guessed it was you."

The waitress was hovering nearby; he glanced at her, then frowned meaningfully at me. "Hello, there," he said, tone that of two old business acquaintances, not in the least surprised to have run into each other this way. But if he knew my name, he didn't use it. It was "Long time no see," and "How *are* you, then?" and no nonsense about waiting for me to answer. When the waitress had taken his order and gone off with it he said in a conversational tone, "You weren't followed here. There's nobody in the restaurant watching you. We can talk."

There is just so much mystery I am willing to put up with. I picked up the other half of my sandwich and regarded him over a bite of it. Youngish fellow, two or three years younger than I. Open-faced, freckled, sandy-haired—the boy next door, the one you knew would never do anything mean or sneaky. Except that here he was being a sneak. "What are we going to talk about?" I asked, my mouth full of tuna fish and cracked-wheat toast. "And who am I talking to, then?"

He made an impatient gesture. "Call me Jimmy.

Names don't matter. What matters is, what were you trying to do at Daleylab?"

"Ah, Jimmy," I said sadly, and put down the rest of my sandwich. "This is stupid," I said. "You go back and tell Chief Agent Christophe that the trick didn't work."

He frowned at me for silence while the waitress brought his ham and cheese sandwich. Then, "There's no trick," he said.

"There's nothing *but* a trick, Jimmy. I was never anywhere near Daleylab, and you and Christophe better know it."

"Don't jerk me around," he said. "They've got your picture."

"It's a fake."

"Fingerprints? They fakes too?"

I said steadily, "Anything at all they've got that says I was trying to break into Daleylab last Saturday night is a fake, because I wasn't."

He chewed on his ham and cheese, studying me suspiciously. I studied him back. Not only was he younger than I, he was taller and a lot better looking. A whole lot better dressed. The white suit he'd worn that afternoon was flashy. This one wasn't flashy, but it was cut nicely out of real English fabric—seventy-five dollars at least, and matching shoes that hadn't come from any Thom McAn I ever saw. He said suddenly, "Nyla thinks your alibi witnesses are lying."

I'd started to pick up the rest of my sandwich. I put it down again. "How do you know what Nyla Christophe thinks if you're not FBI?"

"We're friends," he explained. "I've got a lot of cop friends—not just in the FBI. You ought to know that."

"I know what you did," I said. "I don't know why you did it."

"Why shouldn't I do a favor if I want to?" he demanded. "Get back to your witnesses. Are they lying?"

"No! If they were, would I tell you? But they're not."

He chewed the rest of his ham and cheese in silence, keeping his eyes on me as though some change in expression might resolve the problem for him. I let him keep his quiet. I finished my own sandwich, drank the last of my coffee, waved the waitress over for a refill. He tapped his cup for the same, and when she had gone away again he said, "I didn't think they were, actually."

"I'm glad to hear that."

"Oh, don't come with that supercilious crap with me, Dominic. You're in trouble up to your ass, you know that?"

I hadn't known that. "Christophe told me I could go home!" I objected.

"Why shouldn't she? You couldn't get out of town if you tried. She's not through with you."

"Why not, damn it?"

"Because," he explained, "photos and finger-prints don't lie."

"But I wasn't there!"

He said slowly, "I swear, I think you mean it. I think your witnesses mean it, too, and that's pretty hard to swallow. I think you people might even pass a lie-detector test."

"Why not? We aren't lying."

"Oh, hell, Dominic!" he exploded. "Don't you know you need help?"

"Are you going to help me?" I asked.

"Me? No," he said. "But I know somebody who might. Pay the check, Dominic, and let's go for a ride."

Around this time in August the sun doesn't go down till eight or so, but it was already full dark before we got to where we were going. There wasn't much traffic, once we got out of the Chicago suburbs heading south. We went past cornfields by the mile and small towns by the dozen, and every time I asked this Jimmy person where we were going he only shook his head. "The less you know," he said, "the less trouble you can get anybody in."

"When are we going to get there, then? I'm not a night owl, Jimmy, and I've got a job, and they expect me to be working in the morning—"

"What you've got," he said patiently, as he slowed for a light, "is trouble with the FBI. If you don't get that straightened out, no other trouble is going to matter."

"Yes, sure, Jimmy, but—"

"But quit your bellyaching," he ordered. "We're just about there. It's right outside this town."

"This town," according to the sign on the road, was called Dixon, Illinois, population 2250, Rotary and Lions Club met every Thursday and Friday in the Holiday Inn. We turned off the main street at a square with a World War II 75-millimeter cannon in a little green patch, drove a few blocks, and then Jimmy took a tire-whining left into a private road.

Who the road belonged to it did not declare. There was no cute little "Welcome to Hiddenwell Acres" sign, no name, nothing to identify it and certainly nothing to make us feel at all welcome. On the contrary. What distinguished this road from any other around was the swinging-gate barrier that blocked us at the first turn. There was a little wooden guardhouse next to the gate, and out of it leaned a large, nonwooden guard. "I.D.," he ordered. Jimmy passed him something. What it was I knew not, but it satisfied him. Well, it almost satisfied him. He pored over it for a while, licking his lips. Then he picked up a phone and discussed it with someone on the other end. Then he cranked the barrier up and waved us through.

A quarter of a mile farther along the road split, to loop around a lawn with a fountain. We circled and stopped in front of a veranda with huge white pillars.

I'd seen it before—in, I think, the movie *Gone With the Wind*. And the servants came out of the same film. A cheerful young black man came at us from one direction to bob his head and take Jimmy's car to an invisible parking lot behind a grove of apple trees in fruit. A plump, middle-aged black woman came from another direction to admit us to the house. She didn't greet Jimmy by name, and didn't pay any attention to me at all. She didn't ask questions. She didn't volunteer any answers. The list of things she didn't do was, in fact, very long. What she did do was lead us silently through a huge three-story foyer with a carpeted stairway curving down to the entrance, through a passage, through a little sort of living room, with a fireplace and comfortable couch and armchairs, all unoccupied, through a glass door into, finally, a sort of combination hothouse and gymnasium. It had been hot enough outside. It was twice as hot within. The place was full of tropical plants stretching up to the glass roof, with vines clinging to the trees and a sort of general jungly smell of decaying plants and humid soil.

  In the middle of it all was a swimming pool, long and narrow. And in the pool was an elderly man; and on the elderly man was nothing at all. He was skinny-dipping. It did not seem to concern him. He was doing laps. He splashed to our end of the pool, gasped, "Ninety-eight," swam a sort of sloppy Australian crawl to the far end—"Ninety-nine"—did the last stretch back to us at top speed, arms slipping gracefully into the water ahead of his white topknot, feet frothing up the water behind in a vigorous eight-beat kick. "One hundred," he said, panting, and clung to the edge of the pool. Another young black man, this one grave rather than cheerful, handed him a towel, and he dabbed at his face and grinned up at me. "Evening, gentlemen," he said.

  I made a noise at him. It wasn't exactly a "Good evening," but it was polite. Jimmy did better. He crouched down beside the pool, took one of the old swimmer's wet and slippery hands, and pumped it enthusiastically.

"Ron," he said, from the heart—anyway it sounded as though it came from the heart—"I can't tell you how grateful I am to you for seeing us tonight."

"Not at all," said the man courteously. "After all, Larry, you said it was a significant civil liberties issue."

"Yes, I think it is," said "Jimmy" gamely, carefully not looking to see if I'd picked up on the name. "It's about Dominic here. He has an unusual problem with the FBI. They claim he was detected breaking into a secret government research installation. They have pictures and fingerprints to prove it. But he has unimpeachable witnesses to prove he was a thousand miles away at the time."

Ron had pulled himself out of the pool and was toweling himself dry. He had to be in his seventies, anyway, but when I looked at his tapering torso and absolute lack of any spare tire around the waist, I only wished I could live to be that kind of seventy. He not only looked good, he looked sort of familiar. Then he finished drying himself, dropped the towel on the tiling, and let the black man help him into a white terry-cloth robe. "I don't do private-eye movies any more, Larry," he said, grinning, and I realized why he looked familiar. He was an actor. Had been an actor, anyway. In the movies. Never a big star, but one of those faces you kept seeing until your subconscious remembered it even if the rest of you didn't. Until there was some kind of scandal. Scandal? Trouble, anyway. I couldn't remember the details, but he had been fired. Not just from the job; from the industry. It had been something political, maybe. . . .

Whatever it was, it had happened a long time ago. Right after World War II, right about when I was getting ready to get born; and now old Ron was easily in his seventies and maybe a little more than that. A nice-looking old man, even not counting the slim waist and square shoulders, with an engaging grin and a lock of white hair that kept falling down over his eyes.

So he looked.

Old Ron didn't linger by the pool. He led the way to the room with the couch and chairs. In the five minutes since we had passed through it last someone had lighted a fire in the fireplace and put out glasses and bottles on a sideboard. A third young black man, perhaps the fire-layer and drink-setter-outer, materialized to take our drink orders, while Ron sat in the armchair nearest the fire, raising his bare feet to the warmth of it by resting them on a hassock. You remember it was August? I could understand that his little tootsies might be cold, but surely there was some better way of warming them than by heating up the whole damn room.

When we all had our drinks, he raised his in a toast, swallowed half of it briskly, and then gave "Jimmy" and me that engaging grin again. "Well, Larry," he said, "what kind of a hopeless incompetent have you brought me this time?"

WGN's switchboard was suddenly flooded with calls in the middle of a Cubs game. Every call was a complaint, and every complaint was the same. The broadcast had been drowned out in the top of the third inning by somebody describing a football *game. The complaints were less urgent than the curiosity: who in the world had ever heard of professional football in* **August?**

19 August 1983
9:15 P.M. Larry Douglas

A person in my line of work needs to keep his eyes open. See, I don't have a paycheck every week. There are plenty of weeks when I have a big fat zero, and some when I wind up minus. So I have to make a dollar wherever I can find it, whenever a chance turns up.

When Nyla told me about the poor sap she'd picked up the night before, the way Nyla tells me so many sometimes very useful things, I decided I'd better take a closer look at him. I smelled a possibility, although I wasn't sure yet what it was.

There's always a way to check out the chances if you look for it, and this one was easy. It was no trouble to drop in on his traffic-court hearing—and no big deal to get old Officer Pupp to drop the charges. "If you say he's okay, Larry—"

"I do."

"Then I'll just tell the clerk I had to get back on duty. But tell your pal to watch himself next time."

"I will," I said, and slipped him twenty as we shook hands. That's just a normal business expense for me. In my line of work you want to stay friendly with the cops. It might not keep them from busting you now and then, but at least they probably won't do you any third-degree stuff.

As Mom used to say, I probably take after Grandpa Joe. He was the bank robber, before he came to America and changed his name. Of course, he used a gun. I don't do that, ever, but then when people are so trusting about buying guaranteed flawless diamond rings on a street corner, or investing in warranted sure-to-double-in-value oil stocks over the counter, I don't have to. Unless one of them catches up with me. And as long as I'm tight with Nyla Christophe, that's not likely to happen without at least a little advance warning. So I keep her sweet, in all the ways I can, and, honest, I've got some really good ones.

I keep the Arabs sweet, too, though not in exactly the same way. There are places where I have to draw a line, so I don't do that with them. Any more . . . Well, the other part of that is that they really like their boys younger than I am now, anyway.

Sometimes I think I'd like it better if I were straight, but then I live in the world I've got.

So when I saw what the wimp was into I got the inspiration to get Ron involved. I've kept him sweet, too—a kind of investment, figuring that sooner or later there was a way to make it pay off. When he insulted the wimp, DeSota, I knew I was all right. See, Ronnie's really a mean-natured old grouch, but if you know how to handle him, he'll do almost anything. I know how to handle him. "Ron," I said—grave, serious, open-minded—"you're right. I should have seen it for myself."

He twinkled at me over his Scotch, one eyebrow humorously cocked the way he did. "What am I right about, Larry?" he asked. It was a really nice twinkle. They'd taught it to him back on the MGM lot in the old days, before he got involved in unions and stuff like that. You didn't want to rely too much on the twinkle or the grin, though, because the grin came off like the shutters off Admiral Nelson's gunports, and then *boom* you were shot dead.

"You're right," I said, "that Nicky DeSota here is a turkey who got himself into trouble with the FBI, and I had no right bringing him down here to ask you to get him out of it."

Of course, DeSota's jaw just about hit the floor. But Ron's jaw was the one that counted. It jutted out. The eyes narrowed. The whole face took on the steely look of the marshal who's just heard the outlaw didn't leave town after all.

"I think," he said firmly, "that you ought to tell me what's up, and let me make that decision myself."

"I don't want to cause trouble for you, Ron."

"Trouble, Larry, is something I'm used to," he snapped, and I could almost see him trying to catch a reflection of himself in the French doors.

What could I do? Exactly what I wanted to do, of course. "You're right, Ron," I said, and began to fill Ron in. It took time. Ron is not what you'd call swift. Neither was DeSota. Out of the corner of my eye I could see him glowering at the floor, but he didn't look up or say anything.

And, actually, he had nothing at all to complain about in the way I told his story for him. I explained that it was a clear case of mistaken identity, although the person detected at Daleylab was Dominic's twin, as far as all appearances went. Then I paused, while Ron signaled for another round of drinks, and sat for a moment to take it all in.

"This other guy looked just like him, right?" asked Ron, double-checking.

"Just like him, yep."

"And had the same fingerprints?"

"That's right, Ron."

"But it wasn't him," he finished.

I nodded.

"Then," said Ron, alertly summing up, "it was a clear case of mistaken identity, as I see it."

I gave an admiring little shake of the head, glancing at Dominic to nudge him into doing the same. Dominic wasn't having any. He didn't say anything, but the look he gave me was icy cold. He was not at all pleased with me, Dominic DeSota, but he just didn't understand how you get along with old Ronnie.

Ronnie stood up. "Larry," he said, "you and Nicky will stay for dinner, of course." Of course. It was after ten o'clock at night! Only an ex-movie star would keep hours like that. "Just take it easy while I throw some clothes on, all right? If you'd like some music, just tell Hiram here to switch on the stereo."

And he left us to make up, a task I did not think would be easy.

"What the hell were you trying to pull?" demanded DeSota, as soon as the old man was out of earshot.

I soothed him. "Now, just take it easy. Don't you see what I was doing?"

"I hope not!"

"I was getting him on your side, that's all," I explained. "See, Ron's a deep-dyed liberal. He's committed. Unshakable. He was blacklisted in Hollywood, years ago, for union activities, and—"

I stopped, because the young black man was back in the room. "Some music with the missus's compliments, gentlemen," he murmured, and disappeared again. Some kind of long-hair music came out of hidden speakers, not too loud. I was glad for it; it made it less likely that anybody would be listening to what we said. "Anyway," I finished, "he was lucky. He put his movie earnings into Illinois real estate, and wound up rich."

Dominic was frowning. "Did you say liberal?"

"Yeah, but in his case it's all right, Nicky, because he's rich. Nobody minds a rich man being a little bit of a pinko—they know he won't do anything against the way things are."

"So then what's the use of being here?" he demanded.

"Because if Ron takes an interest in you, he can help you a lot. You got any other offers?"

He shrugged morosely.

I left it at that. I hadn't told him that the other reason nobody minded Ron being a little lefty in his politics was that nobody minded a pinko who was all talk and no action. And that was Ron.

But I wasn't ready for Dominic DeSota to find that out yet.

"This," said Ron gallantly, "is my dear wife, Janie."

"Charmed," she said, when DeSota and I had told her how glad we were to meet her, and then she and Ron led the way into the dining room. It wasn't big. A room that can seat maybe twenty people is big. This one could have served as mess hall for the Grand Army of the Republic. It was *huge*. And around us the music swelled.

I called across the table to Dominic, "You like the sound?" He was turning his head this way and that, the way people do when they haven't heard stereo before. "It's a new system," I explained. "Just listen to that sound! Hear how the violin sounds like it's on one side of you and the rest of the orchestra on the other? Ron's had this stuff for over a year now."

"It'll be on the market for everybody before long," Ron said modestly. "The only thing is that they don't make very many stereo records yet—and most of them more Janie's kind of music than mine." He grinned uxoriously down the long table to his wife, at the far end. She signaled yet another of the young black men to begin serving the salad before she picked up the conversational ball.

"I suspect Mr. DeSota likes the same sort of music I do," she offered sweetly. "Isn't that true, Mr. DeSota? You're obviously enjoying the Beethoven violin concerto."

But Dominic wasn't playing their game. "Is that what it is?" he demanded. "Actually, I was thinking it's the same piece Chief Agent Christophe was playing while she was questioning me."

Ron dropped his salad fork. "Nyla Christophe! You didn't say Nyla Christophe was involved here, Larry!"

"I guess I should have," I said, all open-faced and contrite. "Does it make a difference?"

"A difference! Jesus—I mean, gosh, Larry, of course it does!"

"She can't do you any harm any more," his wife called down the table.

"That's not what I'm worried about! I'd like to do her some! Nyla Christophe," he said, turning back to Dominic, "is one of the worst agents in the FBI. Did you notice she doesn't have any thumbs?"

"You bet," said Dominic. "I wondered how come a—"

"I'll tell you how come," Ron said. "Shoplifting! Then dope! She had three convictions before she was twenty-one years old—the third time meant loss of thumbs, and that's what she got. She was a music student up till then, but she got hooked on that killer weed and had to steal to support her habit!"

"And she got into the FBI?" Dominic demanded, pop-eyed with either wonder or indignation.

"She got religion," Ron roared. "She went to the local office before the bandages were off her thumb. Said she'd been born again, and she wanted to turn in every marijuana dealer and fence she knew in Chicago—and, believe me, she knew plenty of them! They kept her busy fingering and testifying for a year, then the old bureau chief, Federman, he got a special waiver for her to go on salary to infiltrate a bunch of union organizers in Dallas. They got fifteen convictions there, and Nyla was on her way!"

"In a way, Ron," I offered, "it's pretty impressive that somebody like her should make it to chief agent."

"Because she's a felon? Gosh, Larry! Where do you think they get most of their recruits?"

"No, I mean because she's a woman," I said.

"Yeah," muttered Ron. "Well—" He was in a bind there, I knew, because Janie was all for "women's rights," whatever she meant by that. "Well," he said, "the thing is, whatever else she is, what she is now is part and parcel of that whole reactionary gang that's running the FBI. The same ones that framed me, years ago! The ones that're hand-in-glove with the Arabs and that whole fundamentalist bunch in Congress that—"

Dominic interrupted him then. I could have punched Dominic out for doing it, because Ron was just getting to something I really wanted to hear, but Dominic couldn't wait. "Just what I say!" he cried. "Ever since the Arabs and the Moral Might got together they've been turning the clock back! Why, do you know, at my local swimming pool they let the state police come in and raid? Any man who's caught without the top to his bathing suit can get a five-dollar fine!"

Ron darted a humorous glance at his wife. "Should've seen us a few years back in Hollywood, eh, Janie? Men *and* women topless sometimes—and sometimes a lot more than topless."

"Now, Ron," she said, blushing. "Let's just try to concentrate on Mr. DeSota's problem."

I said gratefully, "Thank you." Then I turned to Ron and put the question: "What do you think, Ron? I know this is a serious matter, even if a principle is involved. I don't want you to take any risks—"

Ron looked noble. "It's a serious matter," he declaimed, "and a principle is involved. I'll help you, Dominic."

"You will?" cried DeSota.

"Of course," said Ron benignly. "First thing, I'll write a letter to *The New York Times*. Then, let's see, what do you think, Janie? Shall we try to get a demonstration going? Get some of your friends to march in front of the FBI headquarters in Chicago?"

"If you like, Ron," she said, "although some of them are on peace bonds now. I don't know if they'll want to go to jail."

Dominic looked doubtful. "I don't know if I want anybody to go to jail for me," he said.

"Um," reflected Ron. "Then how about this? Get up a petition? Dominic can take a card table and a folding chair down to the Loop somewhere and get people to sign a demand that the FBI, uh, that they— What exactly do you want them to do?" he asked.

"Well, I don't know exactly," said Dominic. "I mean, I'm not charged with anything."

"But they interrogated you! Beat you brutally!"

"Yes, sure, but you can't blame them altogether. They did have those pictures and fingerprints."

This man was being entirely too reasonable for my taste—or for Ron's. "You're sticking up for them," said Ron. "Shows fair-mindedness. That's good—but don't carry it to any foolish extreme! They're still fascists."

Now, that was more like it. I cleared my throat. "When you say 'fascists,' Ron," I said, "you mean—"

"I mean that the FBI has turned itself into an exact copy of the Gestapo or the KGB," he declared.

"You're against them, then?"

He cocked an eyebrow at me. "Ah, Larry," he said, helping himself to the roast lamb, "I'm not just *against* them, I think it is every American's duty to *resist* them."

"You mean with demonstrations and petitions," I pressed.

"If those are enough, yes," he said bravely. "If not, then with whatever measures are necessary. I think—"

But Janie didn't want him to say what he thought. "Ron, dear," she scolded fondly, "you're keeping Seth from passing the potatoes. Why don't you take some and let him move on?"

"Of course, my love," said Ron, and the subject

was changed. It didn't matter. I was content. As soon as we'd got through the main course I discovered that it was past eleven o'clock, and began organizing DeSota for the return trip.

"Oh, no, Ron, no dessert. No, not even coffee, thanks. Dominic here has to work in the morning, you know. Yes, the dinner was lovely, and thank you! And thanks for your help, Ron . . . and if you'll just get my car out . . ."

"You haven't forgotten anything?" asked Jane hospitably, looking around for hats or briefcases.

I shook my head. "I've got everything I need," I assured her, and it was the absolute truth.

I dropped DeSota at an interurban station. He squawked resentment, because they only ran every hour or so at that time, but, as I pointed out to him, it was getting late and I couldn't be expected to give the *whole* night to saving his dumb ass. It was nearly two when I got to the compound on Lake Shore Drive. I left my car in the underground garage, flashed my pass to the guard, and got in the elevator. I was thinking about Ron. Poor old guy! Just out of touch with the modern currents of politics in America. He had some crazy, sentimental notion about Franklin D. Roosevelt or somebody—I don't know—anyway, he simply didn't understand what was going on.

The thing I always tried to keep in mind was that I could've been some kind of pinko myself, if Gramp had kept his principles when he came to America. Back in Russia he was a bank robber and a revolutionary. When it got too hot for him there he came to Ellis Island, still hanging on to some of the profits from the bank robberies, but leaving all the revolutionary ideas behind. That's how J. Douglas and Sons got started; and J. Douglas and Sons is where the money came from to put me through Yale. But suppose Gramp had had to leave the rubles behind and skedaddle out of the country with nothing but a lot of half-baked political ideas, like his buddy Lenin? And what would I have turned out to be, without those good poli-sci courses at Yale to keep me straight?

Straight as a string, I let myself into the big studio apartment on the fourteenth floor. There were no lights, but the shades on the big picture window were wide open and enough illumination seeped in from the street for me to undress and slip into the bed. I put my arm around my girl, cupping a breast, and whispered in her ear. "Nyla, sweet?"

She woke up easily and fast, as she always did. Her voice wasn't even thick as she asked, "How'd it go?"

"That," I said, bringing another hand to bear, "you can judge for yourself when you hear what I got on my wire recorder."

She turned toward me, nuzzling into my neck. "Are you going to play it for me?"

I said, "Why, yes, honey, I absolutely am. But first there's some other business I'd like to take care of, if you don't mind making a quick trip to the bathroom first. . . ."

She lay relaxed in my arms. "Not necessary," she said. "After all, I knew you were coming, so it's all taken care of in advance. . . . And I see you're ready too." And so I was. If I hadn't been when I slid under the covers, I was by now. Lacking a couple of thumbs had never been a handicap to Nyla Christophe, in bed or anywhere else.

There was a bad time in eastern Iowa. Farmers who through adversity were used to flood, drought, and legislative tinkering with their price supports woke to a new disaster. From Muscatine to the edge of the Quad Cities, twenty miles and more, the sky was covered with a green-gray, oily cloud. When the cloud settled, it blanketed three-quarters of a million acres of prime corn, soy, and mung with a carpet of locusts. Locusts! No one in Iowa had ever seen a locust swarm before! And when they rose to fly on, only stubble remained.

21 August 1983
4:50 P.M. Nicky DeSota

When you're a mortgage broker you don't have any Sundays. Sundays are the days when your customers are off work, so if you want to get the breadwinner at home with the housewife, Sunday is your best bet. It was a beautiful day, with fleecy white clouds sailing over the trees of the Mekhtab ibn Bawzi Forest Reserve and the pool sparkling at me as I drove past. No pool for me that day. No church. No sneaking off to watch the Cubs game. No anything but calculating down payments and points and the pitfalls in transferring a Torrens title; I didn't even get a chance to look at the Sunday paper until almost five o'clock that evening, and that on the interurban down to the city. I caught the 4:38 out of Elk Grove, grabbed a paper as the train began to move off, and spent ten minutes on the really important news stories—you know, the ones in the sports section, about the Cubs and the Sox and how far ahead the Brooklyn Dodgers were in the standings. With only about a month left to play, the Cubs were ten and a half games out. The situation wasn't impossible, no. But it didn't justify a lot of time spent poring over the standings, so before long I turned to the main news section.

Now, of course I hadn't forgotten that crazy drive down to Dixon. I guess I really hadn't been worried about my own position before that. Scared, yes. You can't help being scared when the FBI gets hold of you. But not *worried*, because after all I knew that I wasn't there and I had plenty of witnesses to prove it.

So, in a way, it was Ron's big hot-air promises to help me that really started me worrying. I kept waiting for the phone to ring, and, I don't know, some radio news reporter from the NBC Blue Network or somewhere to ask me what my feelings were about the demonstration in Chicago that day.

Well, there hadn't been any calls. There hadn't been any demonstrations, either, or at least none that made the first couple pages of the *Tribune*. The big news story was about President Daley coming back to Chicago to break ground for his library—that was the *Tribune* for you. (A tiny box at the bottom of the page told about renewed fighting between Lithuania and Russia, with the Russians charging aggression in the League of Nations.) There was also a story about the horribly loud roaring and screaming noises in the sky around Old Orchard Field (the Army Air Force denied any knowledge of what caused them), and all in all we were nearly into the Loop before I got to page seven and the headline that said:

FORMER MOVIE STAR ARRESTED ON
CHARGES OF SLANDERING U.S. & FBI

So old Ron was in the slammer.

Not only was old Ron in the slammer, but when I read the story more carefully the things he was accused of having said—the FBI were "fascists"; it was a citizen's duty to "resist" them—were things he had said while I was sitting right there.

There had only been four people at that table. I didn't suppose Ron had turned himself in, nor that his wife had done it; I knew I hadn't.

My mystery pal Larry Douglas had put the finger on him.

He had deliberately dragged me down there—no, even before that. He had sought me out and got me indebted to him. Then he had taken me down there for the specific purpose of getting old Ron Reagan in trouble. Why? I couldn't guess. I didn't care. The one thing I was sure of was that Larry Douglas was bad news.

I really began to worry about that; but by then it was a little too late.

The *Twentieth Century Limited* was due in at six P.M. exactly. I had left myself plenty of time to get there. But I was almost late, because as I was coming along Randolph sirens screamed up behind me and stopped, six cars blocking the street just ahead of my car. My heart was suddenly in my mouth.

It wasn't me they were after. It wasn't anyone they were after. They were just doing their duty to the rich and famous, convoying a limousine that was a football field long and with hubcaps of silver. Arab, of course, *Big* Arab. I thought for a moment it might be old Mekhtab ibn Bawzi himself, though he hardly ever came out in public any more. No, not quite, but it was his firstborn son, Faisal ibn Mekhtab. Faisal wasn't ever hard to recognize, because you never saw him in public without the egg-sized ruby he wore around his neck and the six hard-nosed bodyguards who never took their eyes off it. Not even the city cops got between the bodyguard and Faisal. What the cops were there to do was to hold us gape-eyed civilians back while Faisal, in white robes and tarboosh, minced across a scarlet carpet to enter a big new A & P supersuq. He was officially opening it. That made sense; he owned the whole chain, after all. The radio reporters, eyes respectfully averted, put a microphone in front of the august lips; camera bulbs flashed; a truckload of musicians struck up a medley of happy songs; and with golden shears, Faisal clipped the scarlet ribbon in the doorway.

It was interesting, kind of, but it took a good twenty minutes before he minced back into his

Cadillac and the whole procession evaporated as
rapidly as it had formed. So I found a place to park,
and got into the station about five minutes of the
hour, with my mind all full of rich Arabs and nasty
FBI women and treacherous Larry Douglases, and
hardly at all of my lady-love, Greta. I didn't always
meet her at the station when she came back from the
New York run, but I tried to when possible. Especially
on a Sunday, like today, when the weather was nice,
and the two of us might take a walk down along the
lakeshore, or go to the zoo. Of course, a stewardess
worked for a living, and if she'd been up all night with
cranky passengers or train-sick kids, then we'd just
jump on the interurban and I'd take her home. . . .

How peaceful those bygone days seemed! I'd had
everything I ever wanted, and hadn't known it.

In the big train room the dispatchers were busy
posting arrival and departure times. It's kind of
exciting being in Union Station, because from there
you can go almost anywhere in the world—anywhere
in America, anyway. There were trains coming in
from Los Angeles and Salt Lake City and New
Orleans and Washington, D.C., and departures for
Boston and Minneapolis and Detroit and Houston.
There were grinning redcaps wheeling bags with
fussy passengers trotting worriedly beside them, and
honeymoon couples being kissed good-bye by their
families, and vacationers dragging themselves across
the terrazzo floor with suitcases full of sandy seashells
and straw hats and damp bathing suits. Apart from
an occasional trip with Greta, and business now and
then to Pittsburgh or Milwaukee, I didn't travel
much. Maybe that's why Union Station always seemed
so exotic to me. And so—I don't know—*competent*.
You can set your watch by the trains; they take off on
the click of the minute, come in just as the clock hand
jumps to the dot.

For which reason I was astonished to see that up

on the train board, next to TWENTIETH CENTURY LIMITED, a dispatcher was putting up the word *delayed*.

I hurried to the crew lounge to see if I could find out why, half hoping that the dispatcher had made a mistake and Greta would be there waiting for me. She wasn't. No one seemed to know why, either. I caught up with another stew just as she was coming out of the women's locker room. She'd worked with Greta a time or two, but had switched to the prestigious Los Angeles *Superchief* run as soon as she'd accumulated enough seniority. She gave me a look of astonishment. "The *Twentieth Century* late? No, Nicky, that can't be; it's never late."

And she went off to make a phone call and came back looking worried. "Funny," she said. "They stopped it in the yards. Put on a new engineer."

"That doesn't sound good," I said, throat suddenly dry—had something gone wrong? An accident? An engineer who had a heart attack, or went crazy, or— There was no limit to the catastrophes my mind could invent.

But I didn't invent the right one.

I sat there for twenty minutes, waiting for something to happen, and when it did happen it was not good at all. It came in stages. Stage one was a trainman, hurrying in, looking scared. "You won't believe this," he called to a buddy as he entered. "They stopped the train in the yards. Took off the stewardesses, the conductor, the porters, the two other trainmen, the engineer, the fireman—only reason they didn't take me, I guess, is that I'm just pulling a relief shift, it's not my regular run. Clean sweep! Said something about conspiracy. . . ."

Stage two was when I recovered from all that enough to hear someone ask who "they" were . . . and heard the answer, by then not unexpected at all: "FBI."

And stage three was when I started to go out of the lounge and two neat young men fell into step beside me, one on each side, efficiently grasping my arms.

Nyla Christophe was standing at the *Official Use Only* door they took me through, her hands locked behind her, looking satisfied. She had every reason for that.

Silly me.

I had failed to see how simple this problem was from the point of view of Chief Agent Nyla Christophe. Eyewitnesses that gave me an inconvenient alibi? No problem. Just arrest the witnesses. A witness in an FBI jail, to all intents and purposes, no longer existed as a witness at all. So there was a nice, simple case to be made on the basis of photographs and fingerprints, and no need to worry about confusing details. No problem at all—for Nyla Christophe.

But for me, oh, yes! Lots of problems! And the worst of them just beginning.

The pilot of a Transcontinental and Western Airline luxury liner, coming into Chicago from the south, called Meigs Field to announce his approach. Clouds veiled the city, but he wasn't worried. Chicago didn't have any of those hundred-story buildings like New York; it had something to do with the fact that the city was built on alluvial soil, no bedrock anywhere near, so it wasn't easy to put up skyscrapers. It made things a little easier for pilots of the big trimotors . . . except that this time, as he looked up, he suddenly saw a huge tower where none should have been. He turned desperately to miss it. When he looked back, it was gone, and all thirty-eight of the rich and adventurous passengers behind him, who chose to take the plane in seven hours instead of the train in fifteen, were cursing his name.

21 August 1983
7:20 P.M. Senator Dominic DeSota

I had drowsed off on the couch, waiting for Nyla to show up from the airport. When she did get to the hotel I guess she just decided to let me sleep. I might have expected it. She always liked to get right into a quick practice session as soon as she checked in, even before she unpacked, even before she used the bathroom sometimes. "How do you get to Carnegie Hall?" she asks, and then gives the answer, "Practice, practice, practice! And when I put it off it just gets that much harder to do, Dom dear." So what woke me was the sound of the Guarnerius from the next room—one of the unaccompanied Bach chaconnes. I recognized it pretty easily. I wouldn't have, even a year or so earlier, because classical music was one of the many things that a career in politics hadn't left time for, but having a love affair with Nyla Bowquist had been educational in a lot of ways. That was only one of them.

I got up and walked into the bedroom. There she was, standing before the fireplace with her back to me, sawing away on the old fiddle with her body swaying in time. I walked up behind her and reached up under her raised arm to cup her right breast. She didn't miss a beat. Eyes closed, bow bouncing over the strings, she said, "Give me two more minutes, honey."

"And what am I supposed to do for those two minutes?" I asked her.

She sang it over her shoulder to the bars of the music:

"Order up some champagne—

"Or turn down the bedclothes—

"Or you could just start getting naked."

I kissed the back of her neck. "I'll try number three," I said. I didn't really start to undress. One of the other things I'd learned from Nyla was that it was more fun when we did it together. I went back into the living room—no, I guess you'd call it something classier than that, the salon, maybe. I knew she wouldn't be two minutes. More like a quarter of an hour. When she's on tour Nyla's always afraid she's going to forget something important—how to finger a passage, or the best way to break a three- or four-note chord. So when she practices she does it all, and it takes time. I sat back down on the huge couch and picked up the phone.

While I was dialing my office number I gazed around. I was glad I didn't have to try to put this hotel bill on my expense account. The taxpayers would never have stood for it. Neither would the IRS, if any normal human being had tried to claim that a four-room suite was a necessary business expense. But that's one of the beauty parts of being a concert violinist. Nyla always claims she needs the extra space to practice before her concerts. As a matter of fact, she more or less does. As a matter of strategy, she never gets asked that question by an IRS auditor, because her hotel suites are always engaged and paid for by the management of the concert hall where she is playing; the bill never appears on her cash flow at all.

When my office answered I asked for Jock McClenny. He recognized my voice, of course, so I just said, "I'm at the usual place, Jock. Anything urgent going on?"

"Not a thing, Senator. I'll give you a shout if anything comes up."

"Fine," I said, getting ready to hang up. I knew he'd call if necessary, and also knew that the chance was very small that anything would come up important enough for Jock to call me at Nyla's hotel. He cleared his throat in a way that stopped me. "What, Jock?" I asked.

"Just that I had this call from the Pentagon, Senator. It's peculiar. Routine call from Sandia, just checking to make sure you were there."

Sandia was a research facility in New Mexico. I sat up straighter. "Well, I'm not."

"Exactly, Senator," he said, and I could almost see him nodding earnestly, pleased that I'd got the point. And pleased, too, that the military had somehow screwed things up again, because Jock always enjoys catching the Pentagon in some kind of goof.

As a matter of fact, I enjoyed that too. I would have been pleased to explore that one a little further, but the sound of fiddling in the next room had stopped.

"Keep on top of it, Jock," I ordered. "Talk to you later."

"Right, Senator," he said—a little enviously, I thought. I didn't blame him. Nyla's a spectacularly good-looking woman, which would account for a certain amount of envy from anyone, but it also happens that Jock is a music buff. He never missed one of Nyla's performances. Sometimes, when I was in the box she'd put aside for me, I'd look down and see him along about the twentieth row, gazing at her with that look of patient adoration.

When I opened the door to the bedroom I wondered what kind of gaze he would have given her as I saw her now—shimmying her hips to slide the dress down over them, bare on top, the Guarnerius safely back in its case. She gave me a haughty look. "You've still got your clothes on," she accused.

"That's easily remedied," I said, and proved it to her with no trouble at all.

* * *

In the normal course of events there was just no way that a married man like me could be having an affair with a married woman like Nyla Christophe Bowquist. Our worlds just didn't intersect. I was a failed physicist who'd gone into law and then politics. Nyla was something special. She'd grown up wild and crazy—she said so herself—and if it hadn't been for the luck of the Juilliard School scholarship auditions she probably would have wound up in jail. Or some worse place.

Instead she wound up N*Y*L*A C*H*R*I*S*-T*O*P*H*E B*O*W*Q*U*I*S*T, with a duplex on Lake Shore Drive—and a husband in investment banking—while I've got a condo on Marine—and a wife who's into ambition. If my wife, Marilyn, had her way, I'd wind up President. If I had my own way, maybe I'd still wind up President, but I'd have a different First Lady. The funny thing is that Marilyn got us together in the first place. Didn't mean to, of course, but she was the one who thought it would be really good for my image if I let them put me on the Chicagoland Arts Council. That's where I met Nyla. We sat next to each other at a fund-raising dinner on a Wednesday, appeared together on Terkel's radio show on a Friday morning, and were in bed together Friday night. Chemistry? That's the word they use, but whatever it was it worked between us.

When we were spent and lying back against the heaped pillows, smoking that after-lovemaking cigarette that tastes the best of all, I took note of the faraway look in her eyes and asked, "What are you thinking about?"

"Us," she said.

"Me, too," I said. I stretched to reach for an ashtray, without quite letting go of her left breast, and when I had juggled it to where we could use it, I added, "I was thinking how different things might have been if we'd met a different way."

"Or at a different time," she said, nodding.

I nodded back. "Like if we'd met before you married Fred—or I married Marilyn. If the two of us had come together by chance, without either of us being married to someone else. What do you think?"

"About what, Dom?" she asked, stubbing out the last of her cigarette.

"Do you think we would have married each other?" I asked.

She lay back for a moment, poking the tip of her tongue into my ear in a friendly way. Then she said, "Of course." There wasn't really any "of course" about it, though. We didn't have that much in common, not counting what we had in bed. I don't know much about music—country and western's about as far as I go—and Nyla actively hated most of what I did in politics. And, for that matter, if we were all that gung ho to be married, there were such things as divorce courts. Neither of us had kids, neither was dependent on a mate financially, and the voters don't worry about a senator's marital history the way they used to. If remarriage after a divorce kept you out of office, Reagan would not be President now.

No, what kept us from being married was only that neither of us wanted to take the chance. That was why Nyla said "Of course" again, very positively, and then sat up. "Now I've got to start thinking about getting dressed. Join me in the shower?"

"Of course," I said, and did. "Of course" is a thing we said to each other a lot, to cover up doubts about things that weren't "of course" at all. We splashed and soaped each other happily in the shower; but not for long, because just as we had finished soaping each other's parts satisfactorily, the bathside phone began to chirp at us.

"Oh, hell," said Nyla. "No, let me get it, Dom." There was another "of course." Of course I let her get it, since it might easily have been from someone who should not know that I was answering her phone—manager, husband, reporter, fiddle fan who'd somehow managed to get the number of her suite—lover's wife, even—but we both knew it was not likely to be any of the above. It wasn't. It was who I suspected it would be, because who else would still be in the office on a Sunday evening? Nyla handed it to me, making a face; she didn't much like Jock. Or at least didn't like the fact that he knew about us. She had left the phone soapy with her soapy hands, and my own soapiness nearly made me drop it. But I managed to say, "Yes, Jock?"

Then I did in fact drop it, or barely caught it by the cord as it was heading for the bottom of the shower stall. "It's about that query from Sandia," he said. "It's from the Cathouse, Senator."

That's when I had the trouble with the phone, because the Cathouse was not usually something we talked about on an unsecured phone. "Yes?" I snapped.

"They've called back, Senator. They say they've checked fingerprints, voiceprint, I.D. picture—everything's a match. They've got this man in custody, and he says he's you. And, Senator, so do they."

A recent widow, sleeping badly in the unaccustomed emptiness of the king-sized bed, half heard and half dreamed a sound of screaming. When she was fully awake it didn't go away. Puzzled, she went to the window. There was nothing there but the quiet lawns of her condo village. She opened the windows—not easily; people in hundred-and-fifty-thousand-dollar condos seldom sought outside air—and the screams were instantly louder, with smells of rotting garbage. Was someone being raped? Murdered? But neither of those were conceivable to her, in the quiet elegance of Cabrini Gardens.

22 August 1983
2:50 A.M. Senator Dominic DeSota

There weren't that many flights from Washington to Albuquerque on a Sunday night, and none of them were nonstop. For a while I thought I'd have to call up the Air Force and get help from them. Jock finally managed to get me on TWA, leaving National at nine o'clock. It was four hours' travel time and two time zones, and luckily I was able to sleep a little between Kansas City and Albuquerque. That was the end of civilian comfort. After that it was military all the way. It didn't seem as though any of the War Department people ever slept. They picked me up outside the sleepy terminal in a staff car and raced through the deserted highways and freeways to the entrance to the Sandia base. My driver was a WAC MP lieutenant. The guards saluted her on sight. They demanded no I.D., but as we pulled away from the guard post an MP personnel carrier started up behind us. It followed us all the way across the base, past the solar-power installation, past the nuclear area, to Building A-440.

I had been in Building A-440 before. It was what we called the Cathouse. The King of the Cats was a Regular Army colonel named Martineau. We'd been fairly friendly, at one set of hearings or another, and I was a little surprised he hadn't phoned me himself. It would have been a reasonably casual and informal thing to do.

As I got out, three MP's stepped out of the personnel carrier and followed me in. I began to perceive that there was nothing casual or informal about this visit. The MP's did not march in step, and they made no attempt to surround me, much less to touch me. But they never took their eyes off me, all the way in the door and through the halls to the office of Colonel Jacob Martineau. "Colonel," I said, nodding to him.

He nodded back. "Senator," he acknowledged, and then, "May I see your papers, please?"

No, not in the least informal. Martineau went over my Illinois driver's license, my senatorial courtesy pass, and the red-tagged plastic with my fingerprints and magnetic coding on it that the War Department gives to certain nuisances like myself, who have no military rank but do have the right, sometimes, to visit classified military installations.

He didn't stop with reading the spots off each and every one of them. He put the WD card in one of those little desktop terminals they use in fancy restaurants when you want to put a two-hundred-dollar dinner check on your American Express card, and when that had checked out he still wasn't satisfied. "Senator," he said, "I'd like you to tell me where we met last. Was it at the Pentagon or here?"

I said levelly, "As you well know, Jacob, it wasn't either one. It was in Boca Raton, at the conference on speculative technology. We were both observers."

He grinned. Relaxing slightly, he pushed my wallet back to me. "You're you, I guess, Dom," he said. "The other fellow didn't remember Boca Raton."

I started to ask a question about this "other fellow," but the colonel was ahead of me. "Hold on a second, please. Sergeant! Have the prisoner brought up to the interview room, please. The senator and I will talk to him now."

He watched the sergeant leave the room before he said, "We've got troubles here, Dominic."

"Because of this fellow who says he's me?"

"He doesn't exactly say that," said the colonel, frowning. "The trouble is, he doesn't say much of anything. At first we thought he was you. Now—"

"Now you don't any more?"

The colonel hesitated. "Now," he said, "I hate to tell you what I do think, but there isn't any other good way to explain it. Senator, I think this other man is a Cat."

A farmer named Wayne Sochsteiffer woke up to the sound of the early news report on radio station WGN, yawned, stretched, plodded over to the window, wondering whether he would have to put water on the beans in the north forty. When he got to the window he yelped in surprise. The north forty wasn't there. What was there was a chain-link fence, a parking lot that looked as though it would hold a thousand cars, and a long, low building that bore the sign: NISSAN MOTORS—YOUR BEST IN QUALITY.

This Wayne Sochsteiffer was mightily surprised.

This Wayne Sochsteiffer was not nearly so surprised as a farmer named Wayne Sochsteiffer who woke up in the same way, looked out the same window, and saw only what he expected to see: his north forty, olive-green in the early morning light. His farm was there. His surprise came when he turned back to the double bed and saw, peering out at him sleepily from her side of the covers, a quite different wife.

22 August 1983
4:20 A.M. Senator Dominic DeSota

The Cathouse personnel didn't seem to notice that it was the middle of the night. The prisoner had, though. He had been sound asleep. The sergeant phoned from the detention section to say that the prisoner begged permission to void his bladder and take a shower before he came up to be interviewed. "Why not?" I said, when Colonel Martineau asked me. "I don't mind being a little considerate. Especially to me."

He opened his lips and laughed silently. It was the kind of laugh you give an incongruity, not a joke. He gave the permission and ordered up coffee, as much for ourselves as for the prisoner, and then we sat looking at each other while we waited.

There didn't seem to be much to say.

We could have chatted about this person who seemed to be me, but both of us had formed the habit of not chatting about Cats. In fact, we never even used the term except in the confines of a classified meeting. As far as I knew, the term had never appeared in writing anywhere. It was the biggest secret in America's most secret defense research facility. It was such a big secret that I hadn't for one minute believed it was true.

Sandia wasn't all secret. There was the solar-power research facility, and that wasn't secret at all; it took up more than half the thousands of sprawling acres of the base. The nuclear-weapons section wasn't exactly a secret, either—only what was going on in it was secret. The world knew that there was a flow of smart bombs and self-piloting missiles coming out of that part.

After that no one knew. Or at least, no one was supposed to know, that there were parts of Sandia a lot weirder than any of that. There was one small section devoted to climate modification as a way of cutting off an enemy's agriculture, and another exploring the possibility of genetic warfare. Genetic. The goodies they were whipping up weren't viruses or chemicals to attack the present population of a foe state. They were DNA spoilers. They were meant to make the enemy's children grow up incompetent and defeatable.

I defend myself by saying that, although this seemed immoral to me, it also seemed as though it wouldn't ever work anyway.

Then there was Psi-War. Even more doubtful, even more peculiar. Inside the Psi-War building we kept a herd that averaged eighteen or twenty wackos and loopies—as young as eight years old, as old as eighty—all very odd indeed. Each one of them claimed some special ability. There were the guys with the "out-of-body" skills; they said they could leave their own bodies and enter another's, even another's thousands of miles away, and see with the other person's eyes and hear with the other person's ears. Wonderful! They could go to an enemy base and sniff out every secret there was! Some of them said they had actually done that, although we had yet to find a secret that could be made to work for us, or that any other evidence suggested was working for anyone else.

Of this whole shebang I was a big, big skeptic. Part of the reason was simple cynicism. The loopies were *so* loopy, and besides they had a nasty little habit of cheating on the tests. Once caught cheating they were on probation; twice caught, they were out. Sooner or later, they were all out. This didn't deter the people who ran Psi-War very much, though. As soon as they decided one weirdo was a fake and sent him on his way, the talent scouts turned up another in some tanktown in Idaho or Alabama and shot him over to us to be checked out . . . and so on, and on.

The other reason I was a skeptic was not cynical at all. On the contrary. It was the opposite of cynicism; my fellow committee members charged me with almost idealism when I hinted at it.

I didn't believe we really *had* any enemies.

Oh, the Japanese and the Germans, sure. They were really tough competitors and our business community hated them as much as old Cato had hated Carthage. They really lambasted us in international trade; but did we want to go to war with them? By "enemies" I mean irreconcilable blood foes, like Adolf Hitler or Josef Stalin had been a while back. They were long gone—in fact, there was a grandson of Stalin's in the Russian diplomatic corps that I played poker with when I got a chance. Nice guy. Such mortal, military enemies simply did not exist. That wasn't so much wisdom and tolerance on our part as it was luck, of course—if the Cold War had got a few degrees hotter some years back, it could have been pretty bad. But we were saved all of that when the Russians and the Chinese escalated their border arguments into a full-scale nuclear confrontation. They stopped after a few bombs, but neither of them was a really worrisome military enemy any more. Their big problem was trying to keep from falling apart entirely.

For all of those reasons, it might seem puzzling that our Joint Committee on Weapons Research Analysis had never tried to cut off funds for even Psi-War. There were reasons for that. The big reason was that these projects were so cheap they didn't matter. Given that it was U.S. national policy to maintain a strong defense—and with President Reagan in the White House there was no doubt about that policy—

there had to be something like Sandia. If Psi-War and genetics and the Cathouse were all a total waste of money, as I rather thought they were, the amounts involved were so pitifully tiny that they simply weren't worth the trouble of defunding. Psi-War and the Cathouse together cost less per year than the upkeep on a single missile silo.

And if any of them should actually turn out to make a workable weapons system . . .

Well, the potential was simply enormous. Especially the Cathouse.

The Cathouse was named after something called Schroedinger's Cat. What was Schroedinger's cat? Well, said the physicist who was testifying before us the first time this came up, Schroedinger was a man who had discovered something called quantum mechanics. Ah, yes, and what was quantum mechanics? Well, said the physicist, basically it was a new way of looking at physics. When that explanation didn't seem quite to satisfy any of us hard-bitten politicos on the Joint Committee he tried again. Quantum mechanics, he said, got its name from Schroedinger's discovery that energy, for instance, didn't come in a sort of uniform endless flow, like water out of a tap (although, he corrected himself, even water out of a tap only *looks* uniform and endless, it being in fact made up of molecules and atoms and even smaller particles)—it didn't come in an endless flow, that was, but in unitary packets called quanta. The basic quantum of light was the photon. Well, we began to feel we might be getting to solid ground there, because even senators and congressmen had heard of photons. But then he dashed our hopes by getting back to the cat. What did the cat have to do with all this? Well, said the physicist, gamely hanging in there in the face of our expressions, that was a kind of mind experiment Schroedinger proposed. You see, there is this other thing called the Heisenberg uncertainty principle. And what was the Heisenberg uncertainty principle when it was home? Well, he said, shifting uncomfortably in the witness chair, that was a little hard to explain. . . .

He was wrong about that. It wasn't hard to explain at all. It was just hard to understand. According to Heisenberg, you could never know both the *position* and the *movement* of a particle. Either you could know where it was, or you could know where it was going. You couldn't know both.

Worse than that, there were some questions that you not only couldn't find an answer to, but there *wasn't* an answer, and that's when we got to the cat. Suppose you put a cat in a box, said Schroedinger. Suppose you put in with the cat a radioactive particle, which has exactly one chance in two of fissioning. Suppose in with the cat and the radionuclide, you put a can of poison gas with a switch that will be triggered if the particle fissions. Then you look at the outside of the box and ask yourself if the cat is alive or dead. If the particle has fissioned, it's dead. If the particle hasn't fissioned, the gas was not released and the cat is alive.

But from outside there is no knowing which is true. From outside, there is a five-tenths chance that the cat's alive.

But a cat can't be five-tenths alive.

So, said the physicist triumphantly, beaming around at us in pleasure at having made it so clear, the point is that *both* things are true. The cat's alive. The cat's dead. But each statement is true in a particular universe. At the point of decision the universes split—and now, forever after, there will be parallel universes. A cat-alive universe, and a cat-dead universe. A different universe every time a subnuclear reaction takes place that could go either way—for it goes *both* ways, and universes are multiplied endlessly.

Senator Kennedy cleared his throat at that point. "Ah, Dr. Fass," he said, "that is most interesting, as an exercise in speculation. But in the real universe we open the box and see if the cat's dead."

"No, no, Senator!" cried the physicist. "No, that's wholly wrong. They're all real."

We looked at each other. "In a mathematical sense, you mean?" Kennedy tried.

"In *every* sense," cried Fass, wagging his head violently. "Those parallel universes, created at the rate of millions every microsecond, are just as 'real' as the one I'm testifying before you in. Or, to put it in a different context, the universe we inhabit is exactly as 'imaginary' as any of them."

So we sat there like dummies, eighteen of us, congressmen and senators from all over the United States, wondering if this man was trying to put us on—wondering what it all meant if he wasn't. A congressman from New Jersey leaned over to whisper in my ear: "Do you see any military application in this, Dom?"

"Ask him, Jim," I whispered back, and when the congressman did the physicist looked astonished.

"Oh, I do beg your pardon, gentlemen," he said. "And ladies, too, I mean," he added, nodding toward Senator Byrne. "I thought all that had been made clear. Well. Suppose you want to H-bomb a city, or a military installation, or anything at all, anywhere in the world. You build your bomb. You take it into one of the parallel universes. You fly it to the latitude and longitude of Tokyo—I mean, of whatever the place is—and you push it back into our world and detonate it. *Boom.* Whatever it is, it's gone. If you have ten thousand targets—say, the entire missile capacity of another country—you just build ten thousand bombs and push them all through at once. It can't be defended against. The other people can't see it coming. Because, in their world, it *isn't* coming . . . until it's there."

And sat back, looking pleased with himself.

And we all sat back too. We looked at each other.

But I do not think any of us really were looking pleased.

Even that might not have sold the committee, except for the one big fact. I've mentioned it already: If this program didn't work, as all of us thought, and most of us hoped, it wouldn't, very little would be lost. For it, like Psi-War, was very, very cheap.

Well, they finally brought this guy in, and I have to say it was one of the most unpleasant experiences of my life. Not painful. Not intolerable. But non-pleasant, wholly without pleasure in any way.

Like most men, I really dislike shopping. Especially for clothes. And one of the principal reasons for that is that I detest those three-way mirrors they have in clothing stores. They are simply unfair. They catch you by surprise. You try on a suit; the salesperson tells you lyingly that it fits as though custom-tailored; he walks you down the store to where three mirrors are linked together, like a medieval triptych. You look into them all unaware, and the first thing you know you're staring at your own profile. I never voluntarily look at my profile. I consider the idea almost obscene. It is not the way God intended me to see myself, and the proof of that is that when I do see myself that way I look perfectly terrible. I don't even recognize that simpering fellow with the funny-shaped nose and the stick-out chin. How he got into the mirror that should have been reflecting me is always a great mystery . . . and yet I am not wholly lost to reality. I know that person is really me. I just don't *want* to know it.

That's how it was in the Cathouse at Sandia.

When they brought this person in he didn't look at me. He didn't look at anybody. They'd let him splash water on his face, at least, but then they'd handcuffed his arms behind his back. Maybe one reason he kept his eyes on the ground was fear of falling. I don't think so. I think there was only one reason, and that was that he knew if he raised them

the eyes he would be looking into would be his own.
Or *my* own. Ours.

I hated it.

It was a thousand times worse than the three-way
mirrors in the clothing stores. It was as bad as it could
be.

This other I had my face, my hair color, even my
little thinning patch on top. My everything. Almost
everything, for there were small differences—he was
maybe six or eight pounds lighter than I, and what he
was wearing was no garment I had ever owned. It was
a one-piece coverall made out of some shiny forest-
green fabric, with pockets all over the chest, and
where trouser pockets would have been if there had
been separate trousers. There were even pockets on
the sleeves and over the right thigh. Perhaps all those
pockets once had held my other self's valued posses-
sions. No more. They had been searched and rifled,
no doubt by the colonel's troops.

I made myself say, "Dominic. Look at me."

Silence. The other Dominic didn't answer, didn't
look up, didn't respond at all—though I could tell
from the stubborn way he set his head that he had
heard me clearly enough. No one else in the room
spoke, either. The colonel watched closely but was
silent; and while Colonel Martineau didn't speak
none of his men were likely to.

I tried again. "Dominic! For God's sake tell me
what's happening."

The other I kept his eyes on the floor for a while
longer. Then he looked up, but not at me. He gazed
over Martineau's head at the clock on the wall,
making some sort of calculation. Then he turned to
me and spoke. "Dominic," he said, "for God's sake, I
can't."

It was not a satisfying answer. Colonel Martineau
opened his mouth to say something, but I waved it
shut again. "Please," I said.

That other me said regretfully, "Well, Dom, old

buddy, as a matter of fact the reason I'm here is that I wanted to tell you something. By 'you,'" he explained, "I don't mean second-person-plural or even single-other-person-than-myself. I mean you-Dominic-DeSota, who is, as you know, also me."

The colonel was looking suddenly furious. It took me a different way. "Oh, Dom," I said sorrowfully to myself, "how many times I've wished to myself that I'd outgrow playing that sort of game. Spit out what you wanted to tell me, why don't you?"

"Because it's too late, Dom," he said.

"Too late for goddam *what*?"

"The thing I was going to warn you about, you know?"

"I *don't* know!"

"But you will. It's happening. And the next time we meet"—he offered a grin, but it looked more as though he were crying—"it won't be me you are meeting." He stopped there, started to speak again, hesitated, glanced at the clock—

And then he disappeared.

When I say he "disappeared" that is the exact right word, but it may give the wrong image. The other Dominic DeSota didn't "disappear" by ducking out of sight into a closet or something. Nor did he turn transparent like an actor in a TV sci-fi show. He just *disappeared*. At one instant he was there. At the next he was not.

And a pair of handcuffs, locked around no wrists at all, clattered to the floor where he had been.

Things like that simply do not happen in my life. I had no reactions preprogrammed for flagrant violations of natural law, and neither did Colonel Martineau. He looked at me. I looked at him.

Neither of us said a word about the disappearance, unless "Holy shit!" is a word. I *think* I heard that whisper from the colonel.

"Any idea what he was talking about, Colonel?" I

asked—just to make sure. "No? I thought not. Well, what do we do now?"

"Beats the hell out of me, Senator," he said. But although a commanding officer of the Army is allowed to say that, he is not allowed to mean it. He called in a sergeant and issued orders for search parties to look for my missing other self; the sergeant looked bewildered and the colonel looked resigned, because we all knew how little use that was going to be. "Do it, Sergeant," he said, and watched the noncom start off. "Well," he said to me at last, "one good thing. He said whatever it was was happening already, so we're sure to find out before long what this is all about."

"I wish I were sure that was a good thing," I said. And, as a matter of fact, when it turned out to be true, ten minutes later, it also turned out not to be a good thing in any way at all. Out of the room we went and down the hall, the colonel's little detachment of troops following in hangdog route step, wondering where they'd screwed the bird. And coming toward us was another detachment of troops, a dozen of them or so. They were in route step, too, but not the least hangdog. They were wearing combat fatigues instead of dress suntans, and they carried funny-looking, short-barreled carbines slung over their shoulders. The carbines didn't stay slung. "Hup," said a noncom when they were half a dozen yards away. The detachment stopped. The troopers sank to their knees. The carbines revolved off their straps and were aimed right at us.

An officer stepped forward from the middle of the detachment. "Holy shit," said Colonel Martineau again, and I didn't have to ask why.

The officer was wearing the same combat gear as the troops, but you could tell he was an officer because he carried a pistol instead of a carbine. There was something else I could tell about him right away, and he confirmed it when he spoke. "I'm Major

Dominic DeSota of the United States Army," he said, in a voice I knew very well, "and you are all my prisoners of war."

He said it clearly enough, but there was a strain in his voice. I knew why. The words were addressed to the colonel, but the man's eyes were stuck on me, and the expression on his face was one I knew well. It was the same expression I wore myself. I said, "Hello, me." The other guy's expression hardened. "I thought you'd disappeared," I went on. "Was that some kind of a joke?"

He jerked his head at a soldier, who stepped up behind me and grabbed my arms. Something cold and harsh bit into my wrists, behind my back, and I knew I'd been handcuffed. "I don't know what you mean about disappearing," the other me said, "but there's no joke. You're all in protective custody."

"For what?" demanded the colonel, accepting handcuffs of his own.

"Just while we straighten things out with your government," the "I" assured us. "We have to explain to them what they're going to do, and you're prisoners until they agree. That's your best option, see? If you don't like it, you do have one other choice. You can offer resistance. Then you won't be prisoners any more, just dead."

A combo driver, hunched high in the cab of his big John Deere, drove slowly down the rows of early beans, thinking of nothing more serious than a cold beer and the Sox game he was missing on TV, when he heard from behind him the zap-zap-zap of high-speed cars passing and the rrrrawr-rrrrawr of sixteen-wheel semis. Out of the corner of his eye he saw a huge diesel bearing down on him. Frantically he wrenched the wheel of the combo. He spoiled a dozen rows, but when he looked back there was nothing there.

23 August 1983
9:10 P.M. Mrs. Nyla Christophe Bowquist

It was really disappointing to be in Dom's hometown without Dom there, but I kept busy. There's always plenty to do getting ready for a concert. There are press interviews. There are cocktails before the performance, mixing with the heavy donors to the National Symphony. Most of all, there are rehearsals. Ten minutes of rehearsal with the orchestra uses up an hour of my time—worrying about it beforehand, trying to remember all the cuts and tempi and intonations we'd agreed on afterward. One would think that rehearsing with Mstislav Rostropovich ought to be easier than most, because Slavi started out as a cellist himself. Not a bit of it. He is an endless fusser. He can drive you crazy fidgeting over the dynamics for one oboe, or the exact number of microseconds a note should be syncopated. I don't mean that I don't like working with him. He has a wonderful sense of humor, for instance. In fact, I love the man.

I'll give you an idea of the kind of gentle joke I get from Slavi Rostropovich. When I'd signed and returned the contract for this performance, his concertmaster called up and said, "Slavi says you can have a choice, Nyla. The Sibelius or the Mendelssohn, which?" I couldn't help giggling.

It was the kind of joke that you have to have been around for a while to laugh at. It had a history. The previous time I played the National Symphony a newspaper feature writer caught me off guard. I guess I was tired. Anyway, I told him what violinists don't often talk about, but what every fiddle player since Paganini has known. There are concerti that are crowd-pleasers because they sound a lot harder to play than they are—like the Mendelssohn—and concerti that are tests of skill because they are a lot harder than they sound—like the Sibelius. So I told this woman that when I wanted to win cheap bravos from an unsophisticated audience I'd play the Mendelssohn, and if I wanted to show off for my colleagues, I'd do the Sibelius.

"Tell Slavi I'd rather do the Mendelssohn," I said to the concertmaster, grinning into the phone. Because, after all, I knew that it wouldn't be either. Sure enough, two days later I got a bunch of flowers with a note in Elena Rostropovich's handwriting that said:

"Not only talented—not only beautiful—but also very sensible! Slavi sends his admiring compliments and asks that what you really play is the Gershwin, since the President will be there."

I wired back that I would be delighted. I was. The Gershwin is one of the greats, as well as being the only violin concerto composed by an American fit to call pigs with. Anyway, I knew that President Reagan wasn't going to want to hear some foreigner's stuff.

Elena Rostropovich was a sweet lady, although I didn't always know what she was thinking. I didn't really know, for instance, if she knew about Dom and me. We were very careful to avoid gossip. Still, she never said a word to me, not even a wink. But when I got an invitation to a late dinner after a concert, I knew that an identical one went to Dominic's home in Virginia. Mine was always for Mr. and Mrs. Bowquist. Dom's was always for Senator and Mrs. DeSota. It didn't matter if our mates were back in Chicago, as Ferdie was almost always and Marilyn DeSota more often than not. So Dom would spend the night before in my hotel suite. We'd both put in a full day's work on the day of the concert, and at eleven o'clock that night we would "discover" each other, with expressions of cordial surprise, at Elena's party. Then she would suggest that, since we were both unattached for the evening, Dom take me home.

Which he unfailingly did.

Those evenings were the best kind of time Dom and I had. We were actually able to appear in public together. Then, later on, when we were in private, there was very little chance of either one of us being caught out by our mates. Anything we did like that in Chicago was pretty risky. There was always the chance of somebody one of us knew accidentally turning up at the wrong time—in a hotel lobby, or an elevator, or the restaurant where we met. Other cities, not much better. Sometimes by good fortune Dom could invent a reason to fly up to Boston or New York or wherever I was on the road, but we were always squeezed for time. No. Washington was the best . . . anyway, the best that I could see any way of our ever having.

Even that wasn't perfect. We knew people in Washington too. Sooner or later, either Ferdie or Marilyn was going to hear a hint, or feel a suspicion. From that moment on it would be only a matter of time. Private detectives? Maybe. Why not? Betrayed spouses don't necessarily play fair.

And then the whole thing would come crashing down on our heads, and what would happen after that would be really nasty. . . .

But, please, God, not yet awhile. "Not ever," said Dom firmly, pulling on his socks at two o'clock one morning, when I had just said that to him.

"It has to happen sooner or later, darling," I said reasonably.

"It does not. We don't have to get caught." He paused in putting on his pants to bend to kiss my navel. "We can go on like this forever. Even if we did get caught—"

I headed off what he was going to say next. Or

tried to. "President Reagan is going to be at the concert," I told him.

"Yes? What about it? Oh," he said, nodding wisely as he zipped his fly. "I see the connection. You mean you wouldn't want to shock the President, right? But if we don't get caught, she won't be shocked, will she? And even if we do, there's always the alternative of—"

"No, there isn't," I said, before he could finish the sentence with "getting married." Because that was the one subject I refused to discuss, ever, with Senator Dominic DeSota. I could stand being unfaithful to a man who loved me. I couldn't stand the idea of throwing him out of my life, in public humiliation.

So I wasn't altogether sorry when Dom had to go off to New Mexico, because he'd been getting more and more insistent about that, and I was running out of easy ways to fend the idea off. And on the night of the concert, as I opened the concerto in that fast, syncopated "allegro *hot*" first movement, his seat in the third row center was empty.

What happened next was totally unexpected, and to explain what was going on I have to explain about the concerto.

Gershwin died young. He'd only begun composing violin music of any kind a couple of years before the taxi caught him crossing Fifty-second Street. Then, out of almost no experience, he produced this *wonder*. It was all his own too. In the early days Gershwin had had to hire Ferde Grofe to do his orchestrations for him, but by the time of the violin concerto he had mastered the art. The woodwinds and percussion were as much idiosyncratically his very own as those heart-melting violin themes.

It had something else to it that I liked, a trick he'd borrowed from Mendelssohn. Mendelssohn didn't want to take the chance that some dummy in the audience would think the pause after the first movement meant the whole concerto was over, and so start to clap. That's not awful in itself, but what makes it troublesome is that then half the audience is flustered because they applauded in the wrong place, and the other half is irritated because those dummies have held up the performance. So Mendelssohn doesn't let anybody make that mistake. There is a sustained note left over from the first movement that continues right into the opening of the second. There is never that moment of silence when the audience fidgets, and the men who are there because their wives insisted on it are looking nervously at their neighbors to see what's expected of them, and up on the stage you hear the rustle and the whispers and the muffled coughs. I've often wished that Tchaikovsky and Bruch and Beethoven had been that thoughtful, and I've been grateful that Mendelssohn and Gershwin had.

Funny, though. This time the soft, almost subliminal tattoo of the drums did not keep the audience from stirring. I saw an usherette lean past Dominic's empty seat to whisper in Senator Kennedy's ear. Slavi was already raising his baton for the start of the second movement, but that didn't keep Jack Kennedy from rising and slinking away up the aisle. As I counted bars to the beginning of my own part, I saw Jackie give me a smile and a tiny, spread-hands shrug of apology. With almost any other Senate wife I would have known that was just convention, but I knew that in Jackie's case she was personally contrite. She was the cultured one in the gallery of Senate wives. She would have made a fine First Lady, I always thought, if her husband hadn't been short-counted in Chicago in 1960.

The disturbance didn't end there.

With help from people like Jackie and Slavi Rostropovich—and, of course, from Dom—I had turned out to be pretty much Washington's favorite society fiddler. So the audience was what they call "social." Meaning, in Washington, governmental—diplomats, legislators, top people from the administration. Even President Nancy was there in her box, with her First Gentleman sitting as always urbane and self-assured beside her. That kind of an audience had special problems. The worst of them was that if something went terribly sour somewhere in the world, half the audience would have to be told about it at once.

It had. They were.

By the middle of the slow movement there were gap-toothed empty seats in every part of the house. When I finished my tricky, and beautiful, crescendo in the third, the applause was lean. It wasn't lack of enthusiasm, I thought. It was lack of people. Slavi looked at me. I looked at Slavi. We both shrugged in baffled resignation.

For decency's sake we took two bows. Then we retired from the stage and didn't come back, giving the audience a chance to escape—as many of them were anxious to do.

As curiosity made many of us on the stage eager to do.

It was worse for Slavi than for me. I was through for the evening and glad of it, while he would have to come back after the intermission to do the second half of the program. It was Mahler, and both of us knew there would not be much of a crowd to sit through that interminable First Symphony.

When we found out what was happening that became a certainty.

The first one to get to us to tell us was my dresser, Amy. Amy doesn't really "dress" me, although I'm sure she would if she had to. What she does is take care of me. She keeps an eye on the Guarnerius when I put it down for a moment; she makes sure I have a dress without stains or wrinkles to wear for the concert, and another for the usual party afterward; she sees that there are always tampons in the side pocket of my music bag. She does all that, and one big other thing. She keeps my husband from getting suspicious when I'm off somewhere with Dom.

She also tells me what I need to know, even if I'm not going to like it. *Especially* if I'm not going to like it. Of all the shocked, scared, and worried expressions backstage that night, hers was the most upset; but she pushed through the muttering, whispering stage-hands and musicians to get to us. "Nyla," she wailed, "Albuquerque's gone crazy!"

Albuquerque was, of course, where the Sandia base was. Where Dominic was. I stopped short. My knees went weak. From behind me Slavi caught one arm. Amy caught the violin and then the other arm, in that order.

"And Dom?" I croaked.

"Oh, Nyla," Amy said, sobbing, "he's the worst of the lot!"

A man named Dominic DeSota, sweating as he moved through the reeds around the old water-detention pond, raised his head from his work. He thought he saw a sudden glow of orange light in the sky toward the southeast, in the place where Chicago had once been. It wasn't an illusion. It was a real burnishing of the low clouds, as though there were a huge, distant fire. He stood up straight, peering. What were those lights off on the horizon? There were streams of white, streams of red, the white lights coming toward him and the reds away. It was almost as though there were cars again! But they disappeared in the wink of an eye and he was alone in the sultry night. He returned to the job of emptying the last trap on his line, where what had once been someone's pet angora hissed and spat. It was no longer sleek, fat, and pretty, but DeSota was glad to see it. It was dinner.

23 August 1983
10:20 P.M. Major DeSOTA, Dominic P.

It was just the purest chance that the first prisoner I took was myself.

I would have seen me sooner or later, of course. We knew I was there. Maybe "I"—that "I" who was now my prisoner—did "me"—the me who nailed him—a favor, because one of the reasons I got command of the first assault detachment through the portal was that Senator Dominic DeSota was there. (Senator! How had that happened? How had I risen so high in his timeline, and only to the damn dumb rank of field officer, and reserve at that, in my own? But that other DeSota's position was going to help me elevate mine. . . .)

"They're ready, sir," said Sergeant Sambok.

"Good-oh," I told her, and followed her back upstairs to the office of the chief scientist. I didn't have time to think about the grammatical games we were learning to play—the "I" that watched "me" through the peepers, the "them" that were "us." I didn't have time to wonder at what I'd wondered at a time or two before, either—namely, at the curious coincidences between that Dom DeSota's life and my own. Our lives were different in tremendous ways. But both of us had wound up involved in the parallel-time situation—and not, of course, just "both" of us, because there were all those other Dominic DeSotas in all the other times. The tech advisors had no time for such questions. I knew that was so, because I'd asked them. All they would say, not counting mathematics, was mumble-mumble, after all, we Dominic DeSotas had genes in common; had boyhoods in common, anyway up to whenever the point of separation was; we'd read the same books and seen the same movies. So naturally we set into similar molds. . . .

"Right in here, sir," said the sergeant, and I walked through the door she held open for me into the office of the operating head of the Cathouse, as these people had amusingly named their parallel-time project.

The Signal Corps lieutenant said, "You're on in thirty seconds, Major."

"Right," I said, and sat down at the desk. It was clean—the chief scientist was one of those security-conscious guys, no doubt. The only thing on it was the Signal Corps microphone with the wires that led to the backpack transmitter on the lieutenant's helper. I tested the drawers. Locked, but we'd take care of that in a minute.

"Break a leg, sir," said Sergeant Sambok, grinning at me through her camouflage makeup, and I was on.

"Ladies and gentlemen," I said into the microphone, "this is Dominic DeSota. Urgent circumstances have led to the necessity for a precautionary action at Sandia Base and nearby. There is nothing for you to fear. In one hour we will make a television broadcast through the local stations. All networks are urged to carry it live, and at that time the necessity for this action will be made clear."

I looked at the lieutenant, who drew his finger across his throat. The corporal with the backpack moved a switch, and I was off the air.

"See you later, Major," the lieutenant said, and followed his crew out of the room.

I leaned back, testing the leather chair. These people did themselves well; there were paintings on the wall and carpeting on the floor. "How'd it go, Nyla?" I asked.

She grinned. "Really well, Major. If you ever get out of soldiering, you ought to get into radio."

"I'm too big to fit into those little-bitty sets," I told her. "Have you notified Tac-Five this building is secure?"

"Yes, sir. Tac-Five says, 'Well done, Major De-Sota.' The follow-on echelons have taken the next six buildings too. The whole area is secure."

"The prisoners?"

"We set up a stockade in the parking lot. Corporal Harris and three men are guarding them."

"Fine, fine," I said, pulling at the locked drawers again. I'd taken over the chief scientist's office, but unfortunately the chief scientist had been off the base at the moment. He had taken his keys with him. An annoyance, not a problem. "Open this up for me, Sergeant," I said, and Sergeant Sambok studied the locks for a moment, gauged the angle of possible ricochets, then placed the muzzle of her carbine a few inches from the lock. As she shot it out, .25 caliber bullets whined across the office.

The drawers opened with no further trouble. Inside was the usual mess of disorderly stuff you find in a neat man's desk, but among the mess were a couple of notebooks and a whole drawer of files. Of course, we'd watched these people pretty closely for months before we opened the portal, but Dr. Douglas would want to look the papers over. "Orderly," I said. Sergeant Sambok nodded, and a private popped in from the hallway. "Take this stuff back to the sally port," I ordered, juggling a slim, expensive-looking gold cigarette lighter engraved *Harrah's Club, Lake Tahoe*. It would have made a fine souvenir, but I put it back and slammed the drawer shut.

After all, we weren't thieves.

Sergeant Sambok was standing by the door, and something about the look on her face made me ask, "What else, Sergeant?"

"Private Dormeyer is AWOL," she said.

"Shit." Her look expressed concurrence with my opinion. "There's no AWOL under combat conditions. If the MP's get him, they'll call it desertion." More concurrence. "Damn it, Sergeant, somebody's got to know where he's gone! Find him. I want to keep this in the company."

"Yes, sir. I'll take care of it myself."

"Yes, you will," I told her. "Take ten minutes to find out where he is. Then meet me at the sally point."

My assault party was the first one through, but we'd attained our objectives. There were three hundred more troops on the base now—ours, I mean, not counting the ones we were taking prisoner—and I had nothing to do any more until it was time for the television broadcast. That wouldn't happen until the TV station in Albuquerque was secure, so that we could get it on the network. I headed down for the sally point in the basement of the building. Once it had been a pistol range, but when our peepers found it, it wasn't used for much of anything.

That made it perfect for us. We got our whole party across before anyone knew we were there.

Sandia was an old military base, in our time as well as theirs. The difference was that in our time it had stayed small. In theirs it had grown immense. There were square miles of desert and hill inside its barbed-wire boundaries.

There were not, however, very many of their troops actually deployed anywhere on the base. The perimeter was guarded more by electrons than by men, with a post only every quarter mile or so along the fence. Of course, that must have seemed like plenty of protection to the base commandant. Outside of a paratroop drop, which would have given plenty of radar warning, there was no way any sizable number of enemies could get up to the wire without being detected in plenty of time to summon reinforcements . . . unless, like us, they came from inside. When I got to the sally port there was already a map of the base tacked up on the wall, with the secured points in red crayon. The key parts had been the Cathouse and its immediate neighbors, the MP barracks, the headquarters, the signals exchange, and the radio station. We now owned them all. The few troops who had thought they were guarding them now realized how badly they had failed, in our stockade.

Troops were still coming in. They weren't needed, but it did no harm to have them—what if the previous occupants, against all logic, decided to fight? Bright floodlights racked along the wall showed the column of twos emerging from nothingness. They broke step, marched to a wall, fell out, were assembled again by their officers and noncoms, and marched off to reinforce the troops already in place.

It was a weird sight. If you positioned yourself right next to the sally portal, in the same plane as the plane of the portal itself, it was even weirder. Toes, feet, legs, fists, bellies, heads appeared in that order. If you got *behind* the portal plane, you could see— what would you guess? Raw meat and guts? The insides of those transported soldiers? Nothing of the kind. You couldn't see anything at all. Because from behind, the whole rectangle of the sally portal was featureless, lightless, unrelieved black. From in front there was nothing much, either. Just the troops emerging from the portal, and behind them the dusty walls of the old pistol range.

"Major?" It was Sergeant Sambok again. She looked around and lowered her voice to say, "I think I know where Dormeyer went."

"Good work, Sergeant," I said.

She shook her head. "He's off the base. He sneaked out somehow. He's gone into Albuquerque. The thing is, he lived—he lives here. In Albuquerque, I mean."

Not so good. But it wasn't her fault. "You did right," I said, and indeed she had. For a reservist, Nyla Sambok was a first-rate soldier. The funny thing was that she'd been a music teacher in civilian life, married to a harpsichord player. They'd both got their scholarships by joining the Reserve and they'd both been activated in the call-up; a lot of reservists were bitter, but Sambok was good enough and soldier enough that I'd requested her to come down with me from Chicago to take over this detachment. The fact that she was a great-looking woman didn't hurt any, either. But I've never messed around with the enlisted personnel. Only thought of it, now and then.

"Tac-Five will be on the horn for you in about two minutes," she went on. "I got the word as I was coming in."

"Fine," I said, "but I've got an idea. Go down to the stockade and bring back Senator DeSota's clothes for me."

Even Sergeant Sambok could look surprised. "His clothes?"

"What I said, Sergeant. You can leave him his underwear, but I want all the rest. Even the socks."

A quick flash of comprehension crossed her face. "Right, Major," she said, grinning, and was gone, leaving me to wait for Tac-Five's call.

Two-way communication across the skin that separates parallel times is harder than one. They had to shut down the portal and collapse the field to get the energy, but when the portal officer nodded I picked up the phone and General Magruder didn't keep me waiting. "Well done, Major," he barked. "The President says the same. He's been following this very closely, of course."

"Thank you, sir."

"Now we go to Phase Two. Are you ready for your television broadcast?"

"Yes, sir." Meaning that I wasn't, actually, but I

would be as soon as Nyla Sambok got back with the clothes.

"The TV station and the microwave links are secure; they'll have the circuits open in half an hour. They've already got the President's tape ready to go, as soon as you do the introduction."

"Yes, sir."

"Good." Then his tone changed. "One other thing, Major. Any sign of rebound?"

"Nothing new, sir. I think we're still interviewing the locals, though."

"Um. Any more unwelcome visitors?"

"No sign of any, sir."

"Keep your eyes open," he said harshly, and hung up. I recognized the tone. It was the voice of fear.

Half an hour later, walking over to the base's television studio in the hot desert night, with the same stars blazing overhead that blazed over my own America, I was feeling some of that fear myself. An MP jeep patrol cruised past, headlights swiveling from side to side. They paused long enough to take a good look at me and my assault-force armband, then picked up speed and moved on. They didn't challenge me. They didn't ask for I.D.

I could have been one of those unwelcome visitors. I could have been that other me who seemed to have been everywhere. And, if I had been, all I would have had to do was get a scrap of green cloth to pin around my sleeve and they would never have known the difference. And then—

And then what would that other me have done?

That was the scary question. So far they had watched and pried. But they had done nothing at all.

I couldn't really blame the MP's for sloppy security, because they obviously didn't see the need for being tight. We had taken over the base without a shot being fired, against opposition that consisted mostly of sleepy-eyed sentries being struck dumb with astonishment when our troops pulled them in. What a way to run America! I wondered what it would be like to live in a country where important bases were guarded by only a handful of Regular Army troops, where there had been no draft or call-up of reserves. If I'd been left to finish my postgraduate courses at Loyola instead of being activated into the reserve, what would I be by now?

A senator, maybe?

It was not the kind of speculation that I could afford to get into, while I still had an important part of my job to finish.

Sergeant Sambok was waiting for me at the studio with Senator DeSota's clothes, as promised. I found a dressing room and slid out of my coveralls. He dressed himself well, that other Dom DeSota; shirt, tie, socks, shoes, pants, sports jacket—everything was good cloth or good leather. The cut was peculiar—his fashions were not the same as ours—but I liked the feel of the silky shirt and the soft, crisp-creased slacks. They could have fit a little better. The other Dom was a good size fatter than I, which was a satisfaction, even if it did spoil the cut of the clothes a little.

When I came out of the dressing room the sergeant wasn't critical. "Looking sharp, Major," she complimented.

"What did you leave him in?" I asked, peering at myself in the mirror, and when she grinned I knew the answer. He wouldn't get cold in that August heat in his underwear, but still. . . . "Take him my spare fatigues," I ordered. "They're in my B-4 bag." Fortunately for him, I liked my fatigues a little loose, so he could undoubtedly get into them.

"Yes, sir," said Sergeant Sambok. "Sir?"

"What is it?"

"Well . . . if you're going to wear his clothes and he's going to wear yours, wouldn't that be a little confusing? I mean, suppose he got to you and knocked you out and changed clothes. How would I know which was which?"

I started to open my mouth to tell her she was a fool. Then I closed it again. She was right. "Good thinking," I said. "Tell you what. I'll be the one who knows your full name, okay?"

"Yes, sir. Anyway, as long as he's in the stockade and you're not . . ."

"That's right," I agreed, but then I felt what I'd been unwilling to let myself feel for the last couple of hours.

I wanted to confront this other self of mine. I wanted to sit and talk to him, hear his voice, find out where our lives had been the same and where they differed. It was an itchy, quivery sort of thought, like getting ready for the first time you do dope, or the first sex; but I wanted it.

I didn't have time to think about it just then, because I was on. The cameramen gaped at my snappy civilian clothes, the signals captain grinned openly, but it was time for my television debut, ready or not.

More not than ready. They've always got to swing a mike into position or switch a camera or send somebody out into the hall to stop somebody else's chattering, but in a moment the corporal who was acting as director cried, "Stand by, sir!" He listened to his headphones for a moment, and then began to count. "Ten . . . nine . . . eight . . . seven . . . six . . . five . . . four . . . three . . ." For the last counts he used his fingers, two fingers, one finger, then the single finger stabbed at me and the green light over the camera went on and the prepared speech began to roll.

"Ladies and gentlemen," I said into the camera, "I am Dominic DeSota." That was no lie; I was. I didn't say I was *Senator* DeSota, though the fact that I was now wearing his clothes might have carried that implication. There wasn't much more to my speech: "An emergency has required this action to take place. I ask that every American listen to this broadcast with an open mind, and with the generous heart of all we Americans. Ladies and gentlemen, I give you the President of the United States."

And the photons of my face and neck and that other Dominic's suit and tie and shirt went flocking into the camera and came out as electrons; as electrons snaked through the cables of the base studio to the microwave dish on the roof, were reconverted to photons of a different frequency, and, as radio signals, were hurled across the valley to the transmitter towers of KABQ, bounced up into the air and through it, to a satellite thousands of miles away in space and showered down on the television sets of the United States. *This* United States. And what they would make of it, and of the President who was not their President, I could only wonder.

The whole Signal Corps detachment was in uniform, but there was still a lot of civilian in their blood. Reservists, called up for the emergency, they were almost all veterans of the networks. They'd arranged themselves some civilian comforts. There was a pot of coffee brewing in the lounge outside the studio, and a plate of packaged cakes and junk foods—someone had liberated the local PX.

I poured myself a cup, listening to President Brown's voice coming over the monitors: ". . . as the President of the United States, speaking to you who are also the President of the United States, and to the American people . . ." He looked nervous but well rehearsed as he read the lines written for him. ". . . at this point in our history we are confronted with a terrible despotism out to conquer the world . . ." and ". . . the ties of blood and common devotion to the principles of freedom and democracy . . ." and on and on. It was a pretty good speech;

I'd seen the text beforehand. But the important thing wasn't anything in his speech. It was the fact that we were in control.

The same voice was coming from a control room just down the hall, door open. I carried my cup down to peer inside. There they had not one but a dozen monitors, almost all of them showing the President's earnest face, saying the same things. But there were also a couple of screens that showed other faces, looking serious and even more earnest: John Chancellor, Walter Cronkite, a couple I didn't recognize. They were doing commentary already. That was a surprise, until I remembered that the President's speech was only four minutes long. It had played once and was being rerun by the stations that had been caught off guard and didn't have an instant response ready; the others were already reacting.

I looked at my watch. Midnight local time. It would be two A.M. in the big cities of the East Coast, but I doubted very many of the population would be sleeping. And in California the citizens would be tuning in for their late-night news and getting a kind of news they hadn't expected.

Served them right. Why should they be fat and happy when we were facing the terrible struggle for the freedom of the world?

Even a commander of assault troops has to sleep sometime. I got nearly five hours. When I woke up it was with the smell of bacon and coffee. I was in the chief scientist's office, making use of the chief scientist's eight-foot couch, and Corporal Harris was setting a tray down next to my head. "Sergeant Sambok's compliments, sir." He grinned. "We occupied the officers' club last night."

The eggs were nearly cold, because they'd been carried, but the coffee was hot and strong. It was just what I needed to get me going.

First stop was the studio again. The soldier-technicians had been joined by three civilians, an old woman, a young woman, and a bearded man of no particular age. I stopped the Signal Corps captain, jerked a thumb at the civilians clustered in front of the monitors, and raised an eyebrow. "Them?" he said. "Them's scientists, Major. Anyway, that's what they say they are, and their orders are okay."

"Doing what?"

He shrugged. "Monitoring responses to the President's message, they say. It's some kind of political-science study, you know?" I didn't know. "Anyway," he said sourly, "there's damn little to study, because there hasn't been diddly-shit coming out of this President they got here."

That wasn't the kind of news I wanted to hear. "You could check with Tac-Five," he added as an afterthought, but I was already on my way back to the Cathouse. The base was nice and calm in the hot desert morning. I wasn't. Dry as the air was, I was sweating into my second-day's-wearing fatigues (maybe I shouldn't have been so generous with my spares!), and beginning to feel worried.

General Ratface Magruder was where you'd expect a general to be at seven o'clock in the morning, namely asleep, but I got Colonel Harlech. He was not a friendly soul. When I asked him about the civilians, he pruned me back to the trunk in half a dozen words. "They're authorized and none of your business, Major," he snapped. "What's the status of your base?"

"All secure, sir." Hoping it was so, because actually I hadn't checked out my own troops. "Still no sign of rebound here."

"Unwanted visitors?"

"Nothing reported, sir." At least not to me. "Sir? May I ask about Dr. Douglas?"

Rusty chuckle. "He's in his tent under guard and scared shitless. What's the current status on enemy signal interceptions?"

He meant listening in on radio and TV. "No clear pattern, sir. They do keep repeating the President's broadcast. He comes through loud and clear."

Colonel Harlech didn't actually say *shit*. He just made a noise close enough to be clear, muffled enough to be deniable. Harlech was one of Magruder's own hotshot warriors, and everybody knew what they thought of the President. Who had opposed a preemptive strike vigorously . . . until the chiefs of staff let him know they had plenty of military prisons for politicians who got in the way of what they considered the essential defense of the United States.

When I got off the cross-time phone with the colonel I debated going back to the studio for a word with the poli-scientists. It would be interesting to hear their theories about why a militarily active U.S. society like ours got a jelly-backed President like Jerry Brown, while this other one, fat and peaceful, had elected the fire-breather, Reagan. But I was a soldier, not a scholar; and there were things I was more curious about than that. I yelled for an orderly, and when Corporal Harris stuck his head in the door, I ordered him to go down to the stockade and bring back the prisoner, Senator Dominic DeSota.

He sat there in my fatigues, looking so much like me that it was embarrassing. I couldn't take my eyes off him, and he was studying me just as hard. He wasn't scared. At least he didn't look that way. What he looked was partly resentful and mostly interested—a quality I have always admired in myself. "You're a ballsy guy, Dominic," I told him. "Tell me. How's this thing going to go?"

He stretched thoughtfully before he answered; he'd been sleeping, too, and on something not as comfortable as the chief scientist's couch, no doubt. "You mean how is President Reagan going to respond to armed invasion?" he asked.

"That's the hard-nosed way to look at it."

"It's a hard-nosed thing to do, Dominic. What do you hope to gain from this?"

"Peace," I said, grinning. "Victory. The triumph of democracy over tyranny. I don't mean *your* tyranny, of course. I'm talking about our mutual enemy, the Russians."

He said patiently, "Dom, I don't have any Russian enemies. The Russians just don't signify in the world—my world. They would have starved if we hadn't fed them after their shoot-up with China."

"You should've let them starve!"

He sighed, disliking me. "So you come along and invade us. Without warning." He shrugged. "You tell me how it's going to go. You're making the play."

"It's going to go our way, Dom." I said and grinned. "The sooner you guys understand that, the easier it's going to be for you." He didn't answer that. I wouldn't have, either. I tried being friendly. "It's our country, whichever side of the barrier we're on," I said persuasively. "You ought to cooperate, because we have the same basic interest, the good of the United States of America. Right?"

"I sure as hell doubt that, Dom," he said.

"Aw, Dom, come on. You might as well take my word for that because, after all, you don't have much to say about it, do you? We've got you by the ying-yang . . . speaking of which," I added, "how's your prostate?"

That surprised him. "What are you talking about? I'm too young to have prostate trouble."

"Yeah," I said. "That's what I thought when they told me. Better have it checked."

He shook his head. "DeSota," he said, looking a lot braver and more determined than I thought I might have in his place—pleasing me, because that made me think maybe I would have—"let's cut out the bullshit. You invaded us without warning, and that's a pretty dirty thing to do. Why did you do it?"

I smiled. "Because it was there. Don't you know

how these things go? We had a problem, and we saw a technological solution. When you get the technology you use it, and we got the technology." I didn't bring up the question of how we got it, which after all was not very relevant. "See, old buddy, you're faced with what we call a nonnegotiable situation. Our President tells your President what we want to do. You let us do it. Then we go away again and that's the end of it."

He gave me a searing look. "You don't believe that, do you?" he asked.

I shrugged. We knew each other well enough to know that neither of us would believe it. I hadn't thought beyond the objective of the exercise—officially—but I knew as well as I do that once we had used their time-line to take care of the major enemies in our own, we would not very likely go away. There would always be other little jobs we could use them for.

But that was too far in the future for me to worry about—though I could see why that other me would worry, a lot. I said, "Get back to the question. Will your President listen to ours without a struggle? In my time the Reagans and Jerry Brown weren't exactly buddies."

"What's that got to do with it? She'll do what she has to do. She's sworn an oath to protect and defend the United States—"

"Yeah, but which one?" I asked. "Our President swore the same oath, and he's carrying it out." Reluctantly—being a wimp; but I didn't say that. "And the best way for old Nancy to protect you folks would be to let us do what we want. Do you have any idea of what the alternative is? We have all the muscle! You want us to push some anthrax into the White House? Smallpox-B into Times Square?" I laughed at his expression. "What's the matter, did you think we were just talking hydrogen bombs? We wouldn't want to mess up a lot of good real estate."

"But biological weapons are—" He stopped,

thinking. He'd been going to say that they were against international law or something.

I explained, "After Salt II we had to do something. We pretty much gave up nukes. So we worked on other things."

"What's 'Salt II'?" he asked; then, immediately, "No, the hell with that, I don't want history lessons from you. All I want from you is for all of you to go the hell back where you came from and leave us alone, and I doubt you'll do that. If it interests you, you make me want to puke."

What a feisty little devil he was! He made me almost proud . . . but also mad. "Bullshit, Dom!" I yelled. "You would have done the same thing! You were getting ready to, one way or another—otherwise why were you working on this Cathouse project?"

"Because—" he began, and stopped. His expression was a good enough answer. He changed the subject. "Have you got a cigarette?" he asked.

"Gave it up," I said with satisfaction.

He nodded, thinking. "I really didn't believe it would work," he said slowly.

"But you were in there trying, boy, weren't you? So what's the difference? We're not doing anything you wouldn't have done if you'd finished your research ahead of us."

"That's—that's doubtful," he said. Honest of him. He hadn't said, "That's untrue."

"So will you help talk your President into it?" I pushed.

No hesitation this time. "No."

"Not even to save a lot of lives, maybe?"

He said, "Not even for that. No surrender, Dom. . . . And I'm not sure I would want to buy a few American lives with a few million Russians, either."

I looked at him in amazement. Was it possible that I—in any incarnation—could be such a soft-headed fool? But he wasn't looking softheaded. He leaned back in his chair, studying me, and suddenly he seemed taller and more sure of himself. "So what's the thing that scares you, Dominic?" he asked.

"What do you mean?" I sparred.

He said, reasoning it out, "Sounds to me like you've got a worry you're not telling me about. Maybe I can't guess what that is. On the other hand, maybe I can. The reason I came down here was because there was another one of us snooping around. He seemed to know what you were going to do. If I were you, I think I'd be real worried about him. Why? Who is he? What's going on?"

I should have known that it was hard to keep secrets from myself. I was never a dummy, not even in this senator incarnation. He'd twigged to the thing that was most on my mind—or one of them.

I said slowly, "He's from another parallel time, Dom."

"I guessed that much," he said impatiently. "Did he visit you before?"

"No. Not exactly. Not him." I didn't want to tell him any more about the visitor we had had—the one we had managed to catch and detain, who was now sitting in his tent under guard on the other side of the portal, sweating with fear that his people would find him and do something bad to him for helping us develop the portal. "But we did have a visitor. Maybe more than one."

"Keep talking."

I said, "Have you ever heard of 'rebound'?"

"Meaning what?"

"Meaning 'bouncing back.' When you go through the skin, or whatever it is, that separates one time from another, there's some kind of conservation effect. Things begin going in the other direction."

He frowned. "You mean other people being thrown back and forth?"

"Not just people. It's complicated. It depends on how badly the skin is torn. Sometimes it's just energy—light, or sound. Sometimes it's gases drifting back and forth, or small things—birds flying, maybe. Sometimes it's a lot more."

"And that's happening here?"

I said unwillingly, "Seems to be, Dom. And not just here."

He stood up and went over to the window. I let him think it out. Over his shoulder he said, "It sounds like you people are really screwing the bird, Dom." I didn't answer that. He turned around, looking at me. "I wish you'd get me a cigarette," he said testily. "This stuff is hard to take calmly."

I debated for a moment whether to hardnose him on that, decided not to. "Why not? They're your lungs." I poked at the intercom on the desk until I figured out which button connected with the orderly room and told Sergeant Sambok to bring up some smokes. "So," I said, "we want to get this thing squared away. Are you going to help us?"

He said simply, "No."

"Not even when it's as risky as I'm telling you? Not even when your country is defenseless against us anyway?"

"You got into it, Dominic. You get out of it by yourself," he said definitely, and turned toward the door as Nyla Sambok appeared with a carton of tax-free PX cigarettes.

And all of a sudden my friendly other self changed from the self-assured name/rank/serial-number-only prisoner to something brand-new.

What the hell had happened to him? He was staring after the sergeant as if he'd seen a ghost. I never saw such an expression of astonishment, and rage, and worry on any human face—least of all on my own!

A man named Dominic DeSota sat before a screen, his fingers busy on a keyboard, analyzing and recording. Without lifting his fingers he spoke into a tiny microphone that curved around his cheek, "Boss? This one's the farthest off yet. There don't seem to be any vertebrates in it at all."

24 August 1983
9:20 A.M. Senator Dominic DeSota

When I got back to my home away from home, the stockade in the J-3 parking lot, I found out I had missed breakfast. I was also missing six of my fellow prisoners. There were a dozen or so of the base's permanent party soldiers still there, including a couple shamefacedly wearing "PW" stencils on their shirt backs and picking up leftover cafeteria trays from where the others had left them. A different soldier, with a green armband, was watching them with an automatic pistol held loosely before him. One of Major DeSota's, no doubt.

But of the few civilians who had shared the canvas cots in the parking lot with me the night before, there were none. This upset the corporal who had brought me back. He motioned me inside the fence while he muttered worriedly to the other guard. It didn't worry me. I had other things on my mind.

I had *one* other thing: Nyla Bowquist!

I don't know how to say how shattering it was to see my dear lover in an Army uniform, with traces of blackout makeup still on her face, a gun over her shoulder, looking at me with no recognition at all.

Now that I had time to think I realized that it was likely enough that there would be another Nyla in their time, just as there was another Dominic DeSota—and, no doubt, another Marilyn (but who would she be married to there?) and another Ferdie Bowquist and a whole other cast of characters. The other Dom DeSota wasn't at all the same as me. There was no reason the other Nyla should be. This one was no famous concert violinist. She wore her hair shorter and her eyes less made up. And her clothes—well, it was an army uniform, after all. My Nyla dressed beautifully, but this one hadn't had the freedom of choice.

But so heartbreakingly similar! And she hadn't known me at all! Or—that was not exactly true—she had known me as a copy of that other Dominic, whom she had known, all right (but not, I thought, in the biblical sense). I wondered if I would see her again. . . .

And wondered instantly if I would ever see my own Nyla again. And wondered at myself! Here I was in the middle of huge, fantastic, and frightening events, and the thing that filled my mind was the woman I was having an affair with—

"You! Prisoner DeSota!" growled the corporal, and I realized he'd been waving at me. "Come on, your people have been moved. I have to take you to the assembly point."

I looked at the other prisoners, who only looked back at me in the opaque, I-only-work-here expression of enlisted men in a situation not covered by orders. "Where's that?" I asked. But the only answer I got was a nasty twitch of the machine-pistol.

It wasn't far. It was right back the way we had come, to the Officers' Club just across from the Cathouse.

I'd been in it before. Many times. It was a sort of lounge where the people working could sit for a cup of coffee and a short conversation away from their desks, or take their latest load of information memos to read over in peace. It looked as it always had, except that there were nine people in it who clearly didn't want to be there. Two of the civilian scientists were pacing back and forth, glaring out the windows.

Colonel Martineau was sitting talking to one of the women, whom I recognized as a mathematician brought down from ITT, and therefore one of my constituents. "Edna," I said, nodding. "Colonel." Just as though I had happened to drop in for a Coke and nothing strange was going on at all.

"We wondered where you were," said the colonel.

"I was being questioned by that nasty other Dominic DeSota. Made me miss breakfast."

"If you have any quarters," he said, "there's a vending machine right out in the hall, and the guard'll let you use it." I didn't, but Dr. Edna Valeska did—just like our own, except that the face was Herbert Hoover's. A soft drink and a couple of Twinkies didn't make a meal, but at least they informed my stomach my intentions were good. Out of habit, Colonel Martineau made a round of the room while I was getting them, checking windows (shake of the head; armed guards outside), checking the other door (locked), listening to the telephone (dead). Then he sat down and watched me eat. "We've all been questioned," he said. "What interested them most seemed to be you, Dom—anyway, that first man who looked like you. The one that disappeared."

"They asked me the same thing," I said, mouth full of lardy sugar. "I didn't see any harm in telling them what I knew—which wasn't much, of course. Should I have stuck to name, rank, and serial number, which I don't have?"

He looked at me in surprise. I was surprised too; I hadn't realized how edgy I was. "I think we have to play this one by ear, Senator," he said, placating me. I grinned to show I was sorry, and Edna Valeska perched on the couch next to me to get into the discussion.

"The good news," she said gloomily, "is that we have proof now that the Cathouse Project works. The bad news is they got it before us, and they're using it; and the even worse news is that there seems to be more than one other time-line involved. There's no other explanation that saves the facts."

"That's the way it looks to me," I agreed, "but who are these other ones?" Shakes of the head. "Christ. I'm not used to this kind of stuff."

Flash of a grin from Edna. "Who is?"

"Well, but it's your project!" I protested. "If you don't know what's going on, who does?"

"I said I wasn't used to it, Senator. I didn't say I didn't understand it—part of it, anyway." She saw my eyes on her cigarettes and plucked one out for me. "For instance," she said, lighting us both up, "we know quite a lot about the time-line of our visitors— the invading ones, that is; the one where you're a major in the army."

"We do?"

"To be sure. They're invading because they want to get at an enemy in their time through the back door—the same as we were preparing to do."

"Dr. Valeska," I said, "we weren't *preparing*. The mission of the Cathouse was to study *feasibility*. There were no operational plans."

She shrugged, dismissing the distinction as without enough difference to matter. "There's one other solid deduction, and one other fact. The deduction is that, although they've got pretty far along with time-crossing, there is at least one other time-line that's got farther. The one that produced the first Dominic DeSota."

I noticed that not only had the others in the room begun to cluster around to listen, but even the guard in the doorway was flapping his ears in our direction. Well, why not? Maybe I could read something from his expression. "How do you know that?" I asked, watching the guard out of the corner of my eye.

"Because these other people—we'll call them Population One—can slip one person through at a time and pull him back from the other side. I don't think Population Two—the invaders—can do that." The frown on the face of the guard made that seem plausible, I thought. Edna Valeska was noticing it, too, I could tell. "So," she said, "there's another player in this game."

"So we might have an ally," I said hopefully. "The Population One people might be as vulnerable as we are, only to Population Two."

The guard was goggling at us now, and the look of worry on his face was comforting. We were talking about things that he didn't want to think about. I turned to smile at him. Mistake. He glowered at me and backed away, his weapon stiffly at port arms, no expression at all on his face any more. But that was a kind of confirmation too.

"On the other hand," said Edna Valeska, "if the Population One people were going to do anything for us they had every chance to warn us. They didn't do that."

That was true enough, and I began to feel as discomfited as the guard. "So what's the other fact we know about the Population Two people—the invaders?" I ask.

"The Soviet Union is their principal enemy."

I said, "Yes, so it seems. But that's hard to believe! After the nuke war, when the Chinese did the decapitation bit in 1960, bombing Moscow and Leningrad—"

"Right, Dom," Colonel Martineau put in, "but, you see, in their time that didn't happen. We've pieced that all together, from the things we found out when we were questioned. The Soviets had only one big outside war. Around 1940, I think. They got into a war with Finland, and the Germans got involved—"

"The Germans!"

Martineau nodded. "The Germans didn't have their revolution. A man named Hitler took power, and the war was pretty bad. The Russians won, and after the war they occupied most of Eastern Europe, under their leader, Josef Stalin."

That was toughest of all to swallow. "Now, wait a minute! I know who Stalin was! He ran the country for a while until his assassination. His grandson's a friend of mine, as a matter of fact. He's the Russian ambassador to the U.S. We play bridge. He's a good friend of—some friends of mine," I finished, not wanting to mention Nyla Bowquist. I caught a glimpse of the guard, more cautious this time, but once again definitely listening. "Old Joe," I lectured, "was killed by some kind of Georgian separatist underground. And the English had had their general strike that turned into a revolution. They went socialist, the way they still are, and the Russian Litvinov got to be boss of the U.S.S.R. because he had good English connections. Had an English wife, as a matter of fact. And then, after 1960, the Germans had their counterrevolution and the kaiserin came back, and now they and Japan are the big competitors. . . ." I trailed off. I wasn't scaring the guard any more. I was just boring him. Not to mention what I was doing to Edna and Colonel Martineau.

The colonel shook his head. "None of that happened in their time," he said. "For the last thirty-odd years they've only had two real superpowers, the Russians and the Americans. And they want to knock out the competition."

The guard wasn't only bored. He wasn't even listening any more. There was a faint stir from the front of the O's Club, and he was watching whatever was happening there. By then all of us in the room had been casting sidelong glances at our living litmus paper to see when what we said produced a reaction, and when it stopped reacting the conversation died.

"Oh, hell," said one of the junior scientists, and shrugged to say that it was a general comment with no specific follow-up planned.

Edna Valeska fretted, "Hell and *damn*. My husband's going to be worried sick. He never wanted me to take night duty. I wish I could let him know I was all right."

"I wish the same thing," I said.

The colonel nodded. "In my line of work my wife's had to get used to this kind of thing—well, not *this* kind of thing, I mean, but not being able to call her all the time. I know it's different for civilians. I bet you're worried about your wife, Dom."

"What? Oh, sure," I agreed, and didn't add, *Her too*.

They fed us again before noon. It was canned spaghetti and meatballs out of the dregs of the Officers' Club kitchen supplies, but there was plenty of milk and decent coffee. "Fattening us up for the kill," said one of the junior scientists gloomily, and, on cue, our new guard came into the room with his machine-pistol at the ready, followed by Nyla. Sergeant Nyla Sambok, that was, with two more armed privates at her side.

She looked us over politely. "If you'll finish your coffee," she said, "we're about ready to take you to more comfortable quarters."

"Where's that?" asked Colonel Martineau.

"Not far, sir. If you'll come along now, please." The voice was Nyla's own. So was the "please"—a nice touch, I thought, under the circumstances. The way her troopers unshipped their weapons to cover us wasn't. Whether we had finished our coffee or not, we moved.

We didn't have far to go. Outside the air-conditioned club the desert heat hit us all between the eyes, but we weren't in it long. Out the door. Across the wide and empty base street. Into the front door of the Cathouse, and clattering down a flight of steps to a big, cluttered basement room. Once it had been a pistol range. Now it was full of people with the green invader armbands, some OD-painted things like generators, but with heavy cables snaking outside to where we could hear diesels thudding away . . . and a tall, rectangular screen of featureless jet black.

That was the first time I ever saw a portal. I didn't have to be told what it was. It was simply a blackness hanging in the air, almost big enough to fill the room from side to side; and it was scary. Colonel Martineau snapped: "Sergeant! I demand to know what your intentions are!"

"Yes, sir," she agreed. "An officer will brief you. This is for your own comfort and safety, sir."

"Bullshit, Sergeant!"

But she simply agreed, "Yes, sir," and walked away. She was no longer around to answer questions, and the armed guards obviously had all their answers in their ammo clips.

I watched her go over to the side of the room, where my good old doppelganger-Dominic was standing, with a man who looked somehow odd. Two ways odd. His face was vaguely familiar; and he seemed to be a civilian in borrowed fatigues, like me. He wore no rank insignia, like me; and like me he did not have a green armband. He was not a prisoner, though, because he was standing before a tall console, making adjustments to some sort of instrumentation. Major Dominic was watching him closely; so was an enlisted man with a carbine. His guard? And if he needed a guard, and wasn't one of us, who was he?

Nyla-the-Sergeant was getting orders from Major-me. She nodded and came back to us. "You'll be going through in just a minute," she informed us.

"Now, hold on, Sergeant!" snapped the colonel. "I demand to be told where you're taking us!"

"Yes, sir," she said. "The officer will explain it all." Martineau subsided, fuming. I took my turn.

"You're Nyla Christophe, aren't you?" I asked sunnily.

Blink of surprise. For the first time she looked at me as though I were a human being, not just a lump of captive meat to be moved around at will. The carbine in her hands remained steady. It wasn't pointed at me, exactly, but it only needed a quarter-turn of her body to zero in on my belly. "That's my maiden name," she agreed cautiously. "Do you know me?"

"I know the one of you that's in my time," I said, and smiled. "She's my . . . friend. She's also one of the world's greatest violinists."

She looked at me curiously at hearing "friend," but I got her full attention when I said "violinist." She looked at me searchingly for a moment. She gave a quick glance toward the major, then back to me. "What are you talking about?" she asked.

I said, "Zuckerman, Ricci, Christophe. They're the top three violinists in the world today. This world. Last night Nyla played with the National Symphony before the President of the United States."

"The National *Symphony*?" I nodded. "My God," she said, "I've always wanted— Are you bullshitting me, Mr. DeSota?"

I shook my head. "In my time you're married to a real-estate developer in Chicago. Last night you played the Gershwin Violin Concerto, with Rostropovich conducting. Two months ago your picture was on the cover of *People*."

She gave me a look, partly puzzlement, partly skepticism. "Gershwin never wrote a violin concerto," she said, "and what's *People*?"

"It's a magazine, Nyla. You're famous."

"It's true, Sergeant," chimed in the colonel, listening intently. "I've heard you play myself."

"Yeah?" She was still skeptical, but she was also fascinated.

I nodded sincerely. "What about you, Nyla?" I asked. "Do you play the violin?"

"I teach it," she said. "I did until the call-up, anyway."

"So you see?" I exclaimed, beaming. "And—"

And that was as far as it went. "Sergeant Sambok!" called a captain, standing by the screen. "Move them out!"

That was the end of it. She was all business then, my Nyla. If she looked at me at all again, it was with the same impersonal interest that the hammer man in an abattoir might give a steer coming up the ramp. "Move on, please," she said to all of us, but this time the "please" meant nothing at all.

"Now, listen, Sergeant," Colonel Martineau began, but she was having no more of it. She gestured with the carbine. The colonel looked at me and shrugged. We moved. We lined up in single file, along yellow lines that had been painted so recently on the floor that parts of them were still tacky. There was a broad yellow stripe just before the ominous blackness, like the wait-here line at a customs counter in an airport. The new captain stopped us there, one eye on us and the other on the vaguely familiar civilian.

"When I give the word," he said, "you'll just walk straight ahead through the portal, one at a time. Wait until you are called; that's important. You'll find the other side is the same level as this one, you don't have to worry about stumbling or anything. Anyway, there will be personnel on the other side to help you if necessary. Remember, only one at a time—"

"Captain!" rapped Colonel Martineau, summoning up one last effort. "I demand—"

"No you don't," the captain told him, not rudely, just as anyone with a tricky job might tell somebody else to butt out until the job was done. "You'll have a chance to make any complaints on the other side . . . sir." The "sir" was an afterthought. The tone made it clear that it wasn't to be taken seriously. The captain was a lot more interested in the civilian at the console than in anything any of us might say.

The civilian was interesting enough, actually. He was obviously making some sort of complex balancing adjustment. It appeared that he was trying to keep a red dot on one scale opposite a green one on another. When the red dot drifted away he turned knobs until he got it back. When they were together he called over his shoulder, "Move them out!"

And Dr. Edna Valeska, looking as though she were praying, cast an imploring look over her shoulder at us, shuddered, and walked into the blackness, where she simply disappeared.

All the other eight of us sighed at once. "Next," rapped the captain, and Colonel Martineau followed. The black swallowed him up with no more trace than it had left of Edna Valeska.

I was next in line.

I was standing no more than six feet from the mystery civilian. He gave me a quick look over his shoulder.

And I twigged. Skinny, far more harassed-looking, but the same man. There was no question about it. "Lavrenti!" I exclaimed. "You're Ambassador Lavrenti Djugashvili!"

His guard snapped, "You crazy? Don't bother Dr. Douglas now!"

"Wait a damn minute," protested the civilian. "You! What did you call me?"

"Djugashvili," I said. "You're the Ambassador of the Soviet Union, Lavrenti Djugashvili."

He looked at me fretfully for a moment. "My name's not Djugashvili," he said, returning to his board. He juggled dials for a moment, before nodding to the captain to scoot me through the portal. "But my grandfather's was," he called, just as I stepped into the blackness.

When I was a kid I had an active fantasy life, and it concentrated on two subjects. One was space travel. The other was sex. The principal reason I wanted to become a scientist, back as a sophomore at Lane Tech, was so I could visit other worlds. I never lost that fantasy, exactly, it just sort of slowly evaporated away over the years.

The other I never lost at all. I had the best collection of dirty books on the Near North Side. Porno flicks hadn't got out in the open yet, but there were places where you could pay two dollars and get into the back room of a coin-machine arcade or a sleazy bookstore and watch grainy black-and-white films from Tijuana and Havana. (For a long time I wasn't entirely sure that a man could make love to a woman without wearing black calf-length stockings and a mask.) I traded lies with all the other guys in the chess club and on the tennis team, and I put myself to sleep every night in the time-honored adolescent way, with my imagination carefully writing the scenario of the perfect seduction: the gossamer negligee, the chilled wine by the bed, the silken sheets. . . .

And then came the Fourth of July. Peggy Hofstader.

Her apartment house was near enough the lake to watch the fireworks, and there was nobody on the roof but us, and I'd managed to score two bottles of warm, nasty-tasting beer. And when the fireworks were blattering out their rackety-bang, all-over-the-sky finale, and I felt Peggy's hand reaching toward where no hand but mine had ever gone before, I realized my bluff was called. Fantasy had suddenly become real. All unprepared, I was making my debut, and what did you do with all those arms and legs and parts and places?

It was a good thing for me that Peggy knew my lines better than I did. I needed all the help I could get.

There wasn't anybody to help me now.

In a wholly different way, I was up against the same shuddery, scary, exciting thing. There was another world on the other side of that blackness.

I took a deep breath. I closed my eyes. And I walked into it.

What did it feel like?

Mostly it felt like nothing at all. I've been to a couple of science fairs where they had air doors separating the rooms, currents of ascending air mixed with water vapor so it looked as though a cloud were hanging in the doorway; they project pictures or advertising messages on them, and you walk right through them. This felt like even less of a world-crossing transition than that. It was just that at one moment I was in a shooting range in the basement of a building, noisy, filled with people, lit by banks of flickering fluorescent lights . . .

And then I took a step, and suddenly I was at the bottom of an excavation. I stood on duckboards, in the hottest August sunlight New Mexico can produce. Scaffolding rose around me, supporting curious machines like TV cameras with round wire shields over where their lenses ought to be. A cherry picker stood idle beside one of them, with a man idly looking down at me from the cup. Scooped-out sandy walls surrounded me. A roaring truck motor was breaking my eardrums just a few feet away.

I didn't have time to study the scene. There were two soldiers standing there to grab my arms and pull me forward. "Into the truck," one of them ordered, and turned to get the next prisoner who came stumbling through. I climbed into the truck—unremarkable Army six-by-six with board seats around the sides and a soldier manning a light machine gun, pointed toward us, squatting on the cab. When all nine of us were aboard, the truck motor roared even louder; the vehicle jerked forward, and we climbed up out of the excavation onto a mesa where two Army helicopters stood by, their rotors slowly turning. "Out," ordered the guard, who had followed us into the truck, and one by one we jumped down as the truck roared away. The guard who did the talking, watching us carefully, backed away to exchange a few words with the pilot of one of the helicopters. We all looked at each other.

We were up in bare, sandy hills. I could see the barracky buildings of an actual Army base a mile or so across the mesa—the original Sandia, I supposed. Nearer there was a tractorless OD-painted trailer body, windows showing that it was some kind of an office, on the lip of the excavation. And across the excavation were two or three other trailers, but not offices: they carried generators, thudding away, and the cables went straight down to the machines at the floor of the pit.

I was gasping from the sun in a minute, and so were the rest of us, but we were all too keyed-up to worry about heatstroke. Edna Valeska tugged at my sleeve. "They had to dig to get down to basement level," she said, pointing.

"What?"

"They wanted to come out in the basement of the building," she explained, "and there wasn't any building here. So they had to dig."

"Oh, yeah." It didn't seem important. To tell the truth, I'd had too many things to react to, I didn't know what was important and what was not any more. I could see two more figures appear out of the black rectangle: Nyla-the-Sergeant, and the man who looked like, but said he wasn't, Djugashvili. They exchanged words, and Nyla turned away to get into a jeep. "What about the scaffolding?"

"At a guess," said Dr. Valeska, "that was a matter of positioning too. They wanted to bug us. To look into the laboratories. Some of them were on the top floor."

It sounded rational enough, though I was no longer sure about what constituted rationality, either. One of the juniors put his finger on the central question.

"What do you think they're going to do with us?" he asked, his voice quavering.

Nobody had a good answer for that. Colonel Martineau came closest. "I think that's what we're going to find out from the sergeant," he said, as Nyla Sambok's jeep spun sand from its wheels while she parked it behind us.

She didn't tell us, though—at least not right away. She was called, scowling, over to the colloquy between the guard and the copter pilots. "Colloquy" was too mild a word; it was becoming a straight-out argument, and they weren't keeping their voices down.

We didn't have to wonder long about the subject of the disagreement. It was like that old puzzle of the missionaries and the cannibals crossing a river. Each helicopter could hold five persons besides the pilot. There were nine of us—nine prisoners—and one guard made ten. Two loads. Only neither of the pilots was willing to take a chance with carrying five of us enemy maniac desperadoes without an armed guard.

"Aw, *shit*," said Sergeant Sambok at last. "Get on with it. You take four, you take four, and I'll keep the odd one here until one of you gets back." And as they grudgingly started loading us into the choppers, she spun and pointed to me. "Leave that one," she said. "I'll hold him for the next trip."

"Sure, Sarge," whined one of the guards, "but the major said—"

"Move it," ordered Nyla. And they did. When the choppers were airborne she turned to look at me analytically. I guess I didn't look like too much of a problem to deal with for a healthy woman with a carbine. She gave a short nod. "No sense frying our brains out here," she said. "Let's get inside the trailer."

The blessed thing was air-conditioned.

It was also empty. Apparently it was for the use of the helicopter people, and there weren't any of them left. She let me go in first and waited until I was well clear of the doorway before she followed. She moved into a corner and expertly flipped a couple of quarters out of her fatigue pocket to me. "There's a Coke machine over there," she said. "I'm buying. . . . Open it and put it down on the table," she added, and then added one more thing, "Please."

She sat back and took a long pull at the Coke, watching me. I did the mirror-image same. At close range, with just the two of us there in the room, she looked more like my Nyla than ever. Oh, sure, wearing some sort of getup for a Halloween party. But Nyla Christophe Bowquist, to the life.

She wasn't, of course. She was Nyla Somebody Else. But whatever name she went by, she looked as pretty and as desirable as my Nyla ever had, and that was very much. I don't mean just sexually, though there was all of that; but there was more than that, too. I *liked* her. I liked the half-humorous perplexed look she gave me. I liked the way she leaned back, with her breasts making her fatigue blouse look like a couturier creation. And when she spoke, I liked the sound of her voice.

"What about it, DeSota? What is that stuff you were telling me?"

"You're a concert violinist, and one of the greatest who ever lived," I told her.

"Don't I wish! I'm a music teacher, Mr. DeSota. I admit I always wanted to be up there with an orchestra. But I never made it."

I shrugged. "You had the ability," I said, "because in my world that's exactly what you did. And one other thing I didn't tell you about you in my time-line . . . and me."

She gave me a funny look. She didn't say the word *what?* She made her eyebrows say it for her.

"We were lovers," I answered. "I loved you very much. I still do."

She gave me a different kind of funny look. There was surprise in it, and suspicion. But it was also tentatively pretty warm. It was almost a singles-bar kind of look, though I didn't think this Nyla was any more of a singles-bar person than my own. I know what the look was. It was the look that Roxane must have given Cyrano de Bergerac when she found out that it was he, and not that dumb hunk Christian, who had written her those lovely letters. And she said: "That's a new one on me, DeSota."

"It isn't a line, Nyla."

She thought for a moment, then looked around and grinned. "Under the circumstances," she said, "it might as well be. Let's talk about something else. What's this about a Gershwin concerto? He died young, you know." I shrugged; I really didn't know much about him. "He left a lot of good stuff," she went on, watching me get up and pace over to the window. "All the pop stuff, of course. And then the *Rhapsody in Blue*, the Concerto in F, the *American in Paris* . . . but honest, he never wrote anything for violin."

I was looking down at the portal, where the not-really-Djugashvili was playing with the same sort of console he had on the other side. I shook my head decisively. "Wrong, Nyla. Absolutely wrong. I'm not expert in classical music, that's for sure. But some rubbed off from hanging around with you—with the other Nyla. The Gershwin I've heard many times. It's full of melodies, which makes it easier for a guy like me. I think I could even whistle it—wait a minute." I walked around, trying to remember the lovely, rippling opening theme Nyla played so beautifully on the solo violin. When I managed to try it I knew I didn't do it justice—but it's the kind of definitively beautiful music, like some of the Mendelssohn and Tchaikovsky, that sounds good even when it's butchered.

She frowned. "I never heard that. But it's pretty nice."

And she pursed her lips to try it herself.

And I leaned forward to her puckered lips and kissed her.

She kissed me back.

I'm nearly sure she kissed me back. I could feel those nice, dry, soft, warm lips opening under mine, but I didn't wait to make sure. I gave her the edge of my fist on the back of the neck, as hard as I'd ever done in judo class.

She dropped like a rock.

That sort of hand-to-hand combat was all theory to me. I'd never done it before, except as ritualized exercise. I hadn't planned to do it then, although one part of my brain, all along, had been screaming to me that Nyla's fatigues and my fatigues were absolutely indistinguishable, bar the fact that she wore a green armband and carried a carbine, and I had neither.

When she fell I was not absolutely sure I hadn't hit her too hard.

But when I put my hand on that familiar breast under that very unfamiliar fatigue blouse I could feel that the heart and lungs were going strong.

"I'm sorry, sweet," I said. I pinned her armband onto my sleeve. I took her carbine off the floor and slung it over my shoulder. And I left without looking back.

At the age of seventy-three, Timothy McGarren had been doorman at Lakeshore Towers since the day it opened its doors and he turned in his retirement papers to the Metropolitan Transport Authority. They were the same day, and both were ten years in the past. He had made the trip from curbside to elevator so many times that he could do it in his sleep, or walking backward. Sometimes, like now, holding the doors for Mrs. Spiegel from 26–A, he actually did do it backward, feeling with his foot for the bottom step. Only there didn't seem to be one. He overbalanced, grabbed for the railing, missed, and dropped into thirty feet of water, with the lights of the Chicago skyline blinking at him over a hundred yards of Lake Michigan water.

24 August 1983
12:30 P.M. Major DeSOTA, Dominic R.

This base we had captured was stuffed fuller of goodies than a Christmas stocking. The goody I appreciated most was the base commandant's office. It had its own private base commandant's dining room, with kitchen attached; and in the base commandant's private freezer the cooks had discovered half a dozen of the thickest, juiciest, most marbled steaks I ever put a tooth to. It came out even. There were six of us to eat them: Lieutenant Colonel Tempe, heading the nuke research detachment; the MP major, Bill Selikowitz; the Signal Corps captain; two other captains who were Tempe's adjutants; and me. We were the most rank on the base—on our side, anyway—and rank had its privileges. We ate off a linen tablecloth with linen napkins and sterling silver, and if the glasses had only water in them, at least they were Danish crystal. Outside the big picture window on the fifth-floor dining room of the base headquarters we could see the sixty-odd buildings we had captured, with Selikowitz's MP's patrolling in their jeeps. It was hot out there, but in our little castle the air-conditioning was working just fine.

We were six happy guys.

One of Colonel Tempe's adjutants was chortling over the dumb projects they'd uncovered—a group of weirdos trying to read the enemy's minds; binary chemical weapons of the kind we'd tried, and discarded, five years before; laser guns that would fry an enemy soldier at a distance of three miles, provided

123

he stood still for at least ten minutes without ambling out of the beam.

That was the comic relief. These people had wasted more money on dumb ideas than we had. But not all their ideas were dumb! By the time we got to the apple pie and ice cream, Colonel Tempe was telling us the serious stuff. The rest of us listened hard; in another forty-eight hours it would no doubt be classified down to a whisper, but we were getting it right from the source. At nuclear weapons these people had us outclassed six ways from Sunday. "Cruise missiles," he said. "Like little jet planes that come in under the radar, too fast to be intercepted, with built-in maps so they always know where they're going. Multiple warheads; you launch them in one piece and they separate, ten miles up, and six different missiles hit six different targets. And *submarines*."

That took me by surprise. "Submarines? What the hell is special about submarines?"

"These are nuclear-powered, DeSota," he said grimly. "Big bastards. Ten thousand tons and better. They can stay underwater for a month, where the enemy can't find them; and each one of them carries twenty nuclear missiles with ten-thousand-mile range. Jesus! Never mind your damn sneak-attack biologicals! If we could get just one of those damn submarines through a portal, the Russians'd have to lie down and die for us!"

Suddenly the pie didn't taste as good any more.

"But we walked right over them," Selikowitz objected.

The colonel nodded. "They weren't expecting us," he said. "Now they know where we are."

"Oh, come on, Colonel," I put in. "They're not going to nuke their own base?" It was meant as an argument, but halfway through it turned into a question.

Nobody wanted to answer it. Not even the colonel. He attacked his pie in silence for a moment, then burst out, "We're doing this all wrong, damn it!

We should've gone right for the top! Hit the White House. Grab their President. *Tell* her what we were going to do, and then it's all over before the Russians and their damn satellites begin to get curious about this damn 'archaeological dig' out in the desert!"

They were all looking at me; I began to wish I hadn't opened my mouth. Who was I to defend the decisions of the Chiefs of Staff? All of us knew how hard the debate had raged, and none of us, especially not me, had had any voice in which way the vote went.

Still—

"Colonel," I said, "let's look at facts. Fact one. It doesn't matter what kind of weapons these people have, they can't use them against our interior because *they can't get at us*. The only way they could do that would be with a portal, and the reason we came here first was to preempt the possibility they'd build one."

"They were nowhere near," complained one of the adjutants.

"They might have made it pretty fast," I said. "Once they knew it was possible, that answered a lot of questions. We couldn't take that chance. Now we've got this base, and there's no way they can retaliate against us—whatever we do."

The colonel looked at me hard, then gave me a frosty grin. "You're a good company man, DeSota," he said, and tapped his empty cup with a fingernail. It rang out, like the bell at the end of a round. It was the very best china.

I was willing to let the argument stop there. The colonel was right. But he was also wrong: we'd taken over Sandia with no casualties at all, not counting one guard with a broken arm because one of Selikowitz's MP's had been a little too rough with the hand-to-hand combat. If we'd stormed the White House, there would have been people dead. On the other hand—

On the other hand, there were too many other possibilities for me to figure out. The weaponry these people had! If we could just take back that submarine—or some of those multiwarhead and cruise missiles—

But we didn't have the power, on this side of the portal, for anything that big. We could take blueprints, sure. Even any of the weapons, part by part. But sooner or later the Russians were going to take a closer look at that big hole in the desert we'd called an archaeological survey site, and if they saw weaponry . . .

"Major?" The pretty private who was filling the coffee cups was also distributing flimsies to some of us. "These came while you were eating," she said.

"Thanks," I said, and couldn't help grinning. There was only one for me, but it was a TWX from the President of the United States!

It said:

> On behalf of the American people I commend you and the officers and enlisted personnel of the 456 Special Detachment, A.U.S., for meritorious service over and beyond the call of duty.

I looked around the table, grinning in spite of myself. No matter that all the others were grinning too—they'd got their own commendations, no doubt. Never mind that the President probably—no, undoubtedly!—hadn't written it himself, doubtless didn't even know my name; it was a canned citation from the War Department, of course. Never mind that the President was the weak-kneed jerk he was—*I* never voted for the son of a bitch. All the same! A commendation, by name, from the President was going to look very good in my 201 file. And there was more. Six medals! A Legion of Merit for me. A Bronze Star for Sergeant Sambok. Four others to pass out to whoever I chose to name.

It was not a bad morning's haul; and the only thing wrong with it was that Bill Selikowitz had got more than the rest of us. He was frowning over something the orderly had muttered in his ear, and when he looked up it was to me. "Dom? My patrols have just picked up one of your guys, coming toward the base at ninety miles an hour in a stolen car, with an Albuquerque cop right behind him. Private Dormeyer. He took off for town without leave, and it looks like he tried to kill a civilian."

What I wanted was Sergeant Sambok, because she knew the whole detachment. I couldn't have her. She was on the other side of the portal, escorting the prisoners, and there was some technical malfunction and the portal was down.

What I had was my adjutant, Lieutenant Mariel, fresh out of OCS and about as much use as two tails on a cow. She was waiting for me in my office. "What—what are we going to do?" she managed to get out, and remembered to add, "Sir?"

"We're going to clean this up," I told her. "Damn it, Lieutenant! I wanted Dormeyer brought back quietly!"

"They couldn't find him," she said abjectly. "I sent Privates Weimar and Milton to his home address, but he wasn't there—and you know, sir, the city's real messed up, with some of our troops guarding communications points, and nobody knows if the enemy's going to react—"

"Save the excuses, Lieutenant," I ordered. I'd forgotten that Dormeyer was a local boy—in our time, anyway. That wasn't too good; a commanding officer is supposed to know his troops. "An adjutant's supposed to know the troops," I told her. "Was Dormeyer acting suspicious in any way before he took off?"

"No, sir! Not that I know, sir. He did get a seven-day compassionate about a month ago, sir—wife was killed in a car smash. I suggested dropping him from the unit because he'd missed training, but you said to keep him in—"

"Get him in here," I said. "I'll talk to him. No, wait a minute—let me talk to the cop first."

* * *

I didn't need this. I didn't want my commendation spoiled. I didn't want old General Ratface Magruder getting on my case because some asshole private got himself into trouble. The one good thing I knew was that Bill Selikowitz turned the whole thing over to me; there wouldn't be anything on paper—

Provided I could handle it. And when I saw Officer Ortiz that began to look possible. He was a big, square, old-time cop who wore his Smokey the Bear hat as if it had grown there and looked around my office as though he owned it. "Never been here before, Major," he said. "I guess you know there's a lot of questions being asked about what you guys are doing."

At least he hadn't come in breathing fire and demanding the perpetrator. I said, easy man-to-man talk, "I guess guys like you and me just have to follow orders and let the people on top worry about why, right? Have a cigar." When he took two I could see the talk was going the right way. I had more than half expected that he would give us an argument on the basis of local law, or jurisdiction, or anything that would make enough trouble so I couldn't deal with the poor slob Dormeyer's troubles myself. I needn't have worried. Ortiz was used to getting along with whoever had the reins of power. He was forty or so, twenty years on the force; he'd seen everything and been fazed by none of it. He'd got a call while patrolling in his radio car in a part of Albuquerque our troops hadn't bothered with, so he entered the home of Mr. and Mrs. Herbert Dingman. He found the elder Dingman's away, their daughter Gloria Dingman hysterical, a Mr. William Penderby groggily coming to on her bed, where he'd been just about strangled by our own Private Dormeyer. It wasn't too big a deal. What made it touchy for Officer Ortiz was that on the way in he'd walked right by Private Dormeyer, sitting dazed at the wheel of the Dingman girl's car, and by the time Ortiz figured out that that was the man to arrest, Dormeyer had jumped the ignition and was on his way back to base. And, no, he wouldn't mind waiting around while I interviewed the perpetrator, only would it be all right if he phoned in to let the station know where he was?

Certainly I wouldn't mind. I didn't slap him on the back, but I walked him to the door, and ordered Lieutenant Mariel to get him to a phone as soon as she got Private Dormeyer into my office.

Give him that much, he wasn't a bad soldier. He'd come out of whatever craziness had driven him up the wall. He stood at a brace and answered all my questions clearly and briefly. Yes, he'd gone AWOL. Reason? Well, he'd been really shaken up by his wife's death and somebody told him that there was an exact copy of every one of us in this time—so he'd gone looking for his copy of her . . . and finding her there, and alive—and with this other guy in her bed!—had been more than he could handle. No, he hadn't killed the man. Gloria had dragged him away and he'd gone outside to sit in the car and cry. And when Officer Ortiz reported that the victim was no worse than bruised I saw daylight.

I sent Dormeyer back to duty with a warning. I did, this time, pat Officer Ortiz on the back; and I turned him over to Selikowitz's MP corporal. "Escort Officer Ortiz back to his car and let him go," I ordered. "Make sure he knows we're here as friends, not invaders." And to Ortiz, with half a wink, "You mind a suggestion, Officer? You'll be the first from your side to come out from our occupied zone, so you're going to get a lot of attention from the TV news people. Don't let them get you for nothing!" And I watched him go with satisfaction, and turned back to the real world.

It was like ice water in the face.

The portal was in service again. Messages were coming through. The hottest one was for me: I was ordered to report to Tac-Five on the double. One of our prisoners, the other Dom DeSota, had escaped to some other time-line, they didn't even know which one, and he'd taken our pet scientist, Dr. Douglas, with him.

The last time I had been on the home side of the portal it was dark night. We followed the tapes along the sandy duckboards, with no more light than the blue riding lights from the trucks that had brought us down, stumbling, choking on the dust, shivering from the desert night-time chill—scared. Up on the mesa the big troop-carrying helicopters were landing with no more lights than the trucks. Hand-held flashlights guided them in with their second-echelon soldiers and the specialists who would follow to set up a portal generator, none of us sure what we would find.

Now it was all different. Hot sun baked the duckboards. A desert wind peeled plumes of sand from the lip of the excavation right down into my eyes. Ratface Magruder was pacing up and down in front of his staff car, waiting for me. He thumbed me inside and we spun sand all the way up to the mesa. There I could see that bulldozers had smoothed away even the skid marks of the helicopters, so that when the Russian satellites came over they would see nothing to make a liar out of the archaeological-excavation story.

One thing was the same. I was scared.

I was scared in a way I had never been before, because fear of getting shot at or having to shoot somebody else is a physical fear that you can turn your mind away from, at least for a while. What I was afraid of now was not a speculation. It was a fact. If the senator escaped, he was at least helped in the escape by the fact that he was wearing GI fatigues. And I had given him the fatigues.

Magruder didn't say a word to me on the way up. He didn't even look at me. He was glaring out the window, his lips tight. I couldn't blame him, exactly; his ass was in the wringer along with the rest of us. I made myself stiff as a statue, hanging with all my strength to the seat belt I didn't dare buckle, to keep from being thrown into him.

Hoping he would forget I was there.

We stopped with another spray of sand and Magruder jumped out. He stood there, glaring. What he was glaring at this time was Sergeant Sambok and the civilian technician, Dr. Willard, assistant to the missing Dr. Douglas. He'd left them standing at attention in the sun while he went down to get me in person. Sunstroke? I don't know how they missed it. It wasn't a thing that General Magruder would have worried about, because the sun would never bother him. He was meaner than the sun. He kicked a clump of buffalo grass, spat, and jerked a thumb at the trailer. "Inside, you three," he ordered.

It wasn't any better inside the trailer. It was cooler, but not so much because of the air-conditioning as because of the chill that came from Magruder. When he looked you in the eye, your eyeballs froze. With all the worry I had myself, I had a little left over for Sergeant Sambok. Maybe even for Dr. Willard, too, because he wasn't even in the service. He'd just happened to be standing on the scaffolding with Larry Douglas when the make-believe me came puffing up with the carbine over his shoulder, pushed Douglas through the upper portal, and jumped after him. There hadn't been a thing Willard could have done about it—though that didn't seem to interest General Magruder—because he was a little guy and, like all the civilians on the project, unarmed.

Nyla Sambok was a different case. She answered Magruder's questions briskly and completely. "Yes, sir, the senator was my prisoner. Yes, sir, I allowed him to overpower me and take my weapon. Yes, sir, I was negligent. No, sir, I have no excuse." —But "completely" is the wrong word, because there was something in her tone, and something in her eyes, that said there was more to it than that. Once I'd sat on a rape court-martial, a nurse captain who'd been caught out on the obstacle course one night by a green draftee who thought that all women really wanted it, no matter how hard they resisted. The captain had looked the same way. Full of resentment and fury, and as much against herself as against the trainee.

Of course, there couldn't have been anything like that with the other Dom DeSota? —And then Magruder turned to me, and I forgot all about Sergeant Sambok's troubles, having plenty of my own.

Not ninety minutes before I'd been sitting in judgment on Private Dormeyer. Up and down the yo-yo goes.

They called him Ratface Magruder for a good reason. Not much chin and a hell of an overbite; and to make it worse he wore a stick-out mustache with more wax in it than hair, under a long, pointy nose. I could almost see the nose quivering as he sat there, thinking, frosting us all as his gaze moved around, tapping with his fingers on the leather cushion of the couch. He kept us waiting while he thought things through.

Then he said, "There are some things you should know."

We waited.

"The first thing," he said, "is that their fucking President hasn't given us an answer to President Brown's message, so we are going to have to implement Phase Two."

We waited some more.

"The second thing is that I had requested a HU-70 troop-carrying helicopter to transfer the prisoners. I was overruled, because somebody was worried about the Russky satellite seeing it, so they sent those chickenshit little choppers instead."

We waited some more, only with a little less

foreboding of doom—was he saying that there was some excuse? Because if they'd sent the right helicopter, all the prisoners would have gone at once, and the problem would never have arisen. It wasn't much of a hope, but it was the best I'd had for a while—and a blighted one, because of course he wasn't excusing us, he was just rehearsing the story he was going to cover his own ass with. He said: "Make no mistake. You three are still in the deep shit. You, DeSota, because you gave him a uniform. Shut up."—as I started to explain—"You, Sergeant, for letting him get your weapon away from you. And you, Willard, for letting that son of a bitch Douglas play around with the portal in the first place without a senior officer present. Not to mention letting the two of them get through."

"General Magruder," said Willard desperately, "I am here as a civilian consultant, and if there are any charges to be brought against me I have the right to have a lawyer present. I demand—"

"No you don't," Magruder corrected him. "What you do, Willard, is you volunteer to accompany these two, who are now ordered to Bolling Field."

"Bolling Field?" cried Willard. "That's Washington, D.C., isn't it? But—"

Magruder didn't tell him to shut up. He didn't have to; he looked at him, and the objections froze on Willard's tongue.

Outside I had heard the flutter of a chopper's rotors. As Magruder opened the door I saw it sitting there, the vanes turning slowly, the pilot peering out toward us.

"That's yours," said Magruder. "It'll take you to the airport where a MATS C-111 is waiting for you. Phase Two is about to begin."

When the old man, peering out of his apartment door, could hear no noises on the stairs he scuttled down to the mailbox. The precious brown envelope from the Welfare was there. He retrieved it, hurried back up the uncarpeted steps, let himself in, and snapped all three locks behind him. Now if he could just make it to the Seven-Eleven, he would have food and money for the next weeks. He did not even feel the faint puff of—something—that touched him; but as he turned he saw that his apartment had been ransacked! In just that minute, the old TV was gone, the shelves over the stove in the kitchen alcove had spilled out their sparse contents, the worn couch cushions were thrown on the floor. Moaning, he opened the door to his bedroom to see if his precious hoard of papers had been touched. . . . There was someone in his bed. A man. With his throat cut and his eyes glassy; the face was contorted in fear and pain . . . and the face was his own.

24 August 1983
4:20 P.M. Mrs. Nyla Christophe Bowquist

I should have been on my way to Rochester for preconcert publicity spots. I couldn't leave Washington. The whole crazy day zipped past flick-*blur*, and my flight time came and passed, and Amy rebooked me on an evening flight, and I told her to cancel that one too. I did what I always did when hopelessly confused and shaken up and worried. I practiced. I propped up the piano reduction of the Tchaikovsky orchestra part in front of the television set, and I played the concert. Over and over; and all the while my eyes kept getting pulled to the screen, where every twenty minutes or so they repeated that insane broadcast from the night before and Dom—dear Dom, my love, my bedmate, my coadulterer Dom— was sitting up there with that greasy smile on his face, introducing that imitation President of the United States, saying those incredible things. Normal programming was abandoned, but there was no real news, either. The alien troops in New Mexico held inside their occupied areas, ours did not attack them, no one in Washington would say anything tangible.

I was not the only person wholly confused and disoriented in Washington that day. Even the weather was miserable; there was some kind of a hurricane working its way up the coast, and what we were getting out of it was muggy heat with spats of soapy rain.

The phone kept ringing. Jackie called twice. Both of the Rostropoviches called; so did Slavi's

135

concertmaster, so did old Mrs. Javits—so did everybody who had any suspicion that I had a personal interest in Senator Dom DeSota, and none of them said anything embarrassing, and they were all very kind. Ten minutes after I hung up on each conversation I couldn't remember anything that had been said. The good thing was that the newspapers didn't call. That much of our secret was safe, Dom's and mine.

I spared a moment to be sorry for poor Marilyn DeSota, sitting in her penthouse with her phones going every minute, and wondering what the *hell* was going on with the man she was married to.

Yes, I spared a moment to be sorry for my lover's wife. It wasn't the first time. It was only the first time that I'd let myself dwell on it for more than maybe half a second—for as long as it took me to tell myself that Dom's infidelity was, after all, his responsibility and not mine.

I made myself believe that, usually.

And Amy kept coming in . . . with tea; with made-up questions about what dress I wanted to wear in Rochester, and did I remember I had a *Newsweek* interview scheduled for tomorrow morning in Rochester, and what the concert manager from Rochester had said when he called and I wouldn't talk to him.

I hadn't forgotten the concert, of course.

In a way, I was working at it harder than I would have been if I'd been on the scene. They were bringing in Riccardo Muti to conduct, and we had a difference of opinion. I wanted to do the Tchaikovsky, and he had agreed to that, but I wanted to play it without the usual cuts. Muti was resisting. That's a conductor for you. Get the damn concerto out of the way so you can get back to having the whole orchestra under your personal thumb, instead of sharing it with some damn instrumentalist. I'd had the same squabble every time I played the Tchaikovsky for a long time, and usually I gave in. This time I didn't want to.

So I played it all the way through, twice, and

drank a couple of cups of cooling tea, and then I played it some more.

The trouble with that was that my fingers thought about the music, but my mind was flying in all directions. *What* was Dom doing? Couldn't he at least telephone me? Was it *possible* that this crazy Cathouse project he'd joked with me about was somehow *real*? And what was I doing with my own life? Every now and then it would occur to me that if I wanted to start having a baby, it was none too soon to get on with it. . . .

But whose baby did I want?

I tried to make myself think about the music, while those sweet, lush, gut-stirring Romantic themes came floating out of the Guarnerius. Tchaikovsky had had his own troubles. With the concerto, for instance. "For the first time one must believe in the possibility of music that stinks in the ear," one critic had said at the premiere. How could you live after a review like that? (But now it was one of the best-loved concerti in the repertoire.) And his own life had been screwed up worse than mine, in the nonmusical ways—politics aside—*maybe* politics aside, because certainly there was a Byzantine flavor to the jockeying around the czar's court. He'd done worse with marriage than I had: tried it once, and had a nervous breakdown as a result. He'd had his twenty-year love-letter torrid romance with Nadejda von Meck without even once meeting the poor woman, running out of the back door of a house when she unexpectedly showed up at the front. Crazy Peter Ilyich! They said that he first intended to become a conductor. But it didn't work out, because he began leading the orchestra with the baton in his right hand and his chin held tightly in his left, because somehow he'd developed the conviction that if he let go of his chin, his head would fall off.

Crazy Peter Ilyich . . .

Spring went my E-string, the second one I'd broken that morning. I grinned in spite of myself, thinking of something Ruggiero Ricci had said to me once: "A Strad you have to seduce, but you can rape a Guarnerius." Only I'd raped it a little too roughly. At once, Amy popped in the door. I didn't ask if she'd been eavesdropping. Of course she had. I handed the fiddle over to her, and she examined it carefully before beginning to take the broken string off. "Might as well put a whole new set on," I suggested, and she nodded. I went on daydreaming while she opened a fresh packet. Crazy old Peter Ilyich, I thought again—only what it turned into was, "Crazy Nyla Bowquist, what are you doing with your life?"

I sucked on my fingertips, thinking. They were sore. They weren't bloody—you can't cut my left hand's fingertips with anything much less than a chisel any more—but they hurt. I was hurting in a lot of places.

I said, "Amy, where do you suppose my husband is now?"

She looked at her watch. "It's pushing five here— going on four back home—I suppose he's still in his office. Do you want me to get him for you?"

"Please." Even when somebody else was paying for it, Ferdie didn't like me running up huge long-distance bills, so we had this special line to use—only Amy was better at remembering all the numbers you had to dial than I was. It took her a minute or two.

"He was on his way to his club," she explained, handing me the phone. "I got him on the car phone for you."

I looked at her in a way that she immediately interpreted correctly. "I'll finish this outside," she said, taking the Guarnerius and the strings and the polishing material, and I said into the phone: "Honey? It's Nyla."

"Thanks for calling, dear," came the warm, soft old voice. "I've been worried about you, with all that's going on—"

"Oh, I'm fine," I said, lying. "Ferdie?"

"Yes, dear?"

"I—uh—it's pretty wild around here today."

"I know it. I've been thinking you might have trouble getting a flight to Rochester. I suppose the airlines are all messed up. Do you want me to send the company jet?"

"Oh, no," I said quickly. What I wanted was not very clear to me, but I knew that wasn't it. "No, Amy's got all that sort of thing under control. The thing is, Ferdie dear, there's something I want to tell you." I took a deep breath, getting ready for the next words.

They wouldn't come out.

"Yes, dear?" said Ferdie politely.

I took another deep breath and tried a different way. "Ferdie, you remember Dom DeSota?"

"Of course, dear." He sounded almost amused. Well, that was a dumb question! There wasn't anybody in the country who didn't know who Dom DeSota was this day, besides which Ferdie had always made it his business to know everybody with any kind of power in Illinois. "It's awful about him," he offered. "I know it must upset you to think about what he's involved in."

I swallowed. Of course he hadn't intended anything—when you've got a bad conscience, even "hello" is a double entendre. I tried to imagine what Ferdie was hearing, from what I was saying. It seemed to me that I was giving an excellent performance of the wife who has something to confess but can't quite get the words out of her mouth, and maybe down inside my head somewhere that was what I was trying to do—to make Ferdie at last so suspicious that he would come right out and ask the questions that I would have to answer.

Only Ferdie wasn't getting suspicious. He was, if anything, getting tenderly, forgivingly amused at his flutter-brained wife who couldn't seem to remember what it was she was talking about. "Ferdie," I said, "there's something I wanted to talk to you about. You see, I've been—oh, what is it, Amy?" I asked, irritated, as she appeared in the doorway.

"Mrs. Kennedy is here to see you," she said.

"Oh, hell," I said. On the phone I could hear Ferdie's fond chuckle.

"I heard that," he said. "You've got company. Well, dear, at the moment we're double-parked in front of the club, and maybe you can hear the horns blowing. Let's talk later, all right?"

"That will be fine, darling," I said, frustrated, scared . . . and mostly relieved. Some day I would have to say it all to him, every word, every truth . . . but, praise God, that day was not yet. And when Jackie came in to tell me that she was going to carry me off to dinner—"Just family, really, but we want you to join us"—I accepted with gratitude.

It wasn't really a family dinner—none of the children were there—not even in the sense of political family, although Jack Kennedy's principal aide and his wife were at the table, because the only other guest was our old friend Lavrenti Djugashvili. Good host and gracious guest, sure, but I was surprised to see him, all the same. That made my presence a little easier to understand, because Lavi was a single man that evening and Jackie didn't like an unbalanced table. "No, dear Nyla," he said, kissing my hand, "tonight I am bachelor, because Xenia has gone back to Moscow to make sure our daughter is taking proper vitamin pills at boarding school."

"So what we are going to have," the senator said, "is just a nommal infommal dinner, because we've all had all the excitement we need today. Albert! See what Mrs. Bowquist would like to drink."

It isn't just wealth. Ferdie is just about as rich as Jack Kennedy, but when we have a normal, informal family dinner we don't usually have it in the dining room with a butler handing the dishes around. We have it in the breakfast room, and Hannah the cook usually puts the dishes on the table in front of us. The Kennedys were never that informal. We had our cocktails in the drawing room, with the portraits of the senator's three deceased brothers looking down at us, and when we went into the dining hall there were old Joe and Rose looking down at us in oil from that wall. The wines were all estate-bottled, and the silver wasn't silver. It was gold.

And, actually, the whole thing did just what Jack Kennedy said he wanted it to do. It made the world real again. It was exactly the kind of small dinner party that marked a hundred nights of every year for me, even to the talk about the weather (hurricane on its way, rain expected to get worse) and Lavi's daughter's school grades, and how truly beautifully (Jackie told me again) I had played the Gershwin, and what a pity it was that the audience had been distracted.

The ambassador took me in, handsome blocky Russian face cheerful and admiring of my dress, the flowers on the table, the wine, the food. I'd always liked Lavrenti, partly because he really enjoyed music. It wasn't always the kind of music I understood. I'd gone once with him to hear some traveling troupe from Soviet Georgia, fifty squat, dark, handsome men bellowing out a-capella songs that seemed to be made up mostly of roaring, with interjections of *Hai!* and *Hey!* every few seconds. They were not my cup of tea, but Lavi's eyes were misting when we left; and I'd seen him affected just as much from the stage, while I was doing the Prokofiev Second. Which says something; because there's marvelous musicianship in that concerto, but the fraction of any audience that finds it touching its heart is minute.

And for nearly an hour we stayed off the subject of the other United States of America's invasion, and especially the subject of my Dom.

Jackie kept it going. She and Mrs. Hart were helping with a fund raiser for Constitution Hall, and the two of them had amusing stories about how Pat Nixon wanted to bring in a country-and-western group, and Mrs. Helms had a pet tenor from Southern Methodist University she wanted to give exposure to. As we were starting on the guinea hen and wild rice Jackie looked over at me and said, "Shall we really rock them, Nyla? Would you like to come and do something like the Berg?"

The senator shifted position uncomfortably—his back was obviously bothering him again—and complained, "The Berg? That's that squeaky-squawky one, isn't it? Do you really like that, Nyla?"

Well, nobody really "likes" the Berg concerto—I mean, it's like "liking" a rogue elephant. You have to pay attention to it, whether you like it or not. But it's a show-off piece, so I need to do it once in a while to keep the other guys impressed. And I can't do it very well at home, because Chicago's Orchestra Hall isn't up to it. It's fine for, say, the Beethoven or one of the Bruchs, which are so melodic and rhythmic that the orchestra doesn't really have to hear itself. But they need to for something like the Berg, and Orchestra Hall's acoustics aren't good that way.

While I was explaining all this to Jack Kennedy, I could see that I didn't have his attention. His eyes were on me, but they were looking right through me, and he was stirring the wild rice around with his fork instead of eating. I assumed it was his back. So did Lavi. "Ah, Senator," he cut in, with that Russian-bear good humor that he used for sympathy, "why not come to Moscow to see doctors? Our Djugashvili Medical Institute, named for grandfather, not me, has best surgeons in world, no question!"

"Will they give me a new back?" Kennedy growled.

"Spinal transplant, why not? Have Dr. Azimof, best transplant man in world. Has done three hundred eighty-five hearts alone, not counting livers, testicles, I don't know what all. Have saying in Moscow, when world's first successful hemorrhoid transplant is done, Itzhak will do it!"

I laughed. Jackie laughed. Everybody around the table laughed, except the senator. He smiled, but the smile didn't last. "Sorry, Lavi," he said. "I'm afraid my sense of huma isn't working very well tonight." He

put down his fork and leaned across the table. "Gary?
Did you say they were flying Jerry Brown in—I mean,
our Jerry?"

"That's right, Senator. They located him in
Maine, but his flight was delayed on account of the
weather."

The senator grimaced, rubbing his back. "Tell
me about the weather," he said, waving to the butler
to take his plate away. "God knows what use Brown
will be," he commented, "but I guess he can at least
give us some background on his opposite number,
over there."

Hart chimed in, "I wish we had a better line on
those other guys. Maybe we could find some more of
their doubles here and get them in on this."

Neither of them were looking at me, but Jackie
was. "Nyla," she said, "you know Dom DeSota, of
course." And I figured out why I had been invited.
Without ever saying an overt word, Jackie was giving
me honorary status as a wife—anyway, a what-you-
might-call fiancée. She could not have treated me
better if Dom and I had been married. She might not
have treated me as well, if Dom and I had been
married, because Dom's reputation was thoroughly
beclouded—

Or maybe not, because she went on, "I think you
spoke to him not long before he left for Mexico."
Tactful! But Dom's chief aide must have been talking.
"I wonder if he said anything about the reason?"

I hesitated. "I don't know if you all know what
was going on at Sandia—"

Lavrenti said, "Oh, yes, I think so, dear Mrs.
Bowquist. Even I had heard something."

"You can speak freely," said the senator. "If it
ever was a secret, it isn't now."

"Well—the senator said something about a double of himself. Exact. I mean, even with the same
fingerprints. They wanted him to confront this other
man."

"Exactly," said Gary Hart triumphantly. "It's just

what we thought, Senator. That man on television wasn't our own Dom DeSota at all."

The Senator nodded. Then he gestured to the butler. "We'll take our coffee in my study, Albert," he said, and then to us, "Let's take another look at this guy on TV."

Even so, it took me a long time to understand what they were saying. We were in the study—not what I would have called a study; it was bigger than my own living room in Chicago, big enough for war councils and off-the-record meetings of a dozen or more. It had four television monitors plus the big screen; it had news-wire CRT's for INS and AP; most of all, it had a videotape machine. Jack Kennedy sat in the corner of the room nearest the air-conditioning exhaust with his cigar, gnawing on his knuckle as he watched the replay of Dom's face, speaking in Dom's voice the words that I could not believe Dom would ever say.

And neither could Jack Kennedy. "What do you think?" he asked the room at large. No one spoke, and I realized the Harts were looking at me.

For a moment I wondered if, after all, they were blaming me for Dom's incredible turnabout. The guilty conscience again, of course.

Then I had a second thought.

"Run it again, will you?" I asked, my voice beginning to shake, and fumbled in my bag for the glasses that I never wore in public. I looked harder at my love's face, studying every line, listening to every tone, watching every gesture.

I said doubtfully, "He looks very thin, doesn't he? As though he were under some kind of strain—or else—"

"Or else," said Hart, "we were right about that, too, Senator. That isn't our Dom DeSota. It's theirs."

"I knew it," piped Jackie, who had moved over to the arm of my chair. I felt her hand on my shoulder, mothering me. I could have kissed her. A constriction

I hadn't known was there fell away from my chest. Oh, Dom! You might be an adulterer, but at least you weren't a traitor! . . .

"I think," announced the senator, "that we might just take a look at that CIA summary now, Gary." He took a folded sheaf of paper from his aide, put his own glasses on, and glanced at the top page.

I wasn't listening. I was too filled with relief. It didn't make everything all right, quite. There was still Ferdie. Not to mention Marilyn DeSota. But at least one sharp, shocking pain had eased.

I wondered what time it was. If I could excuse myself soon and get back to my hotel—if I could call Ferdie still tonight, before he went to sleep—maybe now I could go through with it and tell him what I was so frightened to say. Of course, there was still Marilyn—

Of course there was still Marilyn! What was I thinking of? How could I tell my secret without telling Dom's too? And how could I do that without at least warning Dom first?

Dissolved again in doubt, I tried to pay attention to what Jack Kennedy was saying. ". . . two people," he said. "One was a smart Albuquerque cop. The other was a smart FBI woman they put in shorts on a bicycle, out on the mountain where the other guys had occupied a television transmitter. Neither one had any difficulty getting the enemy soldiers to talk."

"Lousy security," said Hart, frowning.

"Lousy for them. Good for us," said Jack. "Anyway, they didn't say anything—at least they didn't say much—about military matters. But the cop and the FBI woman did get them talking about the differences between their world and ours. I think we have a pretty good idea now of where their history and ours are different."

I tried to listen with comprehension to the rest of what Jack Kennedy was saying. It wasn't easy. What I know about is music; there weren't very many history courses when I went to Juilliard. For that matter, it was hard for me to grasp what was meant by "parallel times," though Dom had explained it to me. As a theory. As reality it was a whole lot harder to accept.

"Their enemies," Jack said, "seem to be the Soviet Union and the People's Republic of China."

He paused, glancing at the ambassador, who sank down in his chair, frowning, without comment. "Which China?" I asked, as anyone would—did they mean the Korean Mandate, or Han Peking, or the Hong Kong Suzerainty, or Manchukuo or the Taiwanese Empire or any of the other twelve or fifteen pieces China had splintered into after the Cultural Revolution?

"Just one China," said Jack. "They managed to hang together, and now—for them—they're the biggest nation on Earth."

We all looked at each other. That was hard enough to swallow. The idea of the Soviet Union threatening anybody any more was even crazier. I tried to read Lavi's expression, but he had none. He was just listening, and after a moment he stretched out a hand and took one of the senator's cigars, though I knew that normally he didn't smoke. He kept his eyes down on it, slowly unwrapping the foil, not speaking at all.

I could see why he was having as much trouble with all this as I was, although for different reasons. It was, after all, the nuclear exchange with the U.S.S.R. that had sparked the Cultural Revolution in China. What it had done to the Soviet Union was even worse. Moscow gone, Leningrad gone, basically the whole country decapitated.

I tried to remember Russian history. There'd been the czars. Then Lenin, who got assassinated or something. Then Trotsky, who got them into a series of border wars with places like Finland and Estonia, most of which he lost. Then Lavrenti's own grandfather for a while—with all kinds of internal famines and insurrections—who started the nuclear project, which got us into the atom-bomb race, which only ended when the Chinese zapped Moscow and the nuclear project, all at once. . . .

But in their time, it seemed, Trotsky never did take over the U.S.S.R., though Lavrenti's grandfather did. There wasn't a series of border wars. There was one big one. They called it World War II, and it was with a man named Hitler, a German, out to conquer the world, and very nearly making it before the rest of the world united against him.

That was a stunner. Germany was just one country! I'd played there! It wasn't anywhere nearly big enough to threaten the whole world!

And besides—there was Lavrenti, sitting across the room from me, slowly igniting his Cuban Claro. Of course, he was nominally a Communist. But the Russians were nowhere near as militant as, say, the English Bolsheviks, with their centers of aggression in all their so-called commonwealth federated republics. Thank heaven Canada and Australia had split off. . . . I shook my head. It didn't make much sense to me.

It did, unfortunately, to Lavrenti Djugashvili. He had smoked the first half-inch of his cigar by the time Kennedy finished with the CIA report, and expected it when the senator stopped and looked inquiringly directly at him. "I take your point," said Lavi. "This is a matter of concern. If this invasion of your country is in the final analysis directed at mine—"

"Not at yours exactly, I think," Jack said quickly. "At the Soviet Union that exists in their time, I would suppose."

"Whose people," Lavi said heavily, "are still my own, are they not?"

Kennedy didn't say anything. He only gave a fraction of a nod.

Lavi stood up. "With your permission, dear Mrs. Kennedy," he said somberly, "I think I must visit my embassy now. I thank you for this information, Senator. Perhaps something should be done, although I do not now see just what."

We all stood up, even us women. It wasn't a mark of respect so much as a sort of declaration of sympathy. When he was gone, Senator Kennedy rang for the butler to serve us nightcaps. "Poor Lavrenti," he said. And then, "Poor us, too, for that matter, because I don't see just what to do, either."

Bad back or not, the senator decided to drive me back to my hotel himself. Jackie came along for the ride. It wasn't a pleasure jaunt. The rain was coming in sheets and the streets were slippery with emulsified oil.

All three of us fit easily in the big front seat. We didn't talk much, not even Jackie, who was helping her husband scan the road nervously—since both his younger brothers had died in car accidents, one drowned, one burned, she was uneasy about cars. I had my own thoughts. It was not much past ten o'clock. Nine in Chicago. Ferdie would surely still be awake. Should I call him? Did I have the right to, for Dom's sake? Did I have the right not to, for Ferdie's sake?

So I hardly noticed when we slowed down with an unexpected traffic jam ahead of us, until the senator leaned forward irritably. "What the hell?" he muttered, trying to peer past the cars stalled right in front of us.

"What is it?" asked Jackie. "An accident?"

It was no accident.

Kennedy swore. Through the windows of the car ahead I saw something coming toward us in the other lane. It was fast and big, but it didn't have the flashing lights of a police car or ambulance. It had no proper lights at all, just a single bright spotlight that *flick-flick*'d back and forth across the road, like the blade of a windshield wiper, and the light illuminated something that stuck out of the vehicle itself.

It looked almost like a cannon.

"My Jesus God Almatty," said the senator, "it's a fucking *tank*."

Jackie cried out—so did I, I'm sure. The senator didn't wait. He backed the big Chrysler around in a quarter-circle high-speed turn, banging the muffler against the curb on the far side of the street, cramped the wheel as far as it would go, and floored it. He skidded out onto the highway maybe thirty yards ahead of the tank, accelerating all the way up to ninety miles an hour on that meandering river road, and I kept seeing that huge cannon sticking out in front of the tank. Aiming now straight at us. The senator felt it, too, because at the first cross street he stood on the brake. We fishtailed to a stop—almost a stop; oh, say, about forty miles an hour—and he manhandled that car around the corner.

A taxi was coming the other way.

I have never felt closer to death. We stopped. So did the other car, but not with anything to spare. Our front bumper was almost touching the taxi driver's door, and the man inside was already rolling his window down to sob and scream at Jack.

Who paid him no attention.

We had stalled the engine. Jack didn't even try to start it again. He opened his door and leaned out, grunting at the twisting he was giving his back, to stare as the tank went past, fast and serious, followed by half a dozen troop-carrying trucks. I could see the gleam of helmets in the street lights as they passed, and behind them was another tank.

"Remarkable," said Jack Kennedy.

"Why are we putting tanks like that on the street?" I demanded. He turned to look at me. Jack is an elderly man, but I had never seen him look quite that old before. He put one arm around Jackie protectively.

"We ahn't," he said. "Those are not ours. We don't have any tanks that look like that."

The veterinarian was twenty-four years old and she was terrified. She soaped herself and rinsed herself six times, as ordered, and came out naked and wet to the farm bedroom where the army captain was waiting. She did not even think about being naked in front of him as he passed the counter wand slowly over every inch of her skin, listening to the sporadic rattle of radiation. "I think you got all the dust," the officer said at last. "You say you found the cattle just like this? And that dust all over everything?" She nodded, eyes big and frightened. "You can get dressed," he finished. "I think you're all right." But he watched her go with fears of his own. Radioactive fallout! Somehow half a square mile had been coated with high-level radionuclides—here, no more than forty miles from Dallas, with no war going on that he knew about and no source of the fallout reported anywhere. It was a puzzle with no answer. And it was a fear that shook him to his bones—what if it had happened forty miles away, in the heart of the city itself?

26 August 1983
6:40 A.M. Nicky DeSota

I was dreaming that Mrs. Laurence Rockefeller had asked me to arrange the mortgage for a six-hundred-million-dollar apartment complex along the lake, only she wanted to start with a down payment of one hundred fifty dollars because all her money was tied up in dimes . . . and then when I finally got the papers ready to sign she couldn't do it because she didn't have any thumbs. And then, as the bumping of the plane landing woke me up, the first thing on my mind wasn't where I was, or what was going to happen to me, but whether Mr. Blakesell had known I was arrested in time to get someone to cover my three mortgage closings. There wasn't anything I could do about it, of course.

There wasn't anything I could do about anything, because I was handcuffed to the back of the seat in front of me. My first long-distance flight in one of those new big Boeing four-engine jobbers should have been a real thrill. What it was was a pain. I mean, real pain. I was aching from being in that same seat for eleven hours, and two intermediate stops, and God knows how many hundreds, or even thousands, of miles; but the big ache had been with me even before they put me on the plane in the first place, wobbling up that ladder with my hands cuffed behind me and that ugly FBI man, Moe Something-or-other, threatening all kinds of doom if I spoke, or tried to get away, or tried to take off the hat and veil they'd made me wear so nobody would know who I was. He

151

knew all about those aches too. He'd given me most of them.

I will say for the FBI boys and girls, they really know how to hurt you without leaving marks.

Across the aisle, the other prisoner was awake inside his own hat and veil. I could see his head moving. His guard was snoring as lustily as my own as we bumped interminably along runways that seemed to go nowhere.

At least I was out of the holding tank in the Chicago headquarters, where I'd spent most of the last—what was it? Days, for sure, though nobody would tell me how many. It had been pretty bad, in there with that bunch of social undesirables—muggers on the way to the concentration camps, currency speculators held for trial—but it was better than the times they took me out to ask me more questions. I hadn't told them anything, of course. I hadn't had anything to tell—but, my God, how I wished I had!

And then Moe had come in, waking me up, and dragged me out. And we'd wound up in this plane, going God knew where.

No. Both God and I knew where, now, because through the veil and the tiny window I could see a gaudy, foreign-looking terminal, with a big sign that said:

WELCOME TO
ALBUQUERQUE, NEW MEXICO
ELEVATION 5196 FEET

New Mexico, for heaven's sake! What in the world did they want with me in New Mexico?

Of course, Moe wasn't going to tell me. The stewardess came by and tugged his shoulder to wake him, and he leaned over to wake the other guard, but all he said to me was, "Remember what I told you!" I remembered. He made us wait until all the other passengers had got themselves out of the plane. Then he made us wait some more, while mechanics came out to turn the big propellors around a few revolutions and a truck backed up with 100-octane gasoline to refill the tanks.

Then somebody waved to us from the terminal door.

Moe unlocked my handcuffs and we left, me trying not to stumble as we clambered down the steep aisle to the stairs, and then down the stairs. The other prisoner followed behind us with his own guard; and they whisked us through an airport terminal that looked as though it had been built as a set for some Latin-American musical comedy. People stared. The overly curious were pushed roughly out of the way—there weren't too many of them, because the FBI goons weren't hard to recognize, and most people turned the other way fast. Into a car, me and Moe on the jump seats, the other prisoner and his guard behind us. A city police car pulled out ahead of us, and we went blasting away, God knows how fast, through city streets and out onto a two-lane highway that snaked away up into the hills.

We drove for nearly an hour. We wound up at a crossroads, two empty highways stretching to the compass points, and a filling station with a motel behind it. The sign over the office said "La Cucaracha Travelers Rest," which was not a name I would have given to a motel.

I also wouldn't have put armed guards in the driveway.

The guards were, however, a little decorative touch that I had begun to get used to. So there were good signs and there were bad signs. The bad sign was that I was still under arrest. The good sign was that I wasn't being taken to Leavenworth or one of the camps, where I would disappear from sight until they got good and ready to let me out—if ever. This was a permanent island in the FBI archipelago. They could not mean to keep me here for very long. They might even let me go.

Alternatively, what part of me might come out of the Cucaracha Motel might be only enough to send home to bury.

I wasn't given enough time to worry. My silent colleague and I were hustled into one of the cabins and ordered to sit on the edge of the bed and keep quiet, while Moe stood inside the door, glaring at us, and the other one stood right outside. We didn't have long to wait, though. The door opened from outside. Moe moved out of the way without looking to see who it was.

Nyla Christophe strode in, her hands clasped behind her.

She was wearing a sun hat and dark glasses. I could not see her expression, but I could tell that she was gazing at us thoughtfully—I could feel the burning, like acid, where her eyes raked across my face. But her voice was only normally unpleasant when she said, "All right, you guys, you can take those dumb veils off now."

I was glad enough to do that, because I was stifling inside that thing in the desert heat. The other fellow moved more slowly and unwillingly; and when the veil was off his expression was scared, resentful, unhappy—all the things I would have expected; but what I hadn't expected was that the face that wore the expressions belonged to Larry Douglas.

What I was absolutely certain of was that Larry Douglas was at least in part responsible for the last four or five days of misery. How, I didn't know. Why, I couldn't even guess. So I was not in the least sorry to see him caught in the same trap he'd helped me into . . . only that just made it all even more confusing! If he had passed on to Nyla Christophe all the things I'd told him when he dragged me down to see that beat-up old movie actor downstate, why was he a prisoner too? And what were we doing in New Mexico?

The good part of that was that Douglas seemed as baffled as I. "Nyla," he said, his voice unsteady with anger he was trying not to show, "what the hell is this all about? Your guys come and grab me, drag me out of bed, won't tell me a word—"

"Sweetybumps," she said cheerfully, "shut up." Even with the dark glasses on he could read enough of her expression to swallow hard. He shut up. "Better," she said, and, over her shoulder, "Moe?"

Rumble from the apeman: "Yes, Miss Christophe?"

"Is the mobile lab here yet?"

"Parked right behind the cabins, all ready to go."

She nodded. She took off hat and glasses and sat in the one lumpy armchair the room possessed, extending a hand without looking. Moe put a cigarette into it, and followed with a light. "It is possible," she said, "that you two guys are in the clear on this particular matter. We need you to check some things out."

"Oh, good, Nyla," cried Douglas. "I knew it was just some mistake!"

And I managed to say, what I am ashamed to admit I hadn't really been thinking about for some time, "What about my fiancée and those others, Miss Christophe?"

"That depends, DeSota. If the tests come out the way I think they will, they'll all be released."

"Thank heaven! Uh—what tests are we talking about?"

"The ones you're going to have right now," she said. "Get on with it, Moe." And she left the cabin, while the other goon came in with an armload of stuff, followed by a man in a white jacket and another armload.

I couldn't help cringing, but it turned out that not even Moe was going to beat me up again. What they had in mind took longer, but was nowhere near as unpleasant—well, it wasn't exactly *fun*. They took my fingerprints and my toe prints. They measured my earlobes and the distance between the pupils of my eyes. They took blood and saliva and skin samples, and then they made me pee into a bottle and move my bowels into a paper cup. It took a long time. The only thing that made it less obnoxious was that my obnoxious fellow prisoner—the mystery-man Larry Douglas, my coconspirator from the Carson coffee shop and fellow traveler to the Reagan place in Dixon, Illinois—was doing the same.

And liking it even less. Neither Moe nor the other guard liked it a whole lot, either. They went outside, watching through the window, while the lab technician took his samples and signs, so Douglas and I were able to talk a little. The first question I asked him was the one I'd been brooding on for a long time: "What the hell are you? Some kind of undercover Fed?"

He had a hangdog look, but even a whipped dog can snarl. "None of your damn business, DeSota," he snapped. He watched my blood being sucked up into a syringe, holding his own arm where the silent lab man had just done the same to him.

"Well, what are you? Nyla Christophe's boy friend, or fink, or prisoner?"

He said simply, "Yes." Then he let down his pants so the lab man could take a chunk out of the flesh of his butt. "If I were you, DeSota," he said darkly, "I'd worry about myself instead of some other guy. Do you have any idea how much trouble you're in?"

I laughed in his face. All the aches and miseries of my body told me how much trouble I was in. "Anyway," I pointed out, "she said we might be in the clear here, so what have I got to worry about?"

He looked at me with pity and contempt. "That's what she said," he agreed. "But did you ever hear her say anything about letting you go?"

I had to swallow hard before I could ask, "What the hell are you talking about, Douglas?" He shrugged, looking at the medic. He let me stew until the man had taken all the little bits and trickles and probings he wanted and departed with them. Neither of the guards came in after that, though we could see them sitting on the rail, fanning themselves as they gazed out across the highway. A streamliner was arrowing along the rail line just across the highway, and I thought with a sudden pang of Greta. I repeated, "What are you talking about? She said she'd probably let us go—"

"Not 'us,' DeSota. 'Them.' The witnesses, who don't know anything. You're a whole different animal. You know a lot."

"I do?" I searched my brain, came up empty. "Good lord, man, I don't even know what she wants with me!"

He said gloomily, "The big thing you know is that there's something to know, and that's the biggest thing of all. How did you manage to be in two places at once?"

"How the hell do I know?" I cried.

"But you know that it happened," he pressed. "So you know that it's possible. So you know that somebody—say a criminal—could do something, say commit a murder, in one place, and have a hundred good witnesses to swear that he was someone else. Jesus, boy! Do you know what that would mean to somebody like me? I mean, somebody who needed that kind of alibi?" he corrected himself.

"But I don't know how it was done!" I wailed.

He said sourly, "So I found out. Wake up, will you? Do you think Nyla's going to let you go home and tell people that such things can be?"

I sat down, shaken.

I could see the logic to what he said. The stories were that the FBI camps were full of people who were unfortunately in possession of information that couldn't be allowed to become public. If I was one . . .

If I was one, my next stop wouldn't be Chicago. It would be a road gang in the Everglades, digging drainage ditches and fighting off alligators—or cutting down trees for that endless road in Alaska. Anywhere. Wherever. The exact place might be in doubt, but what was sure was that, wherever it was, that would be my permanent address, at least until the time came when my secrets were no secrets any more.

Or until I died. Whichever came first. And I was pretty sure that after a year or two in the camps, I wouldn't *care* which came first.

When the shadows of the flagpole outside had nearly disappeared, because the sun was straight up, they brought us ham and cheese sandwiches wrapped in wax paper and terrible lukewarm coffee out of a machine—both from the filling station in front of the cabins. I was starving, but I took no pleasure in them. I slowly put them away, and was ready with the empty cup and wrappings when the door opened to take them out.

Only it wasn't Moe or the other guard come for that. It was Moe, all right, but he stepped aside, and after him entered Nyla Christophe. She had a sloppy grin on her face. In one thumbless hand she held a bottle of champagne, cradled against her chest so it wouldn't fall. "Congratulations, boys," she said. "You passed. You're exactly the same."

Neither Douglas nor I said a word. She pouted. "Aw, hon," she said to Douglas, giggling a little—it wasn't really a reassuring giggle, "don't you see this is my way of telling you I'm sorry. *Glasses*," she said, in quite a different tone, and the second goon stumbled in his hurry to get into the room with his tray of thick hotel tumblers. She jerked her head. The two of them left, and she gave the bottle to Douglas. "That's the way, sweetie," she said, watching him as, looking more at her than at what he was doing, he began to peel the foil off and thumb back the cork. "Glad to see you haven't lost your touch." There was something in his worried (but faintly belligerent) and her tender (but not so faintly mocking) expressions that told me I didn't know all that was going on. Whatever the relationships between them, they were not just a matter of Federal agent and informer.

Then *pop* went the cork.

Douglas poured. Nyla Christophe accepted the first glass, wrapping all four fingers around it securely enough. "Know what I'm talking about?" she asked. With a hiccup—this bottle of champagne, I thought, wouldn't be her first that day. I shook my head. She said, "Thought not. The tests came out perfect. Same blood, same bones, same prints. You're the same guys—and my report's on the way to headquarters, and that's where I'll be before long myself. So let's drink to Nyla Christophe, next maybe deputy·chief of the whole damn bureau!"

I drank her damn champagne. I drank it because I didn't particularly want to make her angry, and partly because a guy like me doesn't get imported French champagne every day, and most of all because I didn't know what else to do. Maybe Douglas was right! Maybe this was so big a thing that Nyla Christophe really could get a big promotion out of it . . . and in that case maybe he was right about the rest of his nasty remarks too.

I wondered what Greta would do when I just never showed up again. Maybe they'd let me write? At least to say good-bye?

It was not good news for me, what Nyla Christophe said, but Larry Douglas thought it was for him. "That's *swell*, hon!" he enthused. "Boy! You'll show them in Washington. And, listen, I've got a lot of ideas for you! This business of establishing two identical identifications—did you ever think what that might mean to the bureau? I mean, infiltrating subversive organizations, for instance? I don't know exactly how it works, of course, but . . ."

Christophe let him go on, a dreamy smile on her face. While he was still talking she came over beside him and ran her hand down his back in a friendly way. "Sweetie," she said affectionately, "you're a real jerk."

He swallowed. "You—you don't want to take me with you?" he stammered.

"Take you? That's the fucking last thing I would do, Larry hon."

He blazed up. "Then let go of me, damn it! You've got no business sweeting me up like that!"

She let her smile grow deeper. She was actually quite good-looking when she wanted to be. I thought I saw actual dimples above the corners of her mouth. "Larry," she said sweetly, "maybe there are some other people who can get on my back for making love to somebody when I don't really mean it, but you're sure not one of them."

I had no idea what she was talking about. He obviously did. His face went gray. "You don't know shit about it," she told him. "It's a lot bigger than you could possibly guess." She glanced at me. "Want to know what's going on?" she asked.

Oh, boy, did I! I didn't have to answer. She knew the answer and went right on, "Let me start from the beginning. Suppose—"

She hesitated. Then she shrugged and grimly raised her right hand, the four fingers spread and the missing thumb nakedly, shockingly obvious. "Suppose I hadn't got into trouble with the law when I was seventeen. Suppose I grew up in a normal way. My life would have been a lot different, wouldn't it?" I nodded, meaning I guessed so but I was too lost to have a useful opinion; Douglas just went on looking stricken and grim. "So there might have been one life in which I grew up just the way I did—the way I am

now, right? And there could have been another one
in which I became, oh, I don't know. A musician.
Maybe a concert violinist."

Her expression didn't really change, but I got the
idea from something in her eyes that she was waiting
to see if I would laugh at that idea. I didn't laugh.
"See, I would have liked that at one time," she said.
"And the thing is that you can't say one of those
possibilities is real and the other is just imaginary. Not
any more. Because they're both real. All the possibilities are real, maybe. It's just that we only live in
one possibility, and we can't see the others."

I darted a glance at Douglas. He was as lost as I
was, and a lot more scared—probably, I thought with
a sinking feeling, because he knew more than I did
about what was likely to happen to us.

"Hell with that," she said suddenly. "Come on, I'll
show you. Moe!"

The door popped open, and the bigger goon
filled the doorway. Nyla pushed past him, beckoning
for us to follow. It was unbelievably hot outside in the
sun. Her footsteps were unsteady—partly sun; partly
high heels in the sand; mostly, I thought, either
champagne or pure delight in her probable future.
She led the way to another cabin, with a previously
unobserved FBI man hulking in front of it. When
Nyla Christophe nodded he threw the door open. She
peered inside, then nodded to Douglas and me.

"Take a look," she invited. "Here's two good
possibilities for you."

I still did not have an idea in the world what she
was talking about, but I did what I was told. There
were two men in the room. One was over in the
corner, gently patting cream onto one of the worst
cases of sunburn I'd ever seen. He had no shirt on,
and he was lobster red to just above his wrists, and
down to a V around his neck. With his hands over his
face I couldn't get a good look at him.

The other was closer, and not moving. He lay flat

on his back on one of the beds, his eyes closed. Snoring. He looked like he'd had a hard time. I don't mean just the routine hard time that you expected when you were an FBI prisoner, I mean he looked half dead. And he looked—

"Douglas!" I yelled. "It's you!"

Douglas didn't say a word. It hit him harder than it did me. He was strangling, eyes popping. I could see he was trying to ask a question, so I asked it for him. "What's the matter with him?" I asked.

Nyla Christophe shrugged. "He'll be okay. Sunstroke and exposure, and he got himself bitten by a rattlesnake. But he's had all his shots, and the doc says he'll be good as new tomorrow. But you didn't take a good look at the other guy yet, did you?"

And so I did. And he turned and looked at me. And the face was sunburned and raw, and the expression was grim, but the face was a face I knew very well.

"My God," I said. "He's got to be the guy from Daleylab!"

"Close," said Nyla Christophe cheerfully, "but he says he's not. He says lots of things, DeSota, things you wouldn't believe; he's been talking steadily ever since the train crew picked the two of them up in the desert last night. He says all those possibilities are really real and that there's plenty more like him around—in one of those possibilities or another. But you're kind of missing the point, DeSota. What he mostly says—and what all the tests say, every one of them—is that he's *you*."

At this hour of the night the big underground parking garage was deserted, and the lawyer wished he hadn't worked so late as he tried to remember where he'd left his car. You never could find a policeman when you needed one! He felt he needed one now—two rapes, a murder, nobody knew how many muggings in the garage in the past few months. Then he rounded a corner and saw two uniformed men patrolling, with tommy guns slung over their shoulders. "Good evening," he said, feeling better at once—until he observed that their uniforms were gray-green shoulder-boarded things, with forage caps quite unlike the checkerboarded ones of the Chicago police force. Worse, when they challenged him he recognized the language. Russian! Instinctively, he turned and ran, his shoulder blades crawling. He heard a burst of shots, but no bullet struck him. And when, stuck at a dead end, he turned, sobbing, to confront them, they were gone.

26 August 1983
7:40 P.M. Senator Dominic DeSota

All that afternoon I had been staring longingly out the window at the pocket-sized swimming pool in the courtyard, sweating by the bucket and my sunburn tormenting me every minute. It wasn't just the sunburn or the heat that tormented me. Somewhere not far from here—but hopelessly walled away from me by whatever it was that separated one time-line from another—my country was being invaded, and somebody wearing my face had gone on television to give aid and comfort to the invaders. I could not remember any case in the history of the United States since the Civil War when any elected U.S. senator had done anything like that. What were my colleagues thinking of me?

What was Nyla Bowquist thinking of me?

I didn't even know what I thought of myself any more. The last forty-eight hours had been the worst of my life. It had been a terrible shock to find out that the Cathouse represented some kind of reality, and that there were infinite numbers of worlds just like my own, many of them with a Dominic DeSota, indistinguishable from me by any test. I had been taken prisoner by one of them. I had knocked out a woman who was, exactly, the woman I loved, and been held prisoner by another copy of her, not quite exact because of her mutilated hands. I had kidnapped a man. I had suffered the shock of invasion of my country *by* my country. And I had suffered the damnedest worst case of sunburn, trudging through

164

the empty desert without food or water, of my life, and it *hurt*.

One way or another, it all hurt . . . and they wouldn't even let me get in that pool to cool off.

It wasn't forbidden, exactly. It was just something that could not be permitted by anyone but that other Nyla, and she was off on some errand of her own. The washbasin in the corner was no substitute. Every half hour or so I would splash water over my bare skin; on the quarter hour I would try gingerly to put on some of that useless sunburn cream they'd dug up for me. Those things gave me something to do. They didn't help much.

What also didn't help was the presence of my involuntary traveling companion, Dr. Lawrence Douglas. Most of that long day he lay unmoving in the bed. That I could understand. He'd gone through most of what I had: the same sunburn, the same endless hours of heat and thirst, wandering through the empty desert. And worse. Not only had he managed to get himself snake-bitten, and had the antivenom shots that were almost as bad as the bite, but he'd been shot full of pep juice of some kind so Nyla No-Thumbs could interrogate him. I hadn't been there to share it, but when they put him back in our room, by then unconscious again, he'd had bruises to add to the burn.

I didn't try to wake him.

I didn't have to wake him. When I turned unexpectedly away from the washstand I caught his eyes on me. He closed them at once, but not in time. "Oh, hell, Douglas," I said wearily, "if you want to sleep, sleep; if you want to wake up, wake up; but what's the use of faking it?"

For another stubborn minute he kept them closed, but he couldn't keep it up forever. He dragged himself out of the bed, looked around for the toilet that didn't exist, and then, without speaking, urinated into the washbasin.

When he finished I snapped, "At least rinse the

damn thing out!" *I* had. He didn't look around, but he turned the taps on full, sloshed the water around, drank, as a dog drinks, lapping the water out of his cupped hand under the tap, all without speaking.

"If you wet your hair, it'll help a little," I told him. "Also I've got some sunburn cream."

He straightened up slowly, then bent again to do as I suggested with his hair. Over his shoulder he muttered something. It could have been "Thanks." I decided to assume it was, and when he turned back to look for the sunburn cream I managed a smile.

He didn't smile back. Even allowing for everything, I have never seen a man look more hopeless, resentful, and depressed.

Of course, I was in no good mood myself. Apart from the things that had happened, I was feeling itches and twitches I didn't like. I felt I was under constant observation, though I could never catch the guard peering in the window. And I felt another itch I liked even less. "Look," I said, "it's no good sulking."

He paused in putting cream on his tomato-colored face to look at me sourly. "So what *is* good, would you suggest?"

"Well, you could satisfy my curiosity about something, because I've been thinking. When I got up on the scaffolding where you were working on the portal and you went through it with me—"

He barked a nasty laugh. "When you forced me at gunpoint," he corrected.

"Yes, all right. When we wound up ten feet in the air on the other side, because you didn't tell me there was going to be a drop," I amplified, for no better reason than to spread a little guilt back on him. "I thought we were going back to my time. Then, while you were sleeping, I thought about it."

He groaned. "DeSota, if you're coming to any point, will you please get there?"

"The point is, what were you doing?"

"Trying to escape," he said shortly.

"To here? But this isn't your own time, is it?"

"This primitive hellhole?" he snarled. "No!"

"Then—"

"Then why didn't I try to get back to my own? Because I don't have one, DeSota! Not any more! There's only one thing I want now, and that's *out.*"

He flung himself back on the bed. "But, listen—" I began reasonably.

He shook his head. "Forget it," he said.

And, along about that time, I did. Not because of what he said. Because a car roared into the driveway and stopped out of sight. I craned my neck to see what was happening. No luck. I heard car doors slam, and distant voices—rumble from a man, higher-pitched, cheerful sound of a woman's voice. A voice I knew well. And a moment later Nyla appeared, walking toward the pool, shedding clothes as she got near. She didn't bother to glance at our window. She got to the edge of the pool, tested the water with a bare toe, slid out of the last of her underwear, and dived cleanly into the pool, the thumbless hands pressed together over her head.

And that other itch that I had not wanted to feel came rushing back to fill my nerve ends with longing.

If Nyla No-Thumbs didn't look at us, we certainly looked at her. I could see one of the guards, half hidden by a porch pillar at the motel office, eyes missing nothing of that handsome, familiar body. Even Douglas lifted himself off the bed to join me at the window. "Hell of a good-looking putain," he muttered.

I could have killed him.

To feel anything of the sort, of course, was purest insanity. I told myself that. I couldn't help it. Because for quite a while now what had been filling the cracks in my mind, the parts I didn't want to explore, was Nyla. Each Nyla. All the Nylas. Nyla Bowquist, my true-love violin virtuosa; Nyla Sambok, girl para-trooper; Nyla No-Thumbs. Nyla Christophe, who was—obviously never married, because who would marry her?—zealot law enforcer, commander of goons and rubber hoses and secret prisons.

And they were all the same one. I didn't need fingerprints or urine analyses to know that. I felt it in my groin, with an intensity seldom matched since I was fourteen years old, peering through the cracked partition to the girls' locker room at the Y.

There were so many incongruities that I didn't know where to begin to look for a handle to them. That first one, the sergeant—she was bad enough, as a shock to my nervous system. But at least, after that first appalled recognition, she made some kind of sense. If she wasn't a concert violinist, at least she was a music teacher; if not a civilian, at least only a draftee. My own beloved could have gone the same way, given a few acts of God one way or the other in her early life.

But this one!

This thumbless one . . . without kindness, without love . . . most of all, without thumbs! I could not recognize my darling in her at all.

But I could recognize my darling's body. My own body knew it at once.

I almost understood that overwhelming itch, because I'd heard of such things—no, not *such* things; but something similar. One of my old political drinking buddies had told me something once, at one of those beery four A.M. sessions when you're exhausted from speeches and handshaking and watching the election results come in, and everybody else has finally gone home. He said he'd caught his wife in an affair with another man. When he couldn't doubt it any more, he was pained and furious—and something else. He was incredibly horny. All through the fights and scenes and confrontations, the biggest thing on his mind was to make love to her, as often and as forcefully as he could. To take this familiar stranger, this hostile love, this person whom he had suddenly discovered that, having thought he knew her intimately and totally, he hardly knew at all—to take her to bed, because the burning and yearning in his crotch outweighed every other feeling he had.

Staring out of that window, I wanted Nyla very badly indeed.

Any Nyla at all.

Grotesque? Of course! I knew just how grotesque it was. And yet I couldn't help thinking—what would it be like without thumbs? In what ways would our lovemaking change? For instance, she did sometimes mischievously tweak my useless little nipples while I was tweaking hers; we had giggled over the differences between hers and mine, and the impossibility of ever knowing whether what tiny tickle I felt when she pinched mine was in any way like what she felt in hers. But, thumbless, she couldn't do that—or not exactly that—or what would it be like, really?

I cannot put in words how badly I wanted to know.

Spang went the window screen as the big guard, Moe, came up from the side and caught me staring. He slapped it with the flat of his hand and I pulled away, tiny flakes of rust stinging my eyes. "Got hopes, have you?" he jeered. "Forget it! She's not for jailbirds like you, even if she is treating you better than you deserve." He disappeared and I heard him unlocking the door. "God knows why she thinks you rate it," he grumbled, motioning us out, "but she brought you some food. And she says you can eat it in the owner's apartment, and it's got air-conditioning."

The food was Mexican, on cardboard plates and just about cold—well, nothing was cold, really, in that part of New Mexico, but no more than room temperature. And the room was, as promised, cooled down to the merely uncomfortable by a wheezing, rattling box in the window of the large living room. It wasn't enough. Our two doubles were there with us, along with the guard, Moe, and body heat was enough to drive the temperature right back up again.

I sat next to the other DeSota and we eyed each other. "Hi, Dom," I offered. He looked surprised.

"They usually call me Nicky," he said. "Say, did you *see* her out there? And they busted me for just going topless!" I opened my mouth to ask him what he meant, but once started talking he kept right on. "Are you really a United States senator?"

"Since 1978, right. From Illinois."

"I've never talked to my senator before," he said, and grinned. "Especially when he was me. What should I call you?"

"Under the circumstances, Dom is good enough. And you? Nicky? That's funny—I mean, I don't know why. Even when I was a kid, my mother didn't call me Nicky."

"My mother didn't, either, but when I was training for the job my counselor advised a change. 'Dominic' sounded too much like 'dominate,' he said, and customers would be put off by it. I'm in mortgages." He hesitated, mouth full of refried beans. "Dom? How'd you get to be a senator?"

Meaning, of course, *when I'm just nobody*. But how do you answer something like that? I couldn't say, "Because I'm a winner and you're a wimp." That would be unforgivable and, worse, untrue, since we were the same person. What had happened in his world to make my gentle fiddle player a ruthless hunter of men, and me a wide-eyed innocent?

I didn't get a chance to find out. In came Moe, lugging a cardboard carton as though it were heavy, and behind him Nyla Christophe. She had her clothes back on now, a skirt and a modestly long-sleeved blouse, though from the way they molded themselves to her I wasn't at all sure she had anything underneath them. "Enjoyed your dinner, fellows?" she asked cheerfully. "Now you've got to sing for your supper. I went in to the Albuquerque office to talk to Washington on a secure line, and it's working out just the way I thought. There'll be orders for us all tonight!"

She nodded to Moe, who put the box down on the floor and began pulling stuff out of it. A big thing with two turntables that he plugged into a wall outlet, a couple of huge reels of magnetic wire, a microphone the size of my fist on a long cord.

The other Larry Douglas, the one who had not come with me through the portal, said worriedly, "Nyla? What kind of orders are we talking about?" She grinned and pointed an index finger up toward the sky. "*Washington?*" he squealed, his voice changing with sudden tension. "But, listen, Nyla, I don't know diddly-shit about any of this—"

"You do now, lover," she said fondly. "Moe? You ready to record?"

"I am now, chief," he reported, having threaded tape from one reel to another. He flipped a switch, and inside the crisscross metal on the front of the box I could see vacuum tubes—*vacuum tubes!*—begin to glow.

"So what we're going to do now," said the woman who wore the coveted body I loved, "we're going to take all your statements over again. Don't go volunteering any extra information," she said darkly, directly at that Douglas. "Just answer what I ask you. The director isn't going to want to hear anything about what you were doing in Chicago, or whether you like the treatment you've been getting. Just the essentials; because I'm going to have this whole thing wrapped up before we get on the plane!"

Considering all the questions I had been asked, considering the circumstances of what all of us had to say, I could not see this particular series of interviews ending much before daybreak. I was wrong about that. Nyla Christophe knew exactly what she wanted to have on the record, and asked only what she wanted to know. Nicky DeSota was up first. On request he gave his name, his address, and something called his Civilian Registry Number. After that there were only two questions:

"Have you ever been inside Daleylab?"

"No."

"Have you ever seen the man present here who resembles you and describes himself as Senator Dominic DeSota before today?"

"No."

Nyla jerked her head and swept him away, and the local Larry Douglas took his place. For no more elaborate an interrogation. It was the same two questions, except that the man present who resembled him was "Dr. Lawrence Douglas." He gave the same answers, and I was on stage.

I took longer. She ordered, "Start with your being advised that someone like you had been captured in a secret military installation in New Mexico and tell us your story." And she just listened, prompting me with what-happened-next sort of questions and nothing more, except that when I got to the soi-disant major-me who had taken me prisoner, she put in, "Was this man the same as the one who allegedly disappeared while in custody? No? Or the same as the one here present? No? So then you say there are at least four of you? Yes? Then go on."

And I went through the whole thing, even my knocking out the other Nyla, except that I didn't mention the kiss, and most of all I didn't mention that she was indeed a Nyla. "Sergeant Sambok" was description enough. I wasn't asked for more. "And then we landed in deep sand, and there was nothing in sight but desert. There was nobody around. It was burning hot. We had to get out of sight as fast as we could, or anyway we thought we did. We headed southeast, as near as we could tell from the sun. We walked for hours, getting thirstier all the time. Then Douglas said he'd heard that some of the cactus had water inside them, and he tried to pull one of them out of the sand, and there was a snake under it." I hesitated, wondering how much detail the woman wanted. I'd heard the rattles before I saw Douglas jump back, with the snake dropping off his sleeve. It wasn't very big, and the fatigue fabric was tough, so not much venom got in. The funny thing was that he hadn't made a sound, just looked more astonished than any other human being I had ever seen. "By then we had come to a railroad line. We just stayed there until the train crew spotted us."

"Right," said Nyla No-Thumbs, nodding to the apeman. He clicked off the recorder and began the laborious task of changing reels. If Nyla had no thumbs, this man was all thumbs, but she was patient. She had dismissed me entirely. She was devoting all her attention to my involuntary traveling companion, who looked uneasy. I could understand why, because there was something in the gaze she bent on him that I could not quite identify. It was almost—but how could that be?—seductive; and at the same time there was an unmistakable threat. She gave him a warm, sweet smile. "You're on next, hon," she said.

If the first three of us had managed to fill only one reel, this Dr. Lawrence Douglas looked likely to fill every one of the half-dozen spares Moe had brought. Nyla's questions were sharp and to the point; from time to time she referred to a notebook to make sure she was missing nothing.

He started with a surprise. "In the first place," he said, glancing at me with considerable dislike, "the time-line I was kidnapped from is Paratime Gamma. That's not my original one, but—"

"Just a minute, hon. What's 'Gamma'?"

"It's what we call it," he said wearily, "because you have to have some way of identifying them. My own is Alpha. This one is Tau. The senator's is Epsilon— that's the one that's being invaded—and the one I was just in, the one that's doing the invading, that's Paratime Gamma."

"Go ahead."

"Paratime Gamma didn't invent the portal. We did in Alpha."

"Who's 'we,' hon? Did you invent it?"

"Nobody invents that kind of thing by himself, not things as complicated as the portal—it's like asking who invented the atomic bomb. I was part of the team, but I was only an après-doc when I came on. The ones who made the theoretical break-throughs were Hawkings and Gribbin in England, and in the United States Dr. DeSota. Got that part straight?"

He wasn't really being sarcastic, just trying to make sure she understood, but off in his corner Moe made a sort of warning growl in his throat. Nyla shook her head without looking at the goon. "Go on," she said, and this time there was no "hon."

He said obediently, "At first all we could do was peep. That means, we could look through the barrier. We could detect radiation, you see; and after a while we began to get real vision. Not for all the paratimes. Some are accessible, most aren't. Dr. DeSota says it's because of resonance effects—we're 'out of tune' with most of the lines. Actually, there is an infinite number of them, of course. When I—uh—when I left, there were about two hundred and fifty that had been mapped, but for most of them we could detect nothing more than a kind of smeary blur. Is this what you want to know?"

"What we want to know, sweetie," said Nyla, "is everything. If you could just peep, how come you're here?"

"No, no," he said, patiently enough, "that was just at first. That was when I joined, along about the beginning of August 1980. In October we were able to send objects through without retrieving them. And by January 1981 we sent a person through. Me." He added ruefully, "I volunteered."

"And how do you do that?" asked Nyla.

He said, still patient—barely patient, "There is not any person in this room who would have the faintest idea what I was talking about if I told you."

Nyla was keeping very good control of herself,

but if I had been Douglas-Alpha I would have watched myself pretty closely. She said shortly, "Try."

Douglas must not have liked the look he saw on her face, because he swallowed and hurried on. "I don't mean you wouldn't understand because you're stupid. I mean there are only two ways to describe it. One is with the words we had to coin as we went along—the portal device generates a stream of green-dip chronons which heterodynes against the natural flux of red-flow chronons. Do you see what I mean? Gibberish, right? And the other way is mathematical and, please, you'd need to know at least basic quantum mechanics to have a hope of following it."

I saw what he meant. So did Nyla, but all she said was, "Tell us what the dates were."

He shrugged. "Dr. DeSota's doctoral dissertation was, I guess, the first rigorous proof that there were quantum effects of the kind Schroedinger proposed. That was about 1977. It's what made me go back for my doctorate. Then he and Elbert Gillespie detected the actual chronons in 1979, and developed the peeper a few months later. Then, like I said, I went through to Gamma."

He stopped, waiting. Nyla was thinking. "So you defected," she said.

"I helped them," he corrected. "I didn't have any choice, did I?"

"And you could help us," she said and smiled, all sex and sunshine again.

"Now, wait a minute!" he objected. "I—! Maybe I could try, but— Look at that wire recorder! If that's the best you can do, you don't even have solid-state technology. I need something to build on, you know!"

She said gently, "How about building on the entire resources of the United States government?" And when he frowned: "You did it for the—what do you call them? The Gamma people—"

"But they threatened to beat the hell out of me—"

He stopped short, gazing at her.

She smiled. She waited a moment to let it sink in. Then she did something I would not have expected. She got up, still smiling, walked over to him and sat on the arm of his chair, her hand on his far shoulder, her body pressed against his head. If I had suspected she wore nothing under the blouse before, now I was sure of it. She toyed with his ear. "We don't threaten," she said silkily. Another pause, while Douglas glared around the room: trapped animal being offered bait. "On the other hand," she went on, her voice softer and huskier, "we do reward. Oh, yes, hon, we reward. I would personally reward you every way I could."

I could almost smell the pheromones steaming out of her.

So could the local Larry Douglas. "Bitch," he whispered, so softly that I could barely hear him, though he was right next to me on the edge of the bed. "You know what she's up to? She's ambitious, old Nyla is. She's going to use this to get right out of the FBI, right up to the top. And when she gets that poor son of a bitch in bed, he'll do anything she wants—believe me, I know!"

He stopped, because Moe was glowering at us.

He hadn't stopped in time. I swallowed, and my saliva had a sudden bitter taste of rage. How crazy that was! I was *jealous*! I was jealous of the little rat sitting next to me, so hotly jealous I could barely keep my hands off him, and for what? Because he had bedded this other Nyla!

Crazy.

It was worse than crazy. I knew it. I didn't care. If I could have pushed a button and exterminated the bastard, I would have done it in a hot minute. Not just him. The one she was whispering to across the room too—especially him! Not just even him. I was willing to extend my detestation to all Larry Douglases, or even look-alikes, like my old acquaintance and drinking buddy, His Excellency the Soviet Ambassador, the Honorable Lavrenti Yosifovitch Djugashvili.

It is a constant wonder to me how crazy a sane person can get.

I was so filled with rage and jealousy inside my own head that I hardly noticed when Nyla sat up straight, scowling. She glared at the window. "Moe," she ordered, "close the damn blinds! I don't want the whole world gaping in here!"

"Chief," he protested, "nobody's looking in—"

"Close them!" And she turned back, all smiles again, to the man who was obviously responding to whatever it was she had been whispering.

And I was on fire.

It was obsessive. I wanted to possess that woman, right then, and I was willing to kill anybody who challenged me for her. I was paying so little attention to anything else that I hardly noticed the faint *thwick* sound that came from nowhere, was distracted only on the surface of my mind when Moe, turning away from the window, seemed to trip and fall forward, crashing into the wire recorder. I did not fully come back to reality until Nyla herself jumped up, face suddenly full of shock and anger, opening her mouth to yell—

There was another *thwick*.

Nyla, too, fell like a brain-shot deer. I could see a tiny feathered dart gleaming out of the thin fabric over one shoulder.

We looked at each other in amazement. And then all questions were answered for me as there was a quick puff of air pressure, like a door slamming closed on a tight, tiny room, and there, grinning at me, was me. That other me that wore the funny coveralls. "Hello, again," he said, nodding. "Here, give me a hand, let's get her out of the way."

The Douglases were quicker at following orders than I; they jumped, however bewildered, and tugged the sleeping woman out of the middle of the floor. Just in time. Another quick, silent pulse of pressure, and a tall, cylindrical metal object appeared on the floor. "Just keep quiet, please," the new Dominic ordered. He pulled open a panel on the cylinder, fussed with what was inside, and looked up, waiting.

A shimmering oval of blackness spread itself before us.

"Looks like it's working," he said, and shrugged. He was smiling. I found myself smiling back—whoever he was, whatever he represented, it was not likely to be worse than what I had here. He glanced around the room. "We'd better not hang around," he said, "but I think we ought to take these two along with us. Let's get the woman through first."

But then I was functioning well enough to help, though it was no great effort for four of us to lift Nyla's sleeping form through the black oval. It was, however, truly eerie—not just to watch her disappear, inch by inch, but to feel unseen hands on the other side catch her and pull her through.

The apeman was a lot harder. But there were four of us, not counting the help on the other side. "Now all of you," ordered the Dominic-in-charge. We obliged: the wimpy Dominic wonderingly, the ratty Douglas resentfully, the snakebitten Douglas fearfully—and me fairly fearfully, too, as I followed them.

Hot dark night, except for floodlights. I came out on a rough platform of wood, with two men in civilian clothes grabbing my arms. "Just move away, please," one of them said, eyes on the spot I'd come from.

In a moment the black cylinder appeared.

In another moment Dr. Dominic DeSota of Paratime Alpha popped into sight. "Got it all," he crowed, looking delighted with himself. "You fellows, welcome to Paratime Alpha—and you, Doug"—turning to the fearful one—"welcome home."

But Douglas-Alpha did not look in the least joyful about it.

Out in the northwest suburbs a householder fin-
ished his second cup of coffee, stretched, found his
White Sox cap to keep the sun out of his eyes, and put it
on. Vacation time was the time to get caught up on the
chores around the house, and the back lawn needed
mowing. As soon as he opened the sliding door to the
patio he stopped short, marveling. "Marcia," he
called, "come look! We've got hummingbirds in the
marigolds! We never had hummingbirds before!" And
he watched his wife's face as she came up to see, first the
polite curiosity, then the smile of pleasure . . . then
the other expression that followed and wiped the smile
away. He could not understand the sudden shock on
her face, until he turned and saw what was eating the
hummingbirds.

27 August 1983
12:30 A.M. Major DeSOTA, Dominic P.

You can't see much out of the windows of an Army transport jet, but as we banked steeply somewhere over the Capitol I could see the whole District spread out under us. It didn't look warlike. They had the floodlights on the White House and the Lincoln Memorial, and there were long lines of car headlights and taillights because everybody in Washington was out to celebrate T.G.I.F. night. . . . No! Right along the Potomac there were only a few lights on the roads, and they didn't look like the usual car traffic. Some were single bright spotlights. Some were the faint glow that comes from the slitted headlamps of military vehicles. I leaned across the aisle to the dozing infantry colonel and tapped his shoulder. "If those are what I think they are," I yelled, "won't the Russian satellites spot them?"

He peered past me to see what I was talking about. "Oh, yeah." He grinned. "They're practicing for the Labor Day parade. What did you think?"

"*Labor* Day?" I gaped at him, but he'd unfastened his seat belt to come next to me, leaning to the window.

"Could you see my battalion on the White House grounds?" he asked, disappointed because we were looking the wrong way. I shook my head. "That's crowd control for the parade," he announced, winking.

"Jesus! Labor Day's not for ten days yet. Do you think the Russians are dumb enough to buy that?"

He shrugged. "If they weren't dumb, they wouldn't be Russians," he offered, and buckled in because the steward sergeant was coming down the aisle to frown at him.

But apart from that one little patch, there was the same old District, all peaceful and busy and happy. All the other roads were the way they ought to be. Even from the air you could see clearly that these people were not worried about any invasions. . . .

And on the other side of the barrier, I knew, there was another Washington, where our first assault wave had gone through and taken all the Potomac bridges.

And what the people in *that* Washington were doing that Friday night I could not imagine.

When we got out at Bolling and showed our orders the transportation clerk offered to get the colonel a staff car, provided he'd drop me off on his way to the White House. It was a good deal for both of us. On the drive in the colonel did everything but bounce around in his seat with anticipation and joy. He had already let me know he was a West Pointer, and I'd seen the Chile and Thailand ribbons on his chest. "This will be the biggest yet," he promised. "You'll get your silver leaf out of it, Major, so cheer up! You don't get promotions for being in a secure zone when an invasion's going on!"

"Yeah," I said, gazing out at the Virginia countryside. What he said was true enough. What he didn't know was that General Ratface was not going to forget me. He couldn't court-martial me after giving me a medal two hours earlier. But he would remember. Some day, sooner or later, I would be caught hoisting a beer in the Officers' Club or spitting on some GI sidewalk, and then the general would sink his teeth into my throat for the kill.

Unless, of course, I picked up a few more medals in this operation. I'm a prudent man. But it looked to me as though the most prudent thing I could do now was to be a hero, first chance I got. . . .

We crossed the bridge right under Arlington Cemetery, with the eternal light flickering on the hillside behind us. Traffic was heavy and civilian, though I knew that right here, on this very structure, our troops were holding the enemy off, just a wrinkle in time away. And ahead of us—

"What the hell is that?" I asked, pointing to what looked like million-candlepower searchlights blinking into the sky.

"Must be time for the Russian satellites to come over," said the colonel. "Those strobes are on top of the White House and the Sheraton Command Center, and if the Russians can make out any details with their optics fried, they're welcome to them. Anyway," he added, grinning again, "they're just more practice for the Labor Day fireworks celebration."

He dropped me at the driveway to the Sheraton Hotel, commandeered for an operations headquarters. When I showed my orders I found out the front door was for full colonels and up only; people like me had to go around to the ballroom entrance, through the parking lots. And the lots were full. Not with the usual tourists' cars and VIP's limousines; there was at least a division's worth of tanks and personnel carriers parked in orderly ranks—and with a few not-very-orderly-at-all vehicles that had been pulled back from the first assault. Some of them had taken heavy fire. One or two were a real surprise, because I couldn't see how they'd got back at all—a turret blown off one medium-heavy, a weapons carrier that seemed to have burned, four or five other vehicles with holes in them that hadn't come from moths. They were all under tarpaulins to keep the orbiting Russian eyes away, and armed guards patrolled that part of the area.

And just beyond the fringe of boxwood hedge were the busy streets of the District, where a million people were buzzing along without a care in the world.

Whatever was happening in the lobbies and bars and restaurants of the hotel, people like me were not likely to find out. Our part of the hotel was the meeting rooms, and they were as close to GI as they could be made. I got a badge to hang on my blouse in exchange for a copy of my orders, and was sent to the William McKinley room for disposal. On the way I passed a ballroom that was full. It was neither a wedding nor a bar mitzvah; what it was full of was troops, mostly in their underwear, changing from the uniforms of their side in which they had been captured to the uniforms of ours in which they would be discreetly transported to the stockades in the Maryland hills.

Prisoners.

I paused, rubbernecking. These weren't the Air Force guards we'd captured at Sandia. These were combat soldiers, and the wounded among them proved it with their dressings. The differences between their uniforms and ours were multiple, but not all that conspicuous at first glance. The basic color of the uniform was the same olive-drab for both. Their chevrons were smaller than ours, and silver-edged where ours were all black. Ribbons were something else—I couldn't see them clearly enough to tell much, and the MP captain in charge of their guards was beginning to give me hostile looks. Besides, my orders had been to report to the William McKinley room at once, and who knew if the door guards had phoned ahead?

If they had, it made no difference. The tech sergeant at the table by the door had never heard of me. She pawed through papers, muttered into a phone, turned the papers upside down and pored over the back of them and finally said, "Take a seat, Major. We'll get to you as soon as possible."

I didn't have any trouble translating that. "As

soon as possible" meant "when we find out who you are and what you're supposed to be doing here." I resigned myself to spending the next considerable fraction of my life on one of the gilt-backed banquet chairs lined along the wall.

It wasn't quite that bad. There were anywhere from fifty to a hundred people going in and out of that room. Hardly any of them paid any attention to me. But it was no more than twenty minutes, and I'd only had my feet stepped on twice as people in a hurry crowded past, when the sergeant came back. "This way, Major," she said. "Lieutenant Kauffmann is ready for you now."

Lieutenant Kauffmann was not only ready for me, he said, first thing out of his mouth, "Where the hell have you been, Major? You're supposed to be over at the White House right now."

"The White—" I began, but he cut me off.

"Right, and you're supposed to be in civilian clothes too. It says here"—he speared a folder out of the stack on his desk—"that you closely resemble a U.S. senator on the other side—"

"Resemble him, hell. I am him."

He shrugged. "Anyway, you're going to assume his identity. After the first wave has secured the White House—"

It was my turn to cut him off. "We're invading the White House?"

"Where've you been?" He groaned again, this time with a different intonation. "They haven't responded to our messages; now we try force. You'll go in civilian clothes, as I said, and take two guards in their uniforms with you. You'll get orders from the portal master, but it looks like they want you to find the President, take her prisoner, and bring her back here."

"Holy shit," I said, and then, "Wait a minute. What if the real Senator DeSota is there?"

"He's not," he said positively. "Didn't you capture him yourself?"

"But he got— I mean, I thought he'd returned to his own time."

Shrug. Translation: *Not my department*. "So," he went on, "get your B-four bag and change into civvies, and we'll get you transportation to—"

"I didn't bring any baggage," I said. "I don't have any civilian clothes with me."

Thunderstruck stare. "You *what*? Christ, Major! How the hell am I supposed to get you fitted out with civvies? Where would I get them? Why the hell—" And then he turned to the sergeant. He had remembered how to get difficult tasks done. "Sergeant! Get this man fitted out with civvies!"

And so it came to pass that twenty minutes later the sergeant and I were getting out of a commandeered Cadillac limousine the size of a house trailer, in front of a store whose neon sign said: FORMAL CLOTHES RENTAL FOR ALL OCCASIONS. The neon was turned off, but the owner had opened up for us. And forty minutes after that we were on our way to the White House, and behind us the proprietor was grumpily closing his store again. "Good work, Sergeant," I said, stretching out in the back seat, which was roughly the size of a football field. I admired the gleam on the rented patent-leather shoes, smoothed down the rented satin cummerbund, adjusted the rented black bow tie. I was, I believed, the very picture of a U.S. senator coming from some formal dinner party for a late-night call on his President. "I guess the tux is the best idea," I observed, "because who knows what the current styles for men are in their time? And formal clothes don't change, do they?"

She said shortly, "We hope." Then we were at the VIP gate, and she was showing documents to the very thorough and skeptical MP, with two other MP's right behind him, looking over his shoulder. They were all armed, but they didn't have to be. Beyond them, square in the middle of the narrow drive, was a personnel carrier with a heavy machine gun mounted in the rear, and it was pointed right at us.

It took me a moment to realize that the White House had changed considerably. The strobes! They weren't there—evidently the Russian satellite had passed and they were no longer needed. That wasn't the only thing.

Even Washington Friday-night people go to bed sometime, and the traffic had been dwindling all along. Not here, though. The traffic jam was all around us, parked on the grass, crushing the roses. The lawn of our White House would be five years recovering from the tanks and half-tracks and personnel carriers that had chewed it up—"rehearsing for the parade," of course.

I could see why they were not letting ordinary civilians in.

I was no ordinary civilian, though. We were waved through at last. The weapons carrier started up and pulled off onto the grass to let us through— another hundred dollars worth of turf down the tube—and our driver took us to a small portico I had never seen before. "Good luck," said the sergeant, hesitated, then leaned forward and gave me a kiss to show she meant it.

That was the last time for quite a while that anybody showed any affection for me.

The only other time I had been in the White House was in Stevenson's second term, and it was nothing like this. Now there weren't any uniformed pages to show me around, nor velvet ropes to keep the barbarians out of the sacred chambers. There weren't any sacred chambers. There were troops in half the rooms, and machinery or weapons in most of the others. A corporal took me swiftly down a service hall and up a broad staircase, not encouraging pauses to gawk. I wound up in a green-draped room with portraits of Presidents Madison and Taft on the wall. It was a strikingly handsome room, not counting the urn of coffee with paper cups that stood on a card table near the door. The upholstered chairs were sparsely occupied—four or five civilians, one of them a woman who looked familiar, as did two of the men, especially the black one I recognized as a former heavyweight prizefighter—and eight or nine soldiers in the dress uniform of the other side, with side arms that looked as though they meant it.

Two of the soldiers got up and came toward me, hulking, huge paratroop types, both with corporal's stripes. "Here's Major DeSota, sir," said my own corporal, saluted, and left.

It is a measure of how fast things were happening that it did not occur to me that corporals did not salute corporals. I said to the bigger of the two, "The first thing I'd like is some of that coffee, Corporal."

He raised an eyebrow as thick as a chevron, then grinned. "Let's get the man some coffee, Captain Bagget," he said. And while corporal number two went over to pour me a cup, corporal number one said, "I'm Colonel Frankenhurst, Major. Do you know your mission?"

It took me a minute to reorient. "Sorry, sir," I apologized. "Uh—only in general terms. I mean, I understand I'm supposed to find this President Reagan, and when I do you two are supposed to take her prisoner and bring her back."

"Shit," he said dispassionately. "Well, it doesn't matter. The captain and I have been rehearsing this for the past forty-eight hours. If we're stopped, I'll do the talking; all you have to do is look like a senator. Can you handle that?" Then he grinned, to show that he had the situation well in hand. "Don't worry about it, Major. First place, we may never go through. They're having trouble with the peepers; these people on the other side move around so fast they can't keep track of them. Last I heard, they weren't going to open a portal before oh-three-hundred anyway."

"That's dumb," observed the captain-corporal, returning with my coffee. "They ought to wait till morning, that way we won't look so conspicuous."

The colonel only shrugged. "Of course," said the captain with a sigh, looking me up and down, "a tuxedo won't look exactly *normal* at eight o'clock in the morning, either."

"Six of one, half a dozen of the other," said the colonel. "Well, DeSota, would you like to meet the other doubles? This is Nancy Davis—of course you've seen her on the TV." Of course I had; she was the star of the *I Remember Mama* remake, and how they'd got her away from her studios and her well-advertised activities raising funds for everything from Animal Welfare to the Right to Life I couldn't guess. "She's the President." Colonel Frankenhurst grinned. "John here is a Washington police captain on special White House duty—in the real world he's an airline pilot from Ohio. And the champ is a senator like you." He watched me shake hands. "Pretty good work getting you all together," he said complacently. "We missed a few, of course. We found the President's personal maid, but she was eight months pregnant—they didn't think anybody would be fooled. And we lucked onto General Porteco, her personal military aide. Unfortunately our guy was just coming out of the DT's and they couldn't trust him to remember his lines."

The other civilian came forward. "I'm not anybody's double," he apologized. "I'm Professor Greenberg—political science. They called me in to try to get a line on what the structure of this other society is like, so I've been interviewing you doubles to see if I can figure out where the differences began. But before I get to you, Major—you've been through once already, haven't you? What's it like?"

So for the next half hour I did the talking. I didn't have that much to tell, after all—what did I know about the other side except for about a quarter of a square mile in the New Mexico desert? But it was more than anyone else present knew, and they all had questions. Professor Greenberg wanted to know how much a Coke cost out of their machines. "Senator" Clay wanted to know how many of their troops were black. "President" Nancy Davis wanted to know what the hit TV shows were, and whether I knew if abortion was legal. Colonel-corporal Frankenhurst wanted, very badly, to know how well those other guys had done in hand-to-hand combat, if any had occurred when we took over their Sandia base.

I did my best. But while I was still trying to remember who the hosts on those other guys' *Today* show were for Nancy Davis, there was noise in the corridor, and the door flung open and in came President Brown and entourage. He didn't look happy.

I hadn't expected him to, because I'd already heard how pissed he was at the disruption of his home life with troops and equipment, not to mention the disruption of his schedule because he had had to cancel every appointment with every person who wasn't cleared to know what was going on . . . which was almost everybody. "There you are," he snapped to sweet-faced, bland-smiling Nancy Davis. "I've got to talk to you, right now!"

She wasn't fazed in the least. Affably, she said, "Certainly, Mr. President. What can I do for you?"

"You can tell me what the hell kind of person you are," he snarled. "You don't respond to my public messages at all! What does it take to get you to act?"

"I guess you mean that other me, Mr. President," she said, smiling. She really had a dimple when she wanted it—a triumph, I was sure, of the cosmetic surgeon's art. "I don't know if I can tell you that. After all, I'm not really the President—here."

"Make believe you are, for God's sake!" he roared. "Do you have any idea what's resting on this? I'm not talking about this cockamamie other world, I'm talking about *here*. The Russians are getting really nasty about the 'parade preparations' and the 'archaeological study site' in New Mexico, and there are too many people involved. It's only a question of time till the word gets out, and what are they going to do then?" As she opened her mouth he said, "No, that's not what I'm asking you—what the hell would you know about that? I'm asking you about *you*. The other you. Would it help, do you think, if I canceled this operation and tried to get you, the other you, on the phone? President-to-President? A one-on-one talk?"

"Why, I think that would depend on what you said, Mr. President," she said thoughtfully.

"I'd say the truth!" he barked. "Might be an interesting change, at that."

"Well," she said slowly, "I rather think, Mr. President, that I'd remember my oath of office. I suppose it's the same one you took. To defend the United States against all enemies, domestic or external—even if they're both domestic *and* external, so to speak. What I would not do, I think, is allow my country to be invaded by anybody at all without fighting back with everything I had—even if the invaders were my own country."

He glared at her, baffled. Then he glared around the room, particularly at the uniformed men. I think that was the only time in my life when I was glad I was a lowly field-grade officer, with no responsibility for high-level planning. I would not have liked to be on the Combined Chiefs of Staff right at that moment.

Then he sank slowly into a chair, gazing into space. One of his flunkies whispered urgently in his ear, but the President shook him off. "So we've got a war on our hands after all," he said.

No one responded to that.

There was a lot of silence in the room. The anxious flunky glanced at his wristwatch, then at Jerry Brown. Without looking at him, the President said, "I know. It's probably academic by now. Take a look out the window and see if it's started."

The aide was a youngish man, no more than thirty-five, but he looked more like a hundred as he moved stiffly toward the long green drapes.

He didn't have to, actually, because by then we

could all hear the racket of truck motors and tank diesels starting up.

Then everybody was at the windows. There were three of them, and instinctively we left the one in the middle for the President's solitary use. He made his way slowly over and stood gazing thoughtfully and silently at the hot August night outside, while all the rest of us crowded around the other two.

What we were looking at was the South Lawn, usually reserved for photo opportunities with visiting heads of state or Easter egg hunts for the Washington children. Someone had built a huge, flimsy tarpaulin structure to shield something from eyes in the street or overhead, but from our window we could see what it contained: the huge black rectangle of a portal, like a movie screen before the picture has started to show, only black. Even though I'd done it before, it was unnerving to look at that thing and imagine plunging into it.

It was even more unnerving when the first squadron of six whippet tanks roared through and disappeared, churning up the already battered grass . . . after them a dozen personnel carriers with combat-ready machine-gunners and Rangers . . . after them a company of paratroops in camouflage suits on foot . . .

The President sighed and turned away. He walked out of the room, his ducklings waddling after, into the corridors that were also beginning to get noisy with the inside part of the operation. And the ones of us still left in the room looked at each other.

Because we knew that we were likely to be next.

It all went pretty briskly after that—as you might expect, because it was all downhill. People were rushing around, flinging orders in all directions; the sparks flew. I felt the tingle. I worked myself up to a fair-to-middling case of jitters, mostly over the question of how I was going to find something so heroic to do that it would placate even old General Ratface

Magruder. Then they hustled us out of the Green Room, up a stair, down a hall, past guards with rapid-fire weapons at the ready . . . and there we were. In the Oval Office itself. Occupying the very seat of majesty.

It didn't look the way any seat of majesty was supposed to look. It looked like moving day, with a little bit of a mad-scientist laboratory for dessert. The big presidential desk had been shoved against a wall. Thousand-dollar armchairs and five-thousand-dollar couches had been stacked against another. And in the center of the room a rectangle of copper tubing surrounded nothing, like an empty picture frame. It filled the center of the room floor-to-ceiling, with the squat boxes of the portal field generator on one side of it and the control panels on the other.

The field was down.

Nothing was happening but yelling and confusion, because that scarey, velvety black nothing did not fill the rectangle. You could see right through it, and what I saw was a full bird colonel whimpering with rage and frustration, while his technicians ripped the panels apart, trying to find the blown fuse that had crashed the portal. Three-quarters of a platoon of assault troops stood glowering before the panel, while their captain helped things along by yelling at the back of the colonel's head. A captain should not talk to a colonel like that. The colonel was too deep in misery to hear it.

It was not a peaceful scene.

The portal master came toward us. She was a major. She wasn't yelling at anyone. Her face showed no expression at all but terminal weariness. She told my corporals, "You're on hold. We only got eight men through before it crashed, and you might be scrubbed. Stay out of the way."

Colonel-corporal Frankenhurst gave us a jerk of the head, meaning *do it*, but tarried to ask, "How's it going on the other side?"

We tarried to hear. Needlessly. It was a dumb question. The portal master didn't try to answer it. She just turned and plodded away; because, of course, she didn't know. She couldn't. Once the troops were through that portal they were gone. They could not be seen or heard. They could not come back to report. They could not even get a message through until a portal generator was through and operational on the other side. If we had had a peeper working . . . but in this rig the peeper field was tied to the portal itself, and neither was working. We didn't know a thing. . . .

And then we did, and it was bad. The operation was a tactical surprise, a complete success in every way but one. We hadn't done what it was set up for. Madame President had been hustled away through an exit no one had mapped.

Within ten minutes two-way traffic was established on all floors, but by then it didn't matter any more. We took prisoners by the score. We had flushed guards and Secret Servicemen out of every butler's pantry and clothes closet. I saw President Reagan's own military attaché, a brigadier general in full-dress uniform, wearing an expression of fury and resentment—"why was it *me*?" We even had the First Gentleman, caught going back for the videocassettes of his old films, but we didn't have the one we wanted.

Madame President had got clean away.

In the first hot dawn light I hitched a ride back to the Sheraton in a White House van, incongruous among the prisoners and guards in my rented tux.

We were going to have to fight for it.

The tear in the screen was tiny. All it let through at first was air, tinged with the viny smell of tomatoes and the sweet, grassy odor of growing corn. They were noticed only as curiosities, in the huge sprawl of Levitt-Chicago, where no crops had grown for twenty years. Then a bird drifted through, unnoticed. It fluttered around, looking unsuccessfully for its nestlings. It never found them. Birdlike, it went about its business of eating and excreting. It made no change in the world at all . . . except that, back in its own time, it had eaten seeds from the kudzu vines. When it dropped them in an ungardened patch of weeds they grew; and for a century afterward that whole section of Illinois was plagued with the sturdy, migrating, unconquerable invasion of kudzu.

27 August 1983
0940 Dr. Dominic DeSota-Arbenz

As soon as the pulseur was airborne and the seatbelt sign went off I was up and running. There was a woman in a purple muumuu who slipped into the aisle just ahead of me, with a quick flick of a triumphant look over her shoulder. But that was all right; she was only heading for the W.C. I was first in line for the phone.

Actually I got there too fast. When I dialed home I got a busy signal, because we weren't at cruising height yet and the pilot hadn't relinquished his disposable radio channels. I kept dialing. I was impatient. I'd been away too long. The first time I went through to another time my wife had kept me awake all the night before with worries—she remembered all too well what had happened to Larry Douglas. But that jump was physically near, at least—Sklodowska-Curie was less than six kilometers from my front door, and that first trip, going to Rho-time, I'd just popped in and popped out again, mostly to test the new suit.

I make it sound easier than it was. I was scared too. But then when we began narrowing down our searches to the times that were actually getting somewhere with paratime research, or at least theoretical quark physics, the area of exploration began to increase geographically too. Beta had a facility just south of San Francisco. Phi had one in Red Bank, New Jersey. It was pop through a portal, pop out, jump on a pulseur, fly a few hours, pop through another portal . . . and I had a wife and a child I really would have liked to see.

The third time I dialed my number I heard the beepers putting me through, and Dorothy was home. She picked up the phone on the first ring. I was never gladder of anything than to see her sweet, calm face peering out at me from the phone.

"You're looking real good, Do," I told her. She inspected my picture at the other end. Because the camera lens on our home phone is over the screen she had a sort of unfocused look, as though she'd forgotten her glasses, but she saw sharply enough.

"I wish I could say the same for you, hon," she said. "Is it going badly?"

I couldn't tell her just how badly over an open phone, but she didn't have to be told. She could see my face. I said, "Middling awful. How's Barney?"

"Missing his daddy, otherwise all right. He cut a tooth." I'd caught her with a cup of coffee in her hand, and she took a sip, looking at me. "It's not just that there's that, uh, problem," she decided. "There's something else on your mind. What is it, Dominic?"

I said, surprised, "You're right, Do. I feel—funny. I don't know why."

She nodded. I was only confirming what she knew. When Dorothy Arbenz came to the institute as an après-doc psychologist I saw at once that she was beautiful, quickly learned that she was very understanding. It only occurred to me later that for the rest of my life she would be reading my mind, or next thing to it, but I married her anyway. She left my subconscious to worry about what I was worrying about and changed the subject. "Are you coming home now?"

"I wish. It isn't a Sklodowska matter any more, hon."

"You're going to Washington?"

"'Fraid so."

She took a deeper swallow of coffee. I'd begun to

be able to read Dorothy's mind a little, too, so I knew what was coming next. "Are you going through again?" she asked.

I didn't answer directly. "It isn't up to me any more," I reminded her. She knew it wasn't an answer, and she knew, as well as I did, that if I went through again, it wouldn't likely be just a little prowl around to see what was going on.

So I blew her a kiss, and she blew me one back, and after I'd hung up I sat before the phone for a moment, thinking about what it was that was worrying me.

I knew what it was. I'd known it at once, I just hadn't wanted to think about it.

There were too many mes.

When I was skulking around Tau and Epsilon I'd seen other Dominic DeSotas, but it wasn't until we had three of us in the same room that the wonder—the grisly, spine-twitching astonishment and dread—really reached me. I mean, they were *me*. Not the one me I'd lived with all my life, but the mes that I might have been—that, in their times, I *was*. I could have been born into a time when science was a dirty word, and wound up a thirty-five-year-old juvenile, furtively sneaking embraces with a coeur-douce I couldn't afford to marry, terrorized by my own government, whipped into line by an oppressive social system that made me ashamed of my own nudity. I could, in fact, have been the Nicky DeSota the back of whose head I could see, a dozen rows ahead, and in some sense I was him. Or I could have given up science for politics and turned out a United States senator. Well, that wasn't awful. It was a pretty good life—wealth, power, the esteem of all who knew me—but there was a sleaziness to it too. There he was, or I was, sneaking into a hole-and-corner adulterous relationship with another woman, because I had a wife I no longer loved and could not rid myself of without terrible heartbreak and recriminations, not to speak of financial and political ruin.

Or I could have taken the military road, like my other avatar the Major, who prided himself on deception and brute-force conquest . . . or I could have died early, for one reason or another, as seemed to have happened to the Dominic DeSota in Rho.

And all those mes were me.

It was scary. It threatened the stability of my life in ways I had never felt before. Everybody always knew that things could have been very different for him somehow . . . but it was a whole other thing to know that, somewhere, they *had*.

I gazed out at the two of them. Even from a dozen rows back I could see that Nicky was having the time of his life in the big widebody, half empty with the light Saturday traffic of the week before Labor Day. So was the senator. I admired them for taking so much joy in what was around them, in spite of the fact that they were both, as far as they knew, marooned in a time as alien to their own as Mars . . . of course, I hadn't come from where they had just come from.

The other thing I could see was that the executive type in 32-C, the one who had already begun spreading out the contents of his attaché case onto his tray, the empty seat beside him, and its tray, was casting irritable glances at the phone.

I turned back and made my other call.

I didn't go through the switchboard at the Sklodowska-Curie Institute. I dialed Harry Rosenthal's private line, and, as expected, when I got him on the phone the wall behind his face was not the one in Chicago; call-forwarding had tracked him to where he was. "You're in Washington," I said.

"Damn right," he fretted. "Waiting for you. Getting calls every five minutes from the Army and the science secretary and the CIA. I wish you were here now, Dom!"

I didn't ask why.

My conversation with Dorothy hadn't been exactly joyous. Neither was this one. I started out with two big worries—the invasion of Epsilon by Gamma, and ballistic recoil. The call didn't ease either of them. It made them worse. "The events we were monitoring," Harry said tersely, "are still proceeding. And as to the other thing—have you seen the TV news?"

"How the devil would I get time to watch television, Harry?"

"You might want to make time," he said gloomily. "There are intrusions popping up all over the place— we can't get instrumentation around fast enough to check them all. But when you get a thunderstorm on three tables of a Sunday-school picnic and clear skies everywhere else, you don't need instrumentation to know what's happening." Then he added a new worry. "The secretary wants to know why you brought those Tau people back."

"But Douglas spilled his guts to them," I protested. "That's policy! You set it yourself—limit knowledge, keep the ones who don't have it from getting it."

He stared at my picture. "You were sent to bring Douglas back, and to rescue one involuntary emigré, the senator. Nobody told you to manufacture four new emigrés. What are you going to do with them now?"

Since I didn't have an answer to that, I was glad to hang up and let the executive type have his turn at the phone.

I made my way back up the aisle to the midships stew coop. On the way I passed the two other Dominics, both of whom wanted to talk. I didn't. I gave a friendly wave to each and kept right on going. They would have to wait. I had to think about what Harry Rosenthal had asked me.

The stews were busily pulling bubbles of scrambled eggs out of the microwave, but when I said, "Steerage, please," they didn't argue. They knew

what they had in steerage. One of them broke off
long enough to put me on the little elevator, and it
carried me down to the X-class passenger compartment below.

Airlines use the below-decks passenger space in
the widebodies for all kinds of purposes. Some put
first-class bars there. One or two filled them with seats
they sold at a cut rate—there wasn't any easy way of
getting out of them if there was trouble, and so they
weren't exactly popular with most travelers. Trans-
Continental used them for couchettes-dormir on long
flights, and sometimes for special purposes on shorter
ones.

We were a very special purpose.

We were even more special than what they
ordinarily euphemistically meant by a "special purpose," which is to say for transporting prisoners.
There weren't any prisoners here, exactly. There
were the two FBI people from Tau and their Larry
Douglas, who had committed no crimes anybody in
our world cared much about. Then there was our
own Larry Douglas. Whose status was pretty murky;
whose trial, if he ever had one, would set about a
million precedents—I'd already heard the lawyers
argue about what "jurisdiction" meant in his case. No
prisoners. The *flic-de-nation* who was sitting by himself, reading an in-flight magazine, wasn't a guard.
Just a precaution.

I came in from the front of the compartment.
There was room for thirty people in it, and our lot
didn't crowd it at all. The FBI woman and her
anthropoid were sitting at the far end of one row,
whispering to each other. More accurately, the woman was whispering and the bruiser was listening
humbly and respectfully. Neither of them looked up.
Their Larry Douglas was across the aisle, wistfully
trying to get invited into the conversation. They
weren't interested. And our own Larry was sitting

with his head down in the first row, imaging hopelessness. He didn't look up either, but I knew he had seen me come out of the elevator.

I looked at him for a moment. What a lot of hell this man had unleashed! When we found out for sure what he was doing—when the people he was working for made the quantum leap from talk to deployment—we had to decide what to do about him. I voted for going after him. It was a close decision. My first impulse was to send him some token of our esteem, like a pack of rabid wolves. Though I didn't say it, it seemed still like an attractive idea.

Though I hadn't said it, he lifted his head and whined, "I couldn't help it, Dom! They were going to torture me!"

I was surprised to hear a contralto laugh from farther back in the compartment. The FBI woman had quit conspiring to listen; it seemed she'd heard that song before. "It's true," he said desperately. "And anyway it's your fault, Dom."

That jolted me. I opened my mouth to ask what he meant, but he was ahead of me. "You could have stopped it! You could have come after me. Why weren't you peeping me the whole time?"

The gall of the man! That was back in the early days of the project, long before we had had the resources to mount both portal and peeper at the same time. "We didn't because we couldn't," I snapped. He gave me a rebellious look.

The bruiser took a hand in the conversation. "What are you going to do with us?" he growled.

The woman looked on silently. It was like hearing a puppet speak when its owner is absent; I was almost surprised to find the ape was capable of articulate speech at all. "As an attorney," he boomed—bigger surprise still—"I got to tell you you're violating our civil rights like a million different ways, Charlie. You been keeping us incommunicado, which is depriving us of our habeas corpus; you ain't read us our rights or charged us with no indictable act or deed; you kept us from the right of consultation with our lawyer—"

"You just said you are a lawyer," I protested.

"Even a lawyer has a right to a lawyer," he said virtuously, "so what the hell about it, Jackson?"

I looked helplessly at the woman. "Is this goon really an attorney?"

She shrugged, grinning. "Says he is. That's how he got into the bureau. Personally I think he bought it from a diploma mill. Anyway, what about it?"

"What about what?"

"What are you going to do about us?" she asked politely. "Because, honestly, Moe's right. You must have some kind of laws around here, and I'm willing to bet you're breaking a whole bunch of them."

She was a lot too close to what I believed myself for me to be comfortable with the conversation. I tried diversion. "What would you do if you were me?" I asked.

"Why," she said, grinning, "I'd save up my money to pay off a hell of a huge damage judgment, once we get to court, and I'd probably start arranging my affairs for the next ten years in the slammer."

And that, too, did not seem at all unrealistic. I mean, given a good lawyer on their side, and a few bad breaks on mine. This sort of thing was not at all what I had been prepared to risk when I signed up for the project.

And it was all so unfair! I'd seen the bruises on Nicky DeSota's body. I'd heard him say what this pair had done to him. Civil rights? What civil rights had they given him?

And yet in their own time they weren't lawbreakers. They were the law!

I said slowly, "I don't think you really know what you're up against."

"Then tell us," she invited.

I hesitated. Then I reached back and picked up the phone. When the head stew answered, I said,

"Will you ask the gentlemen in 22-A and 22-F to step down here? And, oh, yes, how about some breakfasts all around?"

It's a queasy feeling looking at yourself. I'd had it often enough before through the peepholes, looking at one Dominic DeSota or another in one time-line or another—it was even queasier when I couldn't find any Dominic DeSota at all. (Or sometimes no anybody, but I don't like to think about those time-lines.)

The worst part was wondering where I had gone wrong. Or sometimes where I had gone right—but always different. I couldn't say that Senator Dom had gone wrong. Even in the ill-fitting and dirty fatigues, munching his not very good hash browns, he looked like somebody who had made something of his life.

But what about the other one?

He surely did not look like any kind of success. Rumpled business suit—and long pants at that! Imagine long pants in August! He didn't sound that way, either. He talked like somebody whose world wasn't much to begin with, and lately had gone definitely sour.

Still, I could see him livening up before my eyes. When the pulseur took off he was really shaken— closed his eyes, pressed his whole body back against the seat as though he were trying to disappear inside it. I made sure I had an airsick bag ready as we stood on our tail at eight hundred kilometers an hour. I couldn't blame him. He'd never been in a pulseur before, and not too often in even the clumsy old piston-engine walruses of his time.

I did not know if I would have done any better in his place. No, wrong. I knew I would not.

I wasn't sure I would have done as well as the senator, either, though the fact that he had was encouraging. He was next to Nicky, helping him get the plastic off his scrambled eggs, watching me to see what I was going to say. When I didn't say anything for a moment, trying to figure out how to begin, he did. "Dom," he said, "I appreciate being rescued, but I've got responsibilities in my own time. Can you get me back there?"

"I hope so, Dom," I said.

He looked at me appraisingly. "You could have saved a lot of trouble if you'd told me what was happening the first time we met," he offered.

"I do what I'm told to do, Dom," I said. "There's a lot at stake here." The woman snickered; she'd had a lot of practice listening to people talk generalities when the specifics were embarrassing. I flushed. "I'll tell you anything you want to know," I said, "because you all have a right to that much, but let me start with the basics. Accord? You all know by now that there are parallel times. An infinity of them. We can't reach them all, not even by peeping—well, that's what 'infinity' means, after all. The only times we've been able to reach so far have diverged sometime within the last ninety or ninety-five years. Only a few hundred of those, actually, but there are some interesting ones. In some of them the Communists took over the whole of Europe by 1933, with that supreme military genius Trotsky running the country. Then there's a whole set where Franklin D. Roosevelt escaped assassination and lived to become President. So the country was spared the military takeover and the interregnum, when it turned out there was nothing in the Constitution to say who became President when a President-elect died before assuming office, and so Garner and Hoover both claimed the office—until the Army stepped in and imposed martial law. Then there were—"

"Dom," said the senator patiently, "I guess we've got nothing better to do as long as we're on this airplane, but I don't know if history is the thing we're most interested in."

"I was only giving some illustrations."

"Sure. But we understand about parallel times—

well, no, that's a lie. I don't *understand*. But enough to go on: every time some, I don't know, goofatron in the whatsicle splits there's a whole new universe created, right? Something like that? Well, why don't you first come to the nearest one instead of some world that's really a lot different, in a lot of ways?"

"Ah," I said, nodding, "that's a good question." I felt solid ground beneath my feet; I'd been through this with Senate committees and budget planners often enough. "First I'll give you the technical answer: it's because of what Steve Hawking calls 'permeable-fixed n-space contiguity,' if that's any help." I knew it wasn't. Snort from Moe, the anthropoid, varying expressions of polite detachment from the other men. Nyla Christophe was the only one who showed friendly concern, curiously enough. She gave me an encouraging nod as she dexterously scooped up her scrambled eggs. She didn't look at what she was doing, didn't drop a crumb, thumbless or not. And she didn't miss a word. "I'll give you an analogy. Think of the relationship between the time domains as a coiled spring, with each time strung on it, one after another, like a bead. If you number every bead, of course number five is right before bead number six, and right after bead number four—they're neighbors. But the spring is coiled. So time five may actually be touching time number six hundred and fifty-two, and on the other side of that one is maybe time number fifteen hundred and something, depending on what the radius of curvature is. Are you following me so far?"

"Maybe," called Christophe, speaking for all of them.

"Right. Then—I hate to do this—but, you see, the spring isn't curved in normal three-dimensional space. It's in n dimensions, and I don't know what n is. So proximity makes a difference—that's why we haven't been able to reach times where the split occurred more than ninety or ninety-five years ago, except in occasional fugitive glimpses. But the 'nearest' isn't the 'easiest' to reach, or anyway not always. Have I lost you?"

"Just about," said Nicky, smiling for the first time. "But it's fun to keep trying to understand!"

I said helpfully, "If you get a chance, there's an asimov called *The Intelligent Man's Guide to Quantum Mechanics*."

"No, thanks," said Nicky. "But keep on, please."

"Well, that's about enough for theory. Some of you knew that already, of course." I glanced neutrally at our renegade Larry Douglas, who scowled and went back to his orange juice and roll. "So we developed the peeper, and then the portal. I don't want to go into the technology of that stuff. For one thing I can't—"

"But you're the fellow who invented it," called Christophe.

I shrugged. "If it's credit you're giving—well, no. Certainly not single-handed. We had Gribbin and Hawking from England, Sverdlich from Smolensk—and, of course, we had all the French emigré scientists after Bartholomew Two, so we had a solid base of mathematicians and nuclear physicists available. But if you're blaming me— Well, I'll take that." I took a deep breath. "Because what we hadn't counted on was ballistic recoil."

I don't know what sort of reaction I had expected. I got three different ones—four, if you count the flic, who looked worried. Larry looked despondent. The other Larry and the two FBI people looked opaque: the poker face was a Tau trait, I had discovered, probably because it was not a time when you wanted other people to know what you were thinking very often. And the two Dominics looked interested. I took a swallow of my cooling coffee—I hadn't even touched the solid food yet—and tried to explain:

"There's a tension between the worlds. Call it a skin. Once it's punctured anywhere, it is weakened everywhere. It's a little like that heat-sealed plastic wrapping that the meat comes in in supermarkets, you know?" They didn't. "Like the stuff your eggs were wrapped in," I said. "It's in a state of tension. When we puncture it anywhere it takes a lot of power, but then the skin is weaker—thinner—in other places. It's hard to predict just where the other places will be, because the geometry is fractal—well, never mind that; it's just hard. But it thins. At first radiation is all that gets through; then gases. Then—more than gases." I looked at our own Larry. "Since you, uh, left," I told him, "we've come across some bad ones. Large areas open, causing violent storms. And—well, there was one that killed a lot of people. Time Eta had built apartments over an abandoned railroad right-of-way. Two diesels and four or five flatcars came through at eighty kilometers an hour, right into the lobby of a building, before it closed again."

Nicky put his hand up. "Doc? There were some stories about loud noises around a little airfield—could they have been that? From a time where they had rocketships, like this one?"

I started to tell him that a pulseur wasn't a rocketship but a jet, but caught myself in time. "I'd say probably yes," I agreed. "And we don't seem to be able to prevent it. At first we thought it was because of leakage of energy from our portal generators, and if we could control them better we could eliminate the ballistic recoil. But now we think it's really recoil, and there's a conservation law involved. If x amount of energy or matter goes from my time to yours, then x amount has to come back out of it again. Not necessarily back to mine. It may go to a third time entirely. It may go in fractions to several different ones.

"And we can't stop it."

"Jesus," said Nyla Christophe contemptuously.

"You guys are playing with dynamite. Talk about irresponsible!"

Senator Dom cut in. His tone was less accusing, but a long way from really friendly. "Wouldn't it be a good idea to stop all this until you learn how to control it?" he asked.

"A damn good idea," I said fervently. "Only it got out of our hands when Larry got captured in Gamma. We could stop. But we couldn't both stop and keep an eye on them—not to mention the other times that were getting close, like yours, or that looked as though they'd be dangerous if they ever did get anywhere, like Ms. Christophe's."

The senator said temperately, "I'm in no position to blame you for anything, Dom. If we'd moved a little faster, my time might've been the first to break through, and I don't have any reason to believe we'd have done better. But—it scares me, Dom. I wish we'd thought a little more about the consequences before we got started. Those are big risks to take, just for the sake of developing a new weapon."

I lost my temper. Not at him. At myself, mostly, because of course he was saying nothing I hadn't said to myself a good many times over the past months. "You can't stop scientific research because there might be some danger somewhere!" I snapped. "Anyway, who said anything about a weapon?"

He looked surprised. "I only thought that it was obvious—"

"Maybe to savages the military application was obvious! Do you have any idea at all of what paratime means to research in general? Especially in the sciences that can't perform experiments?"

"I don't know exactly what you mean." He frowned.

"Think about it! Sociology, for instance. You can't isolate societies and perform experiments on them. But here we have an infinite number of societies, as like to our own or as different as we could want: we can develop a science of comparative sociology! Or economics, or poli-sci, or any of the social sciences at all. And not just the soft sciences! We had a meteorologist who came in as a research fellow. He went out of his mind when he discovered that your paratime, Nicky, hasn't had an Atlantic hurricane sweep up the coast in thirty years. We've been having them one or two a year and the damage is terrible. Now they think it has something to do with industrialization and urban sprawl; if we know that, maybe we can do something to stop it. And—trade."

The Tau Larry Douglas pricked up his ears. "I don't get what you're saying, DeSota," he said. "What kind of trade between two sets of the same people?"

"Two sets with slightly different histories. Slightly different fads, for one thing—there's a twenty-million-dollar business in hula hoops that came out of our peeping a year ago."

For once there was unanimity among my guests. All looked blank at once. "What's a hula hoop?" asked Larry Tau.

"A kind of a toy, that's all. But I'm not just talking about toys, I'm talking about a lot more valuable things. Think of it this way. If each paratime spends, oh, call it a billion dollars a year, on research and development—and if you can skim the cream of the R and D for fifty different paratimes—then, even with all the duplication, you're bound to find you still multiply your R and D results by a bunch!"

Silence for a moment while they digested that. Then Nicky said slowly, "I guess I can see what you're saying, Dom. You can't find out things unless you try them, so there's a risk in any kind of science; all right. And I guess getting other people's research to add to your own would be a big help, all right. But still—honestly, Dom, I don't really see how you expected this thing to do much for the ordinary slob in the street. Like me."

"It could save millions of lives, for one thing," I said.

"Come on! You mean by defeating an enemy before he defeats you, something like that?"

"No, not that. Maybe that would be true sometimes, but it's not what I'm talking about. Do you know what nuclear winter is? The death of everything because nuclear war throws so much dust into the air that it hides the sun, long enough to kill off nearly all the vegetation and most of the large animals—including human beings?"

They hadn't; but they understood it quickly enough. "Is that what you mean by a benefit?" Christophe said with a sneer. "Killing everybody?"

"Of course I don't. But there are times where it has happened. There are times we have reached where there are no mammals larger than a rat still alive—because the war did happen, five, ten, or more years ago, and the human race simply exterminated itself."

"Lovely!"

I kept a grip on my temper. Not easily. The woman got under my skin—was having the same effect, or some even more penetrating effect, on the senator, because he was looking at her with an expression I can only describe as fascinated. "No," I said tightly, "it isn't lovely at all. It's just a fact. Some time-lines have a virgin planet. The land is there, even the cities are sometimes there, though they're damaged. But there aren't any people to live in them.

"And then there are other times, our own included, where there are people dying and starving for lack of homes and land. Our Africa has been in a drought condition for most of the last decade. Parts of Asia are almost as bad. In other times Latin America has its own famines.

"Suppose we took those starving people without land, and let them emigrate to the empty planets without people?"

Nicky DeSota shouted, "That's *wonderful*, Dom! You've given new life to millions of people! How do they get along in their new world?"

He was ecstatic. I knew exactly how he felt. I'd felt the same thing—once. I said carefully, "Of course, they need support. It's not just the people. They need their animals, sometimes they need machinery, almost always they need doctors and teachers to show them how to farm new kinds of land . . . or, at least, they would. We haven't done it yet."

Crash went Nicky's exuberance. Up went Nyla Christophe's smug contempt. "Do-gooders," she said, shaking her head.

"Why not?" begged Nicky.

"Three reasons," I said. "First, we came across the ballistic-recoil problem. If we can't prevent that, or at least control it, we can't risk any large-scale transfers. We may have to stop using portals at all. And, second—" I looked at my old friend Larry Douglas. "There's the Gamma situation."

He moved sulkily, but didn't speak. He had already told us that he couldn't help giving them the portal. He had nothing to add.

The senator frowned. "You mean the people who took over Sandia."

I said, "It's not just Sandia any more, Dom. There's a shooting war now. It isn't big. It's only in Washington. But the Gammas have occupied all the Potomac bridges, the White House itself, and the National Airport—what you call Hoover Field. And there have been some nasty firefights. We think there are at least five hundred casualties. The first thing we have to do, since that's our responsibility in a way, is put that fire out . . . if we can."

I had the senator's full attention now. "Oh, my God," he said.

I tried to reassure him. "The fighting has died down now," I said. "As of half an hour ago, there wasn't anything more than sniping—of course, a few civilians are still getting killed—"

It did not seem to reassure him at all. "Civilians!" he cried. "But why don't they— I mean, at least they could— Aren't they evacuating the noncombatants, for God's sake?"

"I believe there is some of that, yes," I said, puzzling over his reaction: he had already told me that his family was a thousand miles away, in his Chicago home.

"I've got to get back," he said strongly.

"We're going to do that, Dom," I said. "I think. You understand that it isn't up to me. But that's what I've recommended. In fact, I've recommended that we all go through to Washington, D.C., Epsilon— that's your time, Senator—to show them what is happening, and offer whatever help we can. Almost all, I mean," I added, glancing at our own Larry Douglas, who shrugged, unsurprised.

There was an interruption from the other Larry Douglas. "I don't want to go back anywhere," he said.

"I beg your pardon?"

"I claim sanctuary!" he said forcefully. "I don't want to go back to my own time, because of, uh, political persecution, and I don't want to go skylarking around to get involved in whatever damn wars are being fought anywhere. You got me into this mess. You owe me something. I want to stay here."

The big goon rose threateningly in his seat. So, immediately, did the flic-de-nation, reaching for the holstered dartgun at his side. Christophe put her hand on Moe's shoulders, and the big man subsided at once, though the look he gave Douglas-Tau was murderous.

"We can talk about that later," said Christophe pleasantly. "Let's deal with one thing at a time. You said there were three problems. You've only told us two of them."

"Ah, yes," I said somberly. "The other new

element in the equation. We're being peeped ourselves. We don't know who, or for what purpose. But
it's happening."

Christophe chortled. "Welcome to the club!"

Our Larry said pettishly—brave with the flic
between him and her—"Oh, shut up, you. Dom? Is
this something new since I, uh, left?"

I nodded. "We don't know the source. We can't
trace it back—there's indications that they're using
technology a lot better than anything we've got. But
we get instrument readings from at least fifty places.
Somebody's watching us, and they've been doing it,
now, for about three months."

"So you're in the same spot we were a few days
ago," said the senator neutrally.

"I'm afraid so," I said.

He pursed his lips, thinking it through. "And
what are you going to do now, Dom?" he asked. "Are
you going to send me back to my own time?"

"I think that's what they've got in mind for you,
Dom," I said. "In fact, I think we're all going. You
because you live there. Me and Larry because we can
tell them things they need to know to defend themselves. And the others because—well, because they're
living proof of the existence of other worlds." And
because they're a nuisance, I thought but did not say
out loud: a couple of FBI people and a mortgage
broker, who needed them in our time?

I took a forkful of my scrambled eggs at last.
They were cold and awful, but I didn't have much
appetite anyway.

When the cleaners entered the McCormick Place auditorium to get ready for the Winter Sports Show, the lights disturbed a bat. "How the hell did that get in here?" complained the supervisor; but the big question was how to get rid of it before the show opened. That question solved itself. The bat blundered around wildly. Finally it blundered out through the big loading-dock doors, as snowmobiles were being carried in. No one there thought of it again. No one knew that it was of any importance—until, over the next weeks, feral cats, wide-ranging suburban dogs, and ultimately human beings began dying of the rabies virus the bat had brought with it.

27 August 1983
8:40 P.M. Mrs. Nyla Christophe Bowquist

They kicked me out of my pretty suite in the hotel. Even Slavi couldn't prevent it, because the whole top part of the hotel was taken over by the President and her staff when the White House was occupied; but he made the manager give me a room on the fifth floor. It was all right. There was a bed for me, and a bed for Amy. She didn't mind listening to me practice, and there certainly was no other reason in the world why either of us needed privacy. Not for my dear Dom's visits, because Dom wasn't around. Not even for my phone calls from my husband in Chicago, because there were very few of those. Not even Ferdie could get through the clogged lines to Washington most of the time.

That was a mercy, because I still had not made any sensible decision about what to say to Ferdie.

I hadn't made very many sensible decisions of any kind, it seemed to me. Staying in a war zone wasn't sensible in the first place. Effectively I was trapped. The airport was in enemy hands, so were all the bridges over the Potomac, so might be almost any road leading out of the capital, because the troops of the other guys were turning up in at least patrol strength almost anywhere. By the time I had finished dithering about whether to catch the next flight to Rochester, there wasn't any next flight to Rochester, and there were firecracker sounds from all over the city that were scary.

The radio said the gunfire wasn't serious. I didn't

215

agree. When I looked out the window and saw the smoke from Anacostia, or the top chopped off the Washington Monument because those other guys had thought our guys had an artillery spotter up there, it looked serious enough for me.

So when Jock McClenty knocked on my door I opened it scared.

I didn't expect good news. I couldn't imagine where good news might come from, that mean and rainy Saturday night. When I saw Dom's assistant, with the Secret Service man standing beside him, my first guess was that we were all being arrested. "Mrs. Bowquist," said Jock, "it's the senator. He's back. He's right here in the hotel, and he sent us to bring you to him."

Well, that was it. I cried. *Buckets*. I don't know why, exactly, I guess most likely because I had been storing up tears unshed for so many different reasons that any nudge would spill them over the top. Out of my eyes they came. I was still crying when we got to the penthouse, although it took quite a long time—we had to go clear down to the lobby, pass through city police at one checkpoint and Secret Service people at another before we got into an elevator in a different bank.

Sniffling into the fifth or sixth Kleenex the Secret Service man had given me (how nicely they train those people!), I got out and looked around. It was a suite that made my old suite look like a peasant hut in Cambodia. Duplex. Ankle-deep carpeting. Cathedral-style windows in a salon with fifteen-foot ceilings. The first person I saw was Jackie Kennedy, standing by a window and talking to somebody, and the second person I saw was the somebody himself.

It was Dom DeSota.

"Dom!" I yelled, and hurled myself at him, still sniffling.

It was Dom, all right, but he didn't hug me as Dom would have, he didn't say what Dom would have said to me, he didn't even smell like Dom. He smelled of pipe tobacco and a wholly different brand of after-shave, and most of all he did what Dom would never have done.

He pushed me away.

He did it gently—even kindly—but he pushed me away all the same; and so I wasn't in the least surprised when Jackie put her hand on my arm and said, "Nyla, dear? It's the wrong one."

Well, that was all right, as it turned out, because the right one was there too. He was halfway up the circular stair that went to the President's private quarters on the level above, but when he saw me he came whooping and leaping down and I got my hug after all. He didn't say anything at first. He just held me. I held him back, meaning it—meaning it so much that if Marilyn and Ferdie themselves had been there, cameramen on one side of them and their divorce lawyers on the other, I wouldn't have given up one squeeze or one moment. Then he loosened his arms a little, and looked at me, and kissed me; and then he said, "Oh, love!"—glancing back at the stairs.

At the top of them the President's appointments secretary was standing, tapping his foot. "Go ahead, Dom," I said, understanding. "I'll be here when you get back."

So then he was gone again, and Jackie was trying to explain what was going on on one side of me, and Jock McClenty was doing the same on the other, and I finally got them both to understand that what I wanted more than explanations was a chance to freshen up a little. And a minute later they led me through a bedroom that must have been designed for the Shah of Iran—mirrors on the ceiling and, good heavens, a real Picasso on the wall—into a bathroom that had a washstand with golden knobs.

It was a good thing I had a chance to put myself together, because when I came out of the czar's bathroom into the Shah's bedroom I discovered that it had been turned into a sort of holding pen for all of us.

When I say "all of us," I don't just mean "all of us." I mean more "all" and more "us" than I had ever meant before in my life. My Dom was back—the President had kicked him out for some private confabulation with a couple of generals—and Dom and I were, of course, the big "us" in my life. But there were *three* of him. If you counted in the one whose face we'd seen on the TV, there were four.

And there were two of *me*.

I had had a lot of trouble accepting the fact that there was more than one of the man I loved, but, boy, I didn't know what trouble was until I had to face up to the other one of me. It reminded me of the time, two or three years before, when Ferdie and I had gone off for a weekend in the Wisconsin Dells to try to save our marriage. I took my spayed Siamese cat, Panther, to stay with Amy in her little apartment, along with her spayed female calico, Poo-Bear. It wasn't a happy meeting. The first thing Poo-Bear did was leap up on top of a knickknack shelf, knocking half of Amy's carved wooden animals on the floor, and the first thing Panther did was dive under a bookcase. They didn't hiss or growl or spit. They just stared at each other across the room, all the time I was there—though Amy told me later that within half an hour they were licking each other.

It was a lot like that with me and this other Nyla, although I saw no chance at all that we would ever be licking each other. She sat in one corner, looking at me and occasionally whispering to the man next to her, who looked seven feet tall and half that much wide. Nasty-looking bit of business, he was. I sat on a Queen Anne loveseat with Dom, *my* Dom, holding my hand and my head on his shoulder, while Dom tried to tell me what things, what amazing things, he had been doing since I saw him last. And the two of us, that Nyla and me-Nyla, stared at each other and couldn't stop.

Although I studied her more closely than I had ever inspected any other woman, I didn't notice that she had no thumbs until Dom whispered to me about it. That wasn't the only difference. The expression on her face was different from any I believed I had ever worn—cynical? Wry? Maybe even envious? All the same, she was *me*.

I was very, very grateful for Dom's arm around me.

With all that going on, it wasn't surprising that I didn't notice the other odd thing. The fact that there were three Doms in the room was bad enough; the presence of another Nyla than me was worse. But we weren't the only duplicates. When I finally took my eyes off the other Nyla long enough to pay attention to the others, I saw that the Kennedys were talking to two of what looked like my old friend Lavrenti Djugashvili, and they were looking at me.

"*Shto eta*, Lavi?" I called across the room, impartially to both of them. They both looked baffled.

Dom laughed and tightened his arm around me. "They're not the ambassador," he said. "He's out at the airport, welcoming some Russian scientists that are coming in to meet with us."

"Oh, lord," I said, laughing because it was better than crying, "are there two of *everybody*?"

"Not just two," he said somberly. "An infinity, I'm afraid. But of me and you, there's only one me and one you that matter, and we're together. Let's keep it that way."

So then there were suddenly two more of "us" in the room, although the new two were only imaginary. They were very clear to me, all the same, Marilyn on one side of us, Ferdie on the other, and the expressions on their faces were full of anger and hurt and accusation.

It was fortunate that they were only imaginary, at

least at that moment, however real they would be later on. I closed my mind to them. "If that's a proposal," I said, "I accept. I don't want us ever to be apart again—not counting when I have to go on tour, I mean."

"And not counting election campaigns," he said, grinning. "I promise."

It is astonishing how easily you can make a promise that you will not be allowed to keep.

Still, there were the real Marilyn and the real Ferdie, and we owed them at least a little discretion until we told them what was going on. In spite of everything—in spite of all the weirdness that was happening, not to mention the fact that my country was being invaded right outside the hotel window—I could still worry about propriety. Especially when I noticed Jack Kennedy studying us appraisingly out of the corner of his eye while he talked to Lavi's doubles.

I flushed and sat up. I didn't push Dom's arm away, but I moved a little bit outside of it. Dom came to the same realization I did at that same moment. I felt him lean away.

Then he came back to where our bodies were touching, and the arm was on my shoulders again. Proudly. Almost defiantly. Oh, hell, I thought, we're past the point of being discreet. If our affair had ever been a secret, our secret was no secret any more.

The luxury of the suite wasn't limited to gold bathroom fixtures. There was a kitchen attached to the suite, and a hotel chef, sous-chef, and waiter attached to the kitchen. "Eat up," said Dom—my Dom. "It's all being paid for by the taxpayer." So we ate. I found I had a ravenous appetite. So did the paratime travelers. Apparently they hadn't been fed a lot lately, and they made up for it. And there was conversation too. I didn't take much active part in it, because I was busy listening, trying to make out just what was going on.

Dom did most of the explaining, and Jack Kennedy did most of the asking. "There's a million of these time-lines, Jack," Dom said. "No, not a million. A million million million, maybe. I think the right word is *infinity*."

"Remackable," said Jack. "I had no idea." He was sitting across from us, holding Jackie's hand as Dom was holding mine. I wished that when we were their age we would be as loving, in spite of our rather bad and adulterous beginning. (But there were all those stories about Jack and heaven knew how many women, long ago, and their marriage seemed to have survived.)

"We can only reach fairly nearby ones," said Dom. "Dr. Dom here"—he nodded in a friendly way to the one I had flung myself at, who was dubiously nibbling at a platter of falafel—"knows more about it than I do."

The other Dom swallowed. "They're almost like yours and mine," he concurred, "but there are, of course, some differences. In the one that's invading you, Jerry Brown is the President of the United States."

"Jerry Brown!" said Jack. "That's the haddest thing of all to believe."

"But it's so." The other Dom lifted a forkful of the falafel and said, "This is pretty good. I'll have to see if I can find somebody to make it back home. That's another advantage of paratime, you see, learning different things that improve the quality of life."

"I can't say ours has improved a lot, Dawm," Jack said wryly. "Go on about the other time-lines."

"Well, there are a couple where Ronnie Reagan is President."

"*Ronnie?*"

"Yes, and in those lines Lyndon Johnson was President twenty years ago, and before that *you* were. Only—" He hesitated, as though it were hard to say it.

"Only in that time you were assassinated in office, Senator. By a man named Lee Harvey Oswald."

Jacqueline either swallowed or gasped—the sound was somewhere in between. Jack glanced worriedly at her, then back at Dom. His expression was as divided as her sound. For the top half of his face his eyebrows were quirked with mild curiosity; but his jaw muscles were clenched. "Lee Harvey Oswald? Wait a minute—was it—yes, I remember, the guy who shot the governor of Texas?"

"The same one."

"Remackable," said Jack Kennedy. There didn't seem to be anything else for anyone to say. It was a conversation-stopper. Then Jack shook himself. "My poor wife," he said, smiling and patting Jackie's hand. "Do you know what kind of a widow she made, Dr. DeSota?"

"I, uh, don't remember exactly," that Dom said apologetically, and for some reason I didn't think he was telling the truth. Jack nodded absently. He thought the same, it was clear; but he was saved from having to ask questions by a major with gold braid dripping from his shoulders. He came into the room, fresh-shaved, hair neatly brushed, eyes as weary as any man's I have ever seen; he looked as though he hadn't slept for two or three nights running, and probably he had not.

"Senator DeSota?" he said tentatively, looking from one Dominic to another. "The President will see you now. All three of you, sir," he added. And Dom, my Dom, hugged me, kissed my cheek, and got up to leave me.

I sat down with the Kennedys. I suppose we talked. I'm not sure what we talked about, because my mind was too full of things. Including the other Nyla. Although we had discontinued our staring match, we had not lost interest. She was standing by the buffet table, dexterously if thumblessly slicing bits of cheese for herself and her anthropoid companion. Although

I didn't catch her eyes on me, I was sure that every time I looked toward her she had just looked away. I wasn't in any doubt about that impression, because I was doing the same for her. It almost seemed to me that she was more interested in me than I was in her, or anyway interested in me in a different way. Not just idle curiosity. Purposeful, although I couldn't imagine what the purpose was.

I decided that she and I needed to talk.

I didn't put the decision into practice, though, because just as I was making up my mind to go over to her, Lavrenti Djugashvili, the real one, came in, smiling, mopping his brow, gazing curiously at the other Nyla before coming over to me. "So very confusing!" he said, kissing my hand and then Jacquelyn's. "Such a difficult day!"

"You brought your boys over?" Jack Kennedy asked.

"Oh, yes, of course, Zupchin and Merejkowsky, two brilliant physicists from Lenin Theoretical Studies Institute. Then I was advised my own presence no longer desired," he added wryly.

"Gave you a hadd time, did she?" asked Senator Kennedy sympathetically.

Lavi shrugged. "I speak no evil of your President," he said, spreading his hands to show how fair-minded he was being, "but it is clear to me she does not like Communists, myself very much included."

The senator also demonstrated his fairness. "I don't speak much good of the lady myself," he said, "because she's in the wrong patty. All the same, she's got a lot on her mind, Lavi. They've captured her husband. They've taken over her White House. She doesn't want to be reasonable right now, and most of all she doesn't want to be the first American President since 1812 to have an enemy occupy her capital."

"Oh, yes, to be sure," Lavrenti agreed. "Especially since there is this new activity from the invaders. . . ." He paused, looking at us. "You have not been informed? But even on the television the news is there for all to see! Surely there is such a device somewhere in this palatial apartment? Come, let us find it!"

There was indeed such a device, although it was hidden behind the doors of a carved mahogany breakfront, and, yes, there was plenty of news on it for us.

None of it was good.

We tuned in in the middle of live-action shots of hard fighting. It wasn't in some faraway land. It was only blocks away from us, at the far end of the Mall, all around the Capitol. Tanks and personnel carriers seemed to be coming from around the Supreme Court building, fanning out to take the Capitol in pincers from both sides. There were bodies there. The camera zoomed in to take a closer look at some of them, and I wished it hadn't. Cut to another shot, and we were looking at a file of tanks. Peculiar ones. I did not quite understand why they seemed peculiar until Lavi choked out something—it sounded angry and dirty, but I couldn't tell what, because it was in Russian. He switched to English to say, "Is a new weapon, Dominic!"

And then the proportions sorted themselves out. They were tanks, but they were tiny—not more than six or seven feet long, only knee-high off the ground, and each one with a great gun swinging from side to side over its body like the whip of a scorpion. "Have nothing like this in Soviets," Lavi said plaintively.

"We don't in this America, either," said Jack Kennedy. "Radio-controlled, I bet! Sweet Baby Jesus, look at that sucker shoot!" Because those cannon weren't for show, they were firing on the Capitol, and at each round great mushrooms of masonry and smoke popped out of the Capitol walls.

The scene changed. We were looking at NBC's war room, very much like the election-night headquarters they trotted out every year. Behind Tom Brokaw and John Chancellor was a wall-to-wall situation map of the District of Columbia, and they were explaining what had been happening.

They didn't have to say much. The pictures said it all. Nearly a quarter of the city was now shaded red—red for occupying forces—the area around the Capitol where we had just been looking, the White House, the Ellipse, and most of the space around the Washington Monument, a big section along the river, and spotty areas all over the District. And along most of the perimeters there were flashing red lights that signaled actual combat going on right now.

Brokaw was pointing to the Capitol. "The most recent breakthrough," he said, "began without warning just forty-five minutes ago at First Street and Constitution Avenue. Simultaneously fighting broke out at nearly every other point in the city where our troops face theirs." He named them, one by one, and then began a recap. "Incongruously," he said, "there has been constant telephone contact between the headquarters of the invaders, in the White House, and ours, at an undisclosed location somewhere within the District. It is known that the invaders have captured three Cabinet members and at least three-quarters of the Combined Chiefs of Staff and their immediate staffs, as well as several senators, congressmen, and other major figures of government. Ronald Reagan is himself a captive. All of the hostages, as our government has termed them, have been allowed to make taped voice messages that have been transmitted by telephone. Here is the voice of General Westmoreland—"

I had heard it. I didn't hear it again. I was looking at Nyla Christophe, and this time she was looking back at me. From the little Dom had whispered to me I had expected, I don't know, a kind of Gestapo agent combined with Mata Hari. She didn't look like that. What she looked like was me. She was sitting on her hands, so I couldn't see them. What I could see was a woman of my age, my face, my body— well, no, perhaps she was six or eight pounds slimmer than I, but that certainly was not to her discredit—a woman whom I might have seen look back at me out of my mirror any morning. I knew that she had instilled fear. I had never done that, no, not to anyone at any time; I didn't think it was possible for me to cause physical fear in anyone, ever. But I had not grown up in a world that cut a young woman's thumbs off for shoplifting. She didn't speak to me, though there seemed to be nothing hostile in the way she studied my face. I didn't speak to her, either, though I was beginning to feel that if we did talk, if somewhere the two of us might somehow sit down together over a just-us-girls-together dinner (it would be mostly salads, with perhaps one small cocktail to make it festive), we might, in fact, get along very well.

It gradually became clear to me that she and I were not the only ones staring at each other. Lavi Djugashvili had got up to leave, and now he was hesitating. He was studying the two men named Larry Douglas. He whispered to Jack Kennedy, looked perplexed, shook his head, finally spoke up. "Mr. Douglas? May I have a word with you—with both of you, perhaps?"

"Why not?" said one of them—I had no way of telling which.

"I observe," said Lavi, "that we resemble each other very closely. Is it possible that we are related?"

One of the Larry Douglases laughed. "Hell, man, that's a chintzy way to put it. We are a hell of a lot related, you bet. We have the same two parents, and the same four grandparents."

"You mean Grandpa Joe," said the other one, nodding.

"I mean all of them," said the first one. "Grandpa Joe is only the famous one. He was pretty hot stuff eighty or ninety years ago—robbing banks in Siberia, outwitting the law, all that. He came to America when it got too hot for him in Russia and used some of his bank-robbery money to open a fabric wholesaling business in New York. He got pretty rich."

"Same with mine," cried the other one. "Did yours end the same way? Killed by some guy with an ice pick in his summer home in Ashokan?"

"It wasn't an ice pick, and it was winter, and it was in Hobe Sound," said the first one, "but, yes. They said it was political. He'd taken this money that was supposed to go to the Communist cause, you know. That your story, too, Ambassador?"

Lavi stared at them. Then he said heavily, "Up to a point, yes. Only my grandparents didn't leave Russia. Grandpa Joe stayed on, and he got to be pretty famous, under his party name of Stalin." He passed a hand over his face. "All this," he said, "is very disturbing. Please excuse me. I must in any case return to my embassy, but you two gentlemen . . . this situation . . . one would like to discuss—" He stopped and shook his head.

I could not help it. I stood up and put my arm around him. He was astonished. So was I. But he hugged me back, and we stood there for a moment. Then he released me, stepped back, kissed my hand, and said, "I must go—"

He stopped in the middle of the sentence, frowning.

I am sure I was frowning, too, because I heard what he heard. That inaudible distant exchange of gunfire was no longer either inaudible or distant. It came from the street just below.

Nobody was looking at me. I became aware that the whole room was looking at the staircase going up to the President's private quarters on the floor above. The Secret Service guards at the bottom were no longer standing around, watching us all for any sign of threat. They were moving around the great salon, ordering everybody to back up against the walls. As one came near he called, "I'm Jenner, Secret Service. The President is being evacuated."

"Evacuated!" snapped Senator Kennedy. "What's the problem, Jenner? Are we in danger?"

"Possibly so, sir. If you want to leave, you can go as soon as the President's clear. There's a way out through the underground garage. But stay put while her party is leaving. Please," he added, and then as an afterthought, "Sir."

And down the stairs came the President with her entourage. More Secret Service people, three of them women; some District Police with Captain Glenn leading them; the WAC liaison colonel carrying the nuclear-weapons codes; four or five staffers trying desperately to talk to the President even while she was walking down the stairs, one hand on the banister. And she was answering each one of them. I've never agreed with Nancy's politics, but she really looked presidential, even in retreat.

As soon as the President was in the elevator the remaining Secret Service man called something up to the upper-floor suite, and the people who had been with the President were allowed to come down. One big gaggle of them I recognized at once: Dom, in fact all three Doms, along with the two Russians, and a couple of other no-doubt scientists fresh from their meeting with the President.

They stopped almost at the bottom. I stopped too. There was a sudden mutter in the room, people catching their breath, making sounds of astonishment and concern. I didn't know what it was—exactly. I did think that suddenly there were fewer people coming down the stairs than I thought there should have been, but I wasn't looking at them.

Then there was a sort of chill in the air and a—I guess you should call it a silence. The kind of ear-popping silence that you get in a jet when suddenly you adjust to a pressure change.

Then, "Pardon me," said a voice from behind

me, a voice I knew very well, "but shouldn't you and I have a talk, Nyla?"

"Of course, Nyla," I said, and turned to look myself in the eye. She was smiling.

There was something about that smile that made me look down. She held her thumbless hands together, just at waist level, and peeking out from between them was the sharp, serrated blade of a knife from the buffet table, pointed at me.

Before the man's head was an object—perhaps it should be called an image—about the size of a beach ball. It was composed of points of light. Seen from outside, a galaxy might look like that, if the galaxy were densely enough packed with stars. Most of the points of light were pale blue, but within the sphere were angry tracings of green, yellow, orange, even red, like the radiating lines of gangrene around an infected wound. Over the sphere was a line of what might have been mirrors reflecting the man's concerned face—except that they were not mirrors. Some of the images had longer hair or shorter or less. Some were tanned and some pallid, some fatter, some thin. "Now that we've synched," said the seated man, "I think we can see the extent of the problem. I've measured harmonics up to sixth-order already, and still propagating." He paused to look at the other faces for disagreement. There wasn't any. "If this goes on," he said evenly, "I project a nine-nines probability that within one standard year the disturbances will be effectively both plenary and irreversible."

28 August 1983
12:10 A.M. Agent Nyla Christophe

With all that was going on, no one paid much attention as Bowquist and I moved toward the pantry. If they had looked carefully at her face, they might have seen something that would make someone ask a question, until I told her to smile. Then she smiled. Next to the pantry was a bathroom, and next to the bathroom was the door to the stairs.

No one saw us go through it.

"We wait here a minute, Bowquist," I said, looking at her. She was a good-looking woman. She had ten pounds on me, ten pounds that I had sweated off with a lot of misery on the exercise machines and judo pads, but they looked good on her. She wasn't in any way fat, only rounder than I. What's more, she smelled a whole other way. I use perfume now and then. Why not? Men like it, and I like to have men like everything about me when we're headed for bed. But she wore it as a matter of course; and also there was the way her hair was done. It was a good four inches longer than the way I kept it, and turned into soft waves. "Who's Bowquist?" I asked.

"Ferdinand Bowquist is my husband," she said. She didn't act frightened, though she probably was. I would have been.

"I thought so. Seemed to me you were pretty squeezy with that senator, though."

She didn't answer that. Well, I wouldn't have, either, but for some reason I was glad to see that this pretty, respectable woman wasn't beyond fooling around a little now and then. "What are you going to do with me?" she asked.

I said, "Very little, love. I heard you say you've got a room in this hotel. We're just going to borrow it for a little while."

The door opened. I had expected it to. And through it came Moe, shepherding the two Larrys, as I had expected. The strange Larry was sunk in gloom, but my old bedmate Larry was cranky. "Nyla," he said, "are you crazy? I don't know what you're trying to do, but you can't—"

I said, "Shut up, honey. We're going for a little walk."

It wasn't little, and it wasn't a walk, exactly. It was climbing down those stairs, and it was fourteen stories—twenty-eight flights—while even in that interior well of the hotel we began to hear the sounds of firing in the streets, and now and then in the actual halls outside the fire doors.

It was enough to make a person nervous. It even made my Larry nervous. "Nyla, for God's sake," he gasped from behind me. "What are you getting us into? These people will shoot first and ask questions later!"

I was running out of steam, too, and glad enough to stop for a minute. "Nobody does that, asshole," I said. "They'll look at us and they'll ask, and then what? Whichever side they are, none of us is on the other, are we?" Except for Nyla Bowquist, I added to myself; but who would shoot her? "Anyway, it's only three more floors."

And so it was, but what I hadn't counted on was that Washington in that time must have been a high-crime area. The stairwell doors were the kind that only opened from one side. Worse than that, they were fire doors, sheet steel with hinges that wouldn't melt away in the first blaze. I looked at Moe doubtfully. "Think you can get it open?" I asked.

He didn't answer, unless a dismal grunt was an answer. He backed up across the landing, lunged forward, and kicked the door right at the lock with all his weight, two hundred and some pounds of it—

It didn't budge. The noise was loud, the results nothing. Moe hopped on one foot, rubbing the other and looking sourly at me. I shrugged. "Try again," I said, but before he could either do it or argue about it the door opened. A soldier in olive-green fatigues was standing there, pointing an automatic rifle at us, looking scared, but not as scared as I was.

"Who the hell are you people?" he asked.

How I would have handled it I don't exactly know. Maybe it was because we were in strange surroundings that made him bold, maybe it was just because he had more breath left than the rest of us; but for whatever reason Moe took over on his own. "Easy with the gun, friend," he said with a grin, putting his ankle down. "These are VIP's I'm trying to get away from the fighting. I'm FBI. I'm going to take my badge out of my pocket to show you, and I'll do it real slow—"

And he did; and the soldier was young enough, and dumb enough, to come close enough to look at it, and that was his mistake. *Oof,* he said, as Moe sank the knife into his belly and pulled it up before I could stop him.

So we had the way clear to Bowquist's room; and we also had a weapon; but, most of all, we now had the problem of finally having committed a criminal act that someone would not take lightly in the place where we could be punished for it.

There was a note pinned to the pillow in Nyla's room:

Nyla dear,
They are making me leave the hotel. I'm going to try to get to Senator Kennedy's house to wait for you. I hope you're all right!
Amy

I didn't really care much about the absent Amy. What I saw that I liked was the open closet, with hangers of dresses, slacks, and blouses; and the bathroom with the working shower. I left Moe in charge of the shaken hostages and I got under the shower.

It felt good, and the shower is a place where I do my best thinking. I needed to do that. The situation had taken a turn I hadn't planned on.

It was good that we had a weapon. I'd never seen that particular one before, but it had a safety and sights and a trigger and a banana clip of ammo, and I had no doubt I could handle it. A lot of people don't think that I can use a gun, missing thumbs as I am. Quite a few of them have lost money betting on that, and one or two have lost more than money. When you've fired everything in the FBI armory, you don't have much trouble figuring out almost anything else that is built to explode gunpowder at one end and drive a bullet out of a barrel at the other.

This is not a womanly grace, but then I haven't had much time to concentrate on being a woman.

I'm not talking about making love, because I can dig up at least a dozen men to testify that at being *female* I am first-rate in any league. I mean the other kind of thing. The Nyla Bowquist kind of thing. The hair just right, the tiny touch of makeup that made the eyes brighter, the way of walking on spike heels as though they weren't there at all. This is the kind of thing I think about when I'm standing under the hot shower, with my conscious mind more than half turned off, letting my head wander where it might.

This time it didn't wander far. There was too much to drag it back to reality, and a lot of reality was nasty.

It was bad that now we had a corpse to explain.

As a practical matter, that might not be important—there were plenty of corpses around, with all that gunfire. I didn't like it, though. I've never been an easy killer. I don't like the people who work for me to kill except when absolutely necessary, either, and before long I would make sure that Moe regretted what he had done.

Before long. Not right away; because right away I had other things to do.

By the time I finished rinsing my hair I thought I had something pretty well worked out. I wrapped a towel around my wet hair, not bothering with the rest of me, and pushed the door open. I got three attentive male stares, ignored them, and spoke to Bowquist. "I'd like to borrow some underwear," I told her, politely enough.

"In the drawer," she said, pointing. She was a lot too well bred to say anything about my nakedness, but as I pulled the drawer open I saw her suppressing a smile. Panties, stockings, bras—they were all neatly folded; Amy must have been a treasure. I selected a matching set in white silk and dressed while I talked.

"What we're going to do," I said, "is steal a portal. Then we're going home."

That changed the look on everybody's face. Especially the men. I've noticed about men that while a naked body always interests them, there is something especially exciting about one that's all damp and rosy from the bath; they can't wait to get it sweaty and soiled again. But I took their minds off that pretty fast. Moe nodded, accepting it as a directive. The other Larry looked stunned. And my own Larry snarled, "For God's sake, Nyla, don't you know when you're well off? Stay here! Forget going back!"

I shook my head. "Maybe you can forget it, sweets," I said, "because, to tell the truth, you've got no future back home anyway. But I work for the Bureau, and they expect something from me. I'm going to deliver."

"Aw, hell, Nyla," he grumbled. "Do you want to go back to where you can go to jail for wearing shorts three inches above the knee? This isn't such a bad place! Once they get this war thing straightened out—" Then his mind caught up with his mouth, and the look on his face changed from angry to apprehensive. "What do you mean, no future?"

I said comfortably, "You couldn't figure on protection from me forever, could you? I would say you're just about used up, sweetmeat. . . . Will you hand me those slacks, Bowquist?"

"But Nyla! You and I have something going!"

"Aw, Larry, who are you kidding? You were running your own little rackets, a swindle here, a little larceny there. I don't blame you for figuring out that meeting me was your big break. Screwing an FBI bureau chief was a great way to find out if we were getting close to you. But we were, hon. I just didn't tell you."

"Nyla!" He was beginning to sweat. The other Larry, on the other hand, was beginning to look a little more cheerful: the worse things got for somebody else, the less oppressive his own problems seemed. They were two of a kind—slippery good looks, charm, meanness inside and all.

"No hard feelings," I said, zipping the slacks and admiring myself in the mirror. They weren't as tight as I would have liked them, but then I would be trying to avoid attention, not attract it. I patted his shoulder. "I got what I wanted, too, you know. I would put you definitely in the top ten of all the men I've ever known in the bed department, and besides I knew you'd fink for me. As you did." I took the towel off my head and felt the hair. Still pretty wet. "Bowquist, have you got a hair dryer I can borrow?"

"In the bathroom," she said, getting up to get it, but I stopped her.

"You get it and plug it in for me, Larry," I said, to my own Larry. Resentfully he disappeared and I heard him knocking around in the cabinets. "Now, what we're going to do is make a trade. We've got something they want. They've got something I want."

"What's that, boss?" rumbled Moe, frowning over the difficult concepts.

"What they've got is a portal. What we've got is hostages." I smiled pleasantly at the other Nyla and the other Larry. "Bowquist is the one they'll be most anxious to ransom, I guess," I said, "judging by the way her boyfriend was hugging her. Unfortunately, he doesn't have a portal. Leaves you, Dr. Douglas. I gather they want you a whole lot—"

"Oh, *no*," he yelled. "Listen, don't turn me over to them! I've got a better idea."

"I'm listening," I said, still smiling.

"We'll borrow a portal, maybe—I don't know how, but we'll figure something out. We'll go back to your time. I'll teach you how to build them, just the way I did for the others! The way you wanted me to! I'll work myself to death for you, I swear I will!"

I thought it over. "Might be simpler in some ways," I conceded. "Question is, how do we get to a portal?" I turned to Bowquist. "Maybe that's where you come in," I said. "Do you think if we talked real nice to your boyfriend he could get us the use of a portal, just for a little while?"

"I have no idea," she said, very cool, very remote. These sleazy goings-on were not part of her world. I had to admire her. Part of me wished I could be more like her; part of me was bitterly complaining that I could have been, *would* have been, if things had gone a little differently for me, because after all I *was* her—

"What?"

"I said," she repeated, "that something seems to have happened to your own boyfriend." She was looking at the bathroom door.

It took me a second to understand what she was talking about. Then I realized she was right. The sounds from the bathroom had stopped some time ago, but no Larry came out. I got to the door in nothing flat.

There was nowhere to hide in there, not under

the sink, not even in the shower cubicle, with its curtain pulled back just the way I had left it to show no one inside.

He wasn't there. There was absolutely no way he could have got out. But he wasn't there.

For the first time in a very long time, I was really scared. I turned to Moe, over by the window, opening my mouth to tell him to look under the bed or something. Moe's expression was puzzled—

Then there was no expression on his face at all. There wasn't even a face to have one on.

Like that.

I was looking at him, and then I was looking through him. He wasn't there any more. I saw the window, and the gun he'd taken away from the soldier he'd killed lying on the sill, but of the man who had stood in front of them there was no sign at all.

I felt suddenly naked as well as scared. I don't mean just skin-bare, as when I came out of the shower; I mean helpless and defenseless. I jumped for that gun out of pure reflex.

I never got to it.

The room flicked away. . . .

And I was gone too.

They had crossed over the wet green fields of Ireland and were two hundred miles out over the Atlantic before they finished checking the tickets. It wasn't the most fun job in the world. The passengers were itchy and irritable. They knew something was wrong. There had been the unexplained wait before they left the gate at Heathrow, the whispered conferences among the cabin crew, the unusual request for everyone to show tickets again after they were airborne. It had to be done, though. 640 boarding passes had been issued. 640 tickets had been picked up at the gate. Only 639 passengers were on the plane. Somebody, somehow, had entered the mobile gate at one end and never come out at the other. When every seat in both levels and all six compartments had been cross-checked against the printout, including all eighteen lavatories and nine baggage spaces, they still had no answer, but at least they had a name. "Well," said the purser glumly, "at least we know we didn't count wrong. But what do you suppose they're going to tell the family of this Dr. John Gribbin?"

27 August 1983
10:50 P.M. Major DeSOTA, Dominic P.

Being a major is not really being a major when you have no troops to command, and they had taken mine away from me. There was fighting going on. At a quarter of eleven every gun we had put through the portals began firing at once. The fighting was bloody. I knew this because I was watching the reentry portal under the bridge, and I could see the casualties coming back. But I wasn't taking any part in it. I was standing around with my thumb in my butt, waiting for someone to tell me where I was supposed to go and what I was supposed to do.

The whole operation was beginning to look very bad. Maybe even terminally bad. The new troops going through the portal south of the bridge weren't heads-up, eyes-bright, combat-ready killers. They slouched into the big black square and didn't talk. And the ones coming back—

The medics had their hands full with the ones coming back.

Through the return portal I could hear the sounds of gunfire and the *whomp* of mortars and grenades. Even the air that came through was bad air. It was a hotter, damper August there than in our own time, and it smelled. It smelled of burning and of dust and shattered plaster. It smelled of sewers ripped open with shellfire, and of the diesel stink of the tanks.

It smelled like death.

Under other circumstances, it might have been a

nice night. I could imagine strolling along here by the river, with my arm around a pretty girl, being very happy. It was hot, but what else would you expect of Washington in August? It was sultry, but not unbearable, and though there weren't any stars in the sky, there was the constant *zap-zap* of our strobes, dozens of them now. I did not really think they were fooling the Russian satellites any more, but they were pretty to look at as they flashed against the patchy clouds.

However, the circumstances were bad. I was a long way from being a hero. At least they'd got me some other clothes to wear—slacks and a sport shirt, probably from the nearest K-Mart—so I didn't have to look like a fool in that rented tux any more. But that didn't stop me from feeling like one. What I was more than anything else was in the way. I stepped back to avoid a half-track lumbering back through the portal with a cargo of stretchers, and I bumped into another rubbernecker, as idle as I. "Sorry," I said, and then saw the general's stars on his collar. "My God," I said.

"No," said General Magruder sadly, "it's just me, Major DeSota."

It isn't easy to feel sorry for a general, especially a general like Ratface Magruder. But this was a whole other man than the one who had chewed his way all up and down my ass back in New Mexico. He had a doomed look about him, and it didn't take long to find out why. All it took was asking him, as politely as I could, which aspect of the operation he was commanding, and him telling me shortly, "None of them, DeSota. I've been reassigned. Fort Leonard Wood. I'm flying out in the morning."

"Oh," I said. There wasn't anything more to say. When a general gets pulled out of an ongoing operation to take over a training post you don't have to say another word. I guess my face showed what I was thinking. He grinned at me. It was not a friendly grin.

"If you're still worried about a court-martial," he said, "forget it. There's about a hundred people ahead of you in line."

"That's good to hear, sir," I offered.

He looked at me with surprise and contempt. "Good?" He rolled the word around in his mouth. "I would not have said 'good' about any of this." He glared at the portal, where a limping sergeant was leading a woman with second-lieutenant's bars sewed onto her fatigues and her head wrapped in bloody bandages. He burst out, "That stupid bitch President! Why did she make us do it?"

"She's crazy, sir," I said, currying favor.

"Damn right she's crazy! But," he said darkly, "at least I understand the way she's crazy. She's not a traitor. And that goddam egghead—"

"Sir?"

"That scientist!" he snarled. "I don't mean Douglas, I mean our own guy. You know what he tells us now? We could have saved the whole fucking operation! There's worlds we could have used where there aren't any people at all!"

"No people, sir?"

"Where the whole damned human race blew itself up years ago," he said testily. "He's peeped them. Like where they had an all-out nuclear war back in the seventies or so. Sure, some are too radioactive, we can't use them. But there are some that aren't. We could have gone into one of them. No opposition. Nobody there to give us any. We could have sent a fleet of transports through, flown them over to Russia, set up portals wherever we wanted them. Shit! We wouldn't even have needed bombs! Just push a nuclear warhead through, a thousand of them if we wanted to, all over the goddam country— or what used to be their country. You want a cup of joe?" he finished abruptly.

"Why—"

"Come on," he said, and tramped across the street to the headquarters building. "We didn't know," he said gloomily over his shoulder. "Now it's all fucked up."

Even a general relieved of command gets what he wants. The colonel with the papers in his hand glared at me, but I was shielded by the stars. He didn't say anything as Ratface drew two cups out of the urn and handed me one.

"This new operation, General—" I began.

"Yeah, yeah. We've got her pinned, I think. Only how much time have we got left?"

"Time, sir?"

"The Russians," he explained. "They're getting antsy." He took a long pull of the coffee. It was about two degrees under boiling, and just sipping it seared my throat. He had a throat of cast iron. "The word's getting out, DeSota," he said wearily. "Prisoners talk to their guards, guards talk to their girl friends. Casualties talk to their nurses. They even talk to reporters. We can't keep the lid on much longer— What's the problem, Colonel?" he demanded, looking at the commandant.

The colonel was pawing through his papers. "Excuse me, sir," he snapped, not in an excusing tone, "but is this man Dominic DeSota? Yes? Jesus, DeSota, what the fuck are you doing here? You're in the wrong place! You're supposed to be going through at the sally point—get your ass up to the zoo right away!"

Magruder hitched a ride with me. He didn't ask. He just jumped into the jeep from one side as I was climbing in from the other, and I didn't argue. He didn't say a word as the driver gave it the hammer. There weren't many cars. Civilians had got the word; they weren't venturing out much any more. The traffic lights turned their colors at their own pace, and we went through the intersections with the horn blaring, red or green regardless; and there was nothing to stop us until we turned into the avenue.

Then there was plenty.

The whole of the avenue was blocked. It was like the lineup for an Inauguration Day parade, with all the military might of the republic filling the little side streets, the squad leaders in their gold and crimson helmets pacing restlessly back and forth in front of their vehicles, talking into their shoulder radios, ready to go on signal. Only they weren't getting ready for a parade. They were getting ready to go through the portal after Madame President. And there was another incongruous note. One lane along the avenue had been kept clear to evacuate some of the larger zoo animals, upset by the noise, scared by the commotion. Vehicles like horse vans, but with heavily barred windows, were taking away lions and leopards and gorillas. Behind them the frantic keepers were leading the giraffes and the elephants and the zebras through the hot Washington night. Our driver slammed his horn button. An elephant trumpeted furiously back. "Shit," yelled Magruder in my ear, "we'll never drive through this! We'll walk!"

Even walking was no joy. The combat vehicles were not moving; dodging around them meant dodging out of the way of elephants—and, now and then, away from steamy great heaps of elephant turds. Ratface Magruder moved like a quarterback carrying the ball through scrimmage, yelling over his shoulder at me. I couldn't hear what; I was too busy trying to follow him to the portal inside the zoo gate.

Nothing was going through the portal.

"Shit," yelled Magruder again. "Come on!" And he headed for the zoo cafeteria, where the commanders were huddled around a television screen.

"What's the problem here?" he snarled. A two-star general looked up.

"See for yourself," he said, jerking a thumb at the

screen. "That's a satellite transmission from the League of Nations in Geneva."

A fat man with pince-nez glasses was reading a speech into the cameras; the voice that came with it was a woman's, not his, translating the Russian into English.

"The Russkies?" guessed Magruder.

"Good thinking," said the major general. "That's the Soviet delegate speaking. Notice how sleepy he looks? It's maybe six A.M. there; he must've been up all night."

"What's he saying, sir?" I asked.

"Why," said the general politely, "he's saying they have—what did he say?—incontrovertible evidence that we're planning to attack his country by means of a parallel time. He's saying that unless we discontinue our 'invasion' at once his people will treat it as though it were an attack on their own country. That's a laugh, isn't it? The Russians protecting the Americans from the Americans?"

I swallowed. "Does that mean—?"

"That they'll attack? Yes, that's what it seems to mean. So take a load off your feet. We're holding off on any further troop movements until somebody figures out what we're going to do—and, thank God, that somebody is higher up than me."

Because she was one of the very few who could understand the man's slurred speech, she was the one allowed to guide his wheelchair over the bumpy, ancient walks of the college. But she could not manage the steps. "I'll find someone to help," she said, and bent to listen to the breathy whisper. "Oh, no," she said, "it's no trouble, Dr. Hawking!" And she meant it. Even in the sweltering heat of England's hottest August—it had to be over seventy-five degrees!—helping a world-famous scientist to navigate Cambridge's pretty paths was not an imposition. It was an honor. And a responsibility; and when she came back with a husky crew member and an eager Greats from King's College she cried out in pain. "But he couldn't have got out of the chair!" she wailed. Yet there was the empty chair, straps still buckled, footrest still set high for his shrunken legs . . . but Stephen Hawking was no longer in it.

Yr 11–110 111–111, mo 1–000, da 11–101
Hr 1–010, mn 11–110
Senator Dominic DeSota

You do not get used to jumping from one parallel time to another, even when you know it's happening.

I didn't know.

All I knew was that at one moment I was hurrying down the stairs from the President's penthouse, looking for my lady love. Then, without perceptible delay (though it must have been hours, might have been days), I was lying flat on my back, listening to a honeyed voice whisper into my ear that I had nothing to worry about. That's the kind of thing that starts me worrying. I knew a lie when I heard one, and I was worried.

That is, the reasoning part of my head was worried. My body did not seem to be worried a bit. It was lying there perfectly relaxed. I don't think I had ever been quite that relaxed before, except maybe now and then after a really good toss-and-tumble with Nyla, when we'd lie back with every knot in either body untangled entirely. I don't mean that my state was in any way sexual, just that I was wholly and completely at a condition of physical ease.

There was no reason for that. There was every reason in the world why I should have been tense and scared, and should have shown it in taut muscles and twitchy nerves. There was nothing in sight or sound that was reassuring in the least. I was lying on a hard pallet in a room that looked as much like a morgue as anything else I'd ever seen. There were a dozen other pallets, each with a body recumbent on it. It even smelled medicinal and nasty, as I thought a morgue should.

The person who was whispering sweetly in my ear wasn't reassuring, either. She didn't have any face. Or he didn't; you couldn't tell, because there was nothing but a flesh-colored blankness between hair and chin. It moved a little as the voice spoke but showed no features at all. She (or he) was saying, "You will be well treated, uh, Senator, uh, DeSota, and you will be completely at liberty." And he was looking at me (or she was), though I could see no eyes, because s/he was touching me here, touching me there, and everywhere he (she) touched there was a tingle or a pang.

Something was being done to me. I just let it happen.

And that was another thing. I let it all happen. I don't mean I wasn't shaken up—no, scared—hell, terrified! But whatever my conscious mind told my head to be, my body was relaxed and compliant. It did what it was told. It didn't even need to be told in words; touch and gesture was enough, and instantly my body held still, or turned over, or presented a part of itself for the occasion.

It occurred to me at once that I'd seen something like that before, when Nyla No-Thumbs and the others were zapped into sleepy-by before we were rescued from the New Mexican motel. But they had just been asleep. This was much, much worse. And then I had been only an observer. I had not had this present indignity of having my body roll over and elevate its rump for a final shot.

It was at that point I realized I was naked. I might not have realized it then if the voice hadn't said, "You can get up and get dressed now, and then proceed into the hover."

* * *

My obliging body pulled on a pair of shorts, a pair of tennis shoes, and a sort of T-shirt from a rack—they all fit snugly, less because they were my size than because they were a kind of fabric that didn't care what size I was. Then my body obligingly walked after the (wo)man and out of the doorless cubicle. No, there weren't any doors. No, one didn't magically appear. All that happened was that she/he walked up to the wall, and kept on walking, and so did I—along with seven or eight equally complaisant bodies belonging to people wearing the same beige one-size-fits-all beachwear.

And, as a matter of fact, we were at a beach. Or close enough. We were at a kind of an airport, curious mixture of the shiny-new and the terminally decrepit, on a hot, hot summer day, with the salt-marsh smell of seawater and dead fish strong on the breeze and waves glinting across a roadway. Behind the stump of a flagpole a cement block had letters picked out in seashells embedded in the surface. The snows of winter and summer suns had done them a lot of harm, but I could still make out what they said:

FLOYD BENNETT FIELD

Behind the squat, white building we had just come out of (there was no door in the outside wall, either), a delta-winged plane came in with a ripping sound of jets at a hundred miles an hour, dropped flaps, rotated its engines, and sat down a few yards beyond the building. It rolled a couple of feet and stopped. The building, on the other hand, began to move. It shuddered, picked itself up, and slid over to the plane; while a quarter of a mile off to one side a bloated-bellied blimp was slithering in to a landing at another new white building. I turned to the happy zombie next to me and said, "Dorothy, I don't think we're in Kansas any more."

He gave me an irritated look. Then the look changed. "Don't I know you?" he asked.

I took a harder look at him. "Dr. Gribbin?" I said. "From Sandia?"

"Bloody hell," he said. "And you're the Yank congressman. What the hell is going on, do you know?"

Well, how do you begin to answer a question like that? As I was casting around for an answer, a voice from behind me saved me the trouble. "It's parallel time," said Nicky DeSota eagerly. "Do you understand about quantum mechanics? Well, it seems that Erwin Schroedinger, or maybe it was one of the people who came after him, proposed a long time ago that every time some kinds of nuclear reactions occur, which can go either way, they go both ways. This means that—"

I turned away to keep from laughing. Here was the mortgage broker explaining Schroedinger's famous conundrum to one of the world's great experts on the subject! But Nicky had an advantage Gribbin had not: he had seen it all happen. Another man in the same shorts and blouse was wandering toward us to listen to Nicky expound. I didn't pay attention. I was looking at this strange world around me, wondering why I was there, whether I would ever get back to a sane life in the Senate—well, strike that; but at least in the Senate it was a kind of insanity I was used to— and wondering, most of all, where my love had gone. There were women in our group, but none of them were familiar. And there was another woman, this one wearing the same white overall, gloves and boots included, that the faceless person who was trying to shepherd us into the bus was wearing. The one with a face was talking to the bus driver, but when she saw us approaching she jumped and hurried away as though we were lepers.

I didn't then know how apt that thought was.

I turned back to Nicky and Gribbin. "We'd better get on that thing," I said.

Gribbin gave me a puzzled look. Then the look deepened, as he glanced from Nicky to me. "You two chaps are the same!" he cried.

Nicky grinned. "That's part of it," he agreed. "Didn't you notice? You two are the same too." And he was pointing to the other man, standing with his jaw hanging; who took one look at Gribbin, another at Nicky and me.

He felt his own face as though he had never noticed it before. "Bloody hell," said the second John Gribbin. Which summed it all up perfectly.

Whatever kind of happy pills they had given us, it was apparent that they were beginning to wear off. My fellow sheep were beginning to talk back to the faceless shepherd, not always politely. But as the drug level in my body declined, my rational self-confidence seemed to increase. Like Nicky, I had had this experience before. It didn't make it pleasing. It did make it a little less nerve-racking.

As far as I could tell, Nicky and I were the only two so fortunate in that bunch. None of the ones who had been with us in Washington were here now. I could live with that easily enough as far as it concerned the other Dom, not to mention the two Larry Douglases and the Russians. The fact that Nyla wasn't with me was a lot harder to take. I wanted very much to ask somebody if I would ever see Nyla again, but everybody else had questions of his own, and they were a lot more scared and angry about it than I. "What's going on here?" demanded one of the Gribbins, and the faceless person said:

"You'll be briefed on the hover. Please get on now; it's waiting." And as she, or he, turned away, a man on the other side grabbed her (or his) sleeve. He had the kind of scowl that says, *I don't know what I'm into, but when I find out somebody's going to pay,* and he was insistent.

"I'm needed at the lab!" he protested. "There's a

top-level meeting *right now,* and if I'm not there it's going to cost us half our grant for the next fiscal year—" He stopped indignantly, because the faceless one was laughing at him.

"The things you people worry about," he/she said indulgently. "On the hover! Now. Please."

I decided there wasn't any better alternative than to do as asked, so I boarded the thing. I took a seat up near the front, just behind the glassed-in compartment that held the driver, and Nicky slipped into the one next to me.

When the faceless person called it a hover I translated that into "ground-effect machine." So it was. I'd never been in a hovercraft, but when I felt the throbbing and bouncing underneath us, and we began to slippy-slide over cracked concrete toward the road, I knew.

I use the word *road* loosely. That's what it had been. It had not been maintained for a long, long time. It stretched wide and empty before us, heading straight for a distant city skyline. But I could see the purpose of the hovercraft; nothing on wheels could have handled the potholes and the curling edges of asphalt. The biggest holes had been roughly filled, the jaggedest edges bulldozed away, and someone had pushed off onto the side an occasional boxy old heap of rust that had once been an automobile. There were places where the cattail marsh had so completely reclaimed the roadbed that I could not see asphalt at all, only mown bulrushes with birds scattering out of our way as we whirred toward them. I stared at that remote skyline every time the hover turned enough to bring it into sight. Something about it looked familiar. . . .

Bouncing around with excitement in the seat next to me, Nicky DeSota cried, "It's New York! Gosh! I've never been in this part of New York!" He nudged me, grinning. "Did you notice? This thing's air-conditioned!"

"That's nice," I said; because all that he said was true, and interesting, but I was watching what was going on up ahead of us. The driver's compartment was closed off from our part of the van with a glass window. It had its own entrance, and the wo(man) who had led us to the bus was inside it. What I was watching was what s/he was doing. What she was doing was revealing herself to be a she. She ducked her face into her hand and pulled, and—wow!—that flesh-colored blankness slipped off. There was an actual face there. In fact, rather a pretty one. She wriggled out of the top of her jumpsuit, revealing more proof of femininity, and then she turned to look back at the fifteen or twenty of us in the hovervan.

"Good morning," she said through an intercom.

Next to me Nicky cried, "Good morning!" So did a couple of the others, like fifth-graders on a school trip—which was about the way I felt.

"By now," she said, "your tranks should be wearing off, so let me explain what has happened to you. There is good news and there is bad news. The good news is that within the next ooty-poot days you will be able to move freely anywhere in the world you like, and it is rather a nice world. The bad news is that you will never leave it." She smiled sweetly. There was a moment's silence, then questions called out from all over the bus. The sweet smile did not fade. "I have not turned on your phones yet," she said, "so I can't hear you just now. Take a few minutes to talk among yourselves. Then I will give you a short talk on what has happened and why, and what you can expect, and then there will be time for questions. The trip to your hotel will take about totter-tot minutes."

She gave us a last smile and turned back to the driver.

It is hard to give a coherent and consecutive account of the trip—there was too much going on. Probably if I could remember being born it would be just as hard to describe it, because I was overwhelmed

with the revolutionary newness of it all. We all were—
or all but Nicky. I envied him the way he took it all in
stride and exulted in the wondrous new strangeness
of it.

I could not share it. More than anything else, I
was wondering if I would ever see Nyla again. . . .

Any Nyla.

By the time the woman began her orientation
talk we had left the salt water behind. We were gliding
along a wide avenue between rows of fallen-down
frame buildings and burned-out one-story stores.
Two or three times we slowed to let another hovervan
pass in the opposite direction, the drivers waving at
each other. The ones going out were all empty. There
were no other human beings in sight. I saw turtles as
big as meat platters sunning themselves along the
road, and once a coiled snake that I was nearly sure
was a rattler. It did not move, though its head was
raised and the beady eyes stared at us. I saw a fox
chasing a rabbit, frantically zigzagging along what
had once been a sidewalk, until the whoosh from our
fans blew both of them over and I lost them behind
us.

And I listened.

The first part of what she told us was a sentence
of exile. "Uncontrolled exploitation of the paratime
portal," she said reprovingly, "will lead to chaos, so we
have stopped it. We have transported the principal
experimenters, as well as all persons who were in
displaced times, to this planet. At the same time we
have rendered all paratime research centers unin-
habitable by means of induced radiation. We had no
choice in this matter. The alternative was destructive
to everyone."

I stretched and yawned. We were going up a
slight incline, with tall, unkempt trees reaching out
over us from both sides. Ahead of us was a circle with
twenty-story apartment buildings, the tallest I'd seen

close at hand. They had all the windows broken out, and ivy climbed their sides. "Until dye years ago," the woman was saying, "this planet was uninhabited by humans. There was a long war, they called it the World War, and somebody started using biological weapons. It wound up with everybody dead. All primates, in fact—there aren't even any gorillas left—but nearly everything else survived." She glanced at the back of her wrist as though she were consulting notes. "Oh, yes, you don't have to worry about the disease any more; that's one of the things you were inoculated against at Reception. And, of course, for all the organisms you all carried—shocking mix of bugs you people had." She dimpled a smile at us. Maybe there was some tranquilizer left. We smiled back. "Anyway, some of the paratimes began using the planet for colonization purposes—people who were displaced from their homes for one reason or another, usually drought or something of the sort. And, of course, there's always a few people who just want to pioneer. But that makes it good for you, because there's a whole infrastructure waiting for you. You won't have to go out and gather roots! This is one of the few cities that we've got working—more or less working—though, so mostly you'll want to resettle on farms. After all, food is the most important thing!"

This time nobody smiled back. Whatever any of us had been back home, it wasn't farmers.

I began to wonder just what socially useful skills a former United States senator, with a law degree and not much else, might have to offer in a new world.

We slid down a long hill toward a taller building still, a skyscraper with a clock at its top. (One face told me that it was a quarter past three, another, missing a minute hand, only said that it was somewhere between ten and eleven.) There were rusted trolley tracks under us, and just ahead an elevated train structure, also rusty. I didn't like the idea of snaking under it and through its pillars. But the driver knew what he was doing. We slowed to a crawl for a couple dozen blocks, then picked up speed again as the tracks veered off to the sides.

"Are there any questions?" the woman asked brightly.

Nicky was first off the mark. "What's a 'totter-tot'?" he called.

The woman looked puzzled. "What?"

"You said it would take totter-tot minutes. I *think* that's what you said."

The pretty face cleared. "Oh, I was forgetting. You're all decimal, aren't you? Let's see, that would be, um"—she glanced at her wrist again—"the whole trip will take about forty and five minutes. About, um, twenty minutes more. Any other questions?"

One of the Dr. Gribbins had his hand up. "A big one, miss," he said. "I'm a quantum-dynamicist. I don't know bugger-all about pushing a plow."

"Of course," said the woman sympathetically. "That's a real problem, here. What we really need are farmers, construction workers, and engineers. There will be retraining programs, though." She smiled brightly at fifteen people who had suddenly stopped smiling back.

There were mutterings back and forth in the van, but no clear-cut questions came out of it. Probably none of us wanted to know the answers to the questions we had yet to ask. Personally I was craning my neck to see ahead, because I had caught a glimpse of a bridge. It scared me. I did not think I wanted to cross the East River on a bridge that had not had a coat of paint for half a century.

The woman was still smiling. "If any of you would like to start work at once, there are job openings in your hotel. We need cooks, cleaners, chamber-workers, and so on. You have to be self-sufficient for that sort of thing, you see, during the period of quarantine. And you will be paid for your work."

I wasn't listening. I was bracing myself as we seemed to be heading for the crumbling approach to the bridge, then relaxed as we turned away—then braced myself again as we slowed down at the water's edge. Were we going to take a ferry? Swim across? Stop here, with the promised land just visible across the water, moldering skyscrapers and all?

It was none of the above. We didn't stop. We slid down a muddy, bulldozed bank to the river; and we slid right on across the water, exactly as easily and surely as we had been gliding over the pitted old city streets. At the far end was the remnant of a pier. Nude bathers were sitting on the end of it, gazing at us incuriously. They were far more interested in one of their own, who had surfaced a few dozen yards away, pushing back his goggles and spluttering with pleasure as he waved the four-foot fish flopping on the end of his spear.

At least we were now in a part of New York where I had been before. I recognized Canal Street, though the signs were long rusted away. I didn't know any of the side streets we wound through—navigation was harder in densely built Manhattan—but I did recognize, or almost recognize, Fifth Avenue when we reached it. It was puzzling that there was no Empire State Building at what otherwise definitely looked like Thirty-fourth Street, and curious that over the next wide intersection there was the remains of a spidery traffic-control booth, elevated above the street.

We stopped there for a moment, while both the driver and the guide put their flesh masks back on. "Almost there," the woman called cheerily. "It's called the Hotel Plaza. A little moth-eaten and moldy, maybe—but, my, what a beautiful view you get of the Central Park wilderness!"

* * *

By the time we were checked into rooms in the old hotel and given a meal, a lot more had been explained to us. We had a new identity. We were "Paratemporally Displaced Persons" or Peety-Deepies for short. We were in quarantine for a week, long enough for the nasties in our circulatory systems to surface, if any had been missed by the shots and sprays we'd received while asleep. And, although we would get out of the hotel in a matter of days, we would get out of this particular paratime never.

We were there for keeps.

It took a lot of the joy out of the old Plaza Hotel. The woman hadn't lied to us. It was a nice place, basically. It had even been a nice place, I remembered, in my own A.D. 1983. A stately old dowager of a place with historic associations—Scott and Zelda Fitzgerald had lived there, and had gone to play at midnight in the fountain outside.

Of course, it had not been maintained for sixty years. There hadn't been anybody alive in this world to maintain it. That showed. There was a funny, nasty smell in the ground-floor restaurant, as though animals had denned there now and then. (They had.) A quarter of the windows were gone, though most of them had been temporarily replaced by some sort of plastic film in the process of getting the place ready for us to occupy. The water from the plumbing ran rusty now and then, and there were whole floors where it didn't run at all. And the furnishings were deplorable, especially the beds. Cotton had turned into mold, mold had turned into dust, the springs of the mattresses had turned into rust. Before we slept that night Nicky and I had to sweat and struggle new bedding up from the stacks in the lobby: bare wooden slats to stretch across the sides of the bed, still raw and sap-smelling from the sawmill, and clever air mattresses to put on the slats, compartmented and very comfortable . . . once we had puffed ourselves scarlet to fill each of the compartments with lungpower alone. We didn't have to worry about blankets, of course. Not in New York in August, in a hotel that had never known what air-conditioning was.

Not everything in the room was a moldering antique. One thing was very new. At first I thought it was a television set, although it was a little puzzling that a sort of keyboard was attached. When Nicky experimentally pushed the "On" switch the screen lighted up, rosy background with sharp black letters that said:

HELLO.
WHAT IS YOUR P.I.D.?

Since neither of us knew what a P.I.D. was we couldn't satisfy its curiosity, and it stubbornly refused to satisfy any of ours. No matter what other keys or buttons we pushed nothing happened; the only key that worked was the one marked "Off."

The day went fast. By the time the sun went down we had made our bed-sitter suite habitable—more or less habitable. That is, we'd collected towels and pillows and extra sets of clothing and soap and all the other things that insured survival. We had discovered how to open the plastic-sheet windows to let some air in—mixed blessing, because with the air came hordes of mosquitoes out of the rank vegetation in what had once been well-groomed Central Park. The lights in our room attracted them, so we turned the lights out.

We were tired. I showered and brushed my teeth, and while Nicky was doing the same I gazed out at the view of the park, as good as our guide had promised, if somewhat stranger. Just before us in the park was a busy scene, temporary buildings with people moving around and vehicles; but a quarter of a mile farther was only blackness. Bright stars shone in the sky, a sight I had never seen from New York City in my lifetime.

It was a dead city. Only the little space around the hotels was the focus of infection where life was beginning to invade it again.

And it was an empty city—for me it was a wholly empty city, because Nyla Bowquist wasn't there.

It struck me as a sad wonder that Nyla had been in that hotel, maybe in that very room, in our own time. I knew that she stayed in the Plaza when she played at Carnegie Hall, only a few blocks away. Perhaps she had stood at that very window. What she would have seen was manicured lawns, a playground, a lake, hansom cabs lined up at the entrance to the park, and a million cars, taxis, and trucks creeping along the streets that bounded it. What I saw was the bubble-shaped temporary structures, and the lights of a blimp floating down to a landing on one of the clearings. . . .

I became conscious of Nicky standing behind me, still damp from the shower, running a comb through his hair. "Isn't it wonderful, Dom?" he asked.

I looked at him with resentment—unjustified resentment, because it certainly was not his fault that he wasn't Nyla. "What are you talking about, Nicky? It's *exile*. We're stuck here forever."

He said, with audible sympathy in his voice, "I know it's tough on you, Dom, because you had a lot to lose. Me, maybe not so much. But it's not just exile. It's a whole new world. Eden! They've given us a new start in life."

"I didn't want a new start in life," I said, "and anyway, they didn't do it for our sake."

"Well, sure, Dom," he said, turning modestly to slip on a pair of pajama pants. "But you have to admit they've put a lot of effort into this. Just fixing up this part of the city for us—do you have any idea what kind of work that means? Getting the water running again when some of the pipes would have ruptured? Starting an electrical generating system? Just cleaning up the garbage—and I don't mean just rotted-out bedclothes. There must have been people in this place when they all died. Bodies. Skeletons, anyway, and somebody had carted them all off before we got here."

"They probably wanted all that for their own purposes, anyway," I objected.

"But we're getting the benefit of it," he pointed out.

"We're being exiled here, sure. That's for their own good too. They were worried about what would happen to them if this paratime stuff went on, not us."

He looked at me thoughtfully as he climbed into his bed. "They didn't have to go to all this trouble," he said. "I mean, transporting us here, feeding us, housing us, giving us clothes—"

"Sure they did! How else could they have stopped research?"

"Well," he said, settling himself under the sheet, "I can think of some people who would have taken care of it a different way. They could have just killed us, you know. Good night, Dom."

After the French-Indochinese wars there were a whole bunch of tribes that couldn't get along with the new governments. Some of them came to America. There was one colony of hill people who wound up in my own state, eighteen hundred refugees who hadn't ever seen a train, a television set, a gas stove, or a vacuum cleaner. Talk about culture shock! But it wasn't learning how to drive cars and run lawnmowers that threw them the hardest. It was the things we take for granted. How to pop open a beer can. How to use a credit card. Why the red light meant stop and the green light meant go. Why you should not urinate other than in an approved receptacle, even if you modestly went behind a tree. When I led the state's congressional delegation down to welcome those

Meos, just outside of Carbondale, I was sorry for them, and a lot amused by them.

If any of them had been with me in the Plaza, they could have gotten even. I was as lost and confused as they, and this time it was harder to see the humor in it.

Nicky and I spent the whole first day just learning rudimentary survival skills in the new world. At the end of the day what I had mostly learned was that it was even harder than it looked. It helped a lot that we had that console in the room, because it was not only a television set but a phone, a computer, and an alarm clock. Once we found out what our Personal I.D.'s were—any ten-letter word or phrase we chose; I picked "Nyla my love"—we could unlock its memories and skills, and patiently it taught us most of what we needed to know. From the menus it offered us we could find the answer to almost any question, even to some we had not thought to ask. It told us, for instance, that our room and board wasn't exactly free. We had been given a credit to draw on, but sooner or later we would have to pay it back or starve. How could we pay it back? Well, there were jobs in the hotel if we wanted to get a head start: making beds, cleaning out rooms on the floors not yet finished, serving food, moving furniture. Then when we were released from quarantine there were a thousand projects that needed workers, all over the continent, even all over the world—a whole technological infra-structure needed to be completed. The volunteer colonists who had preceded us had done a lot, but there just were not enough of them to do the job.

Nor could I see where I was going to be of much help. What they needed was pipefitters, construction workers, motor mechanics, electricians—people with the skills to build and fix. There weren't any openings for U.S. senators. There weren't very many for quantum physicists, either, which seemed to comprise a large fraction of us Peety-Deepies. The ones that were most useful, I thought, would be the cats—the people who were out of their own time—mostly the twenty-two-year-olds of the invading army, of whom hundreds were in our hotel and thousands more scattered around the other temporary quarters in the city.

One of the things the comset in our room would do for us, once we learned how to ask, was to locate all the other Paratemporally Displaced Persons. The master list was purely alphabetical, and that was hopeless—there were nineteen Stephen Hawkings alone, not to mention nine Dominic DeSotas. (Fortunately only four of us were still in the city, the others having completed their quarantine and reassignment and gone on somewhere else.) But there was also a list reordered by time of origin. There were nearly sixty from my own time. . . .

But none of them was Nyla Christophe Bowquist.

When we went down for our morning bloodletting on the third day Nicky was nervous. It was an occasion for some nervousness, in a way, because it was important to us to be healthy. Heaven knows, we *seemed* healthy. We had arrived from our various paratimes positively reeking of germs and viruses and nastinesses of every kind, but our hosts did not tolerate disease. Smallpox, tuberculosis, cancer, and the common cold no longer existed in their worlds, nor did flu or venereal disease or even the caries of tooth decay. They didn't want them brought in. So they had given us any number of shots while we were still unconscious, and they checked the results with a drop of our blood twice a day. What was important about it was that clean blood meant privileges. If we were still clean today, we could switch from the backbreaking labor of shifting furniture to the more refined tasks of serving food. If we stayed clean through the morrow, we would even be permitted to go out into the street! At least as far as the other hotels on the street, so that we could look for lost friends from our own time, if not actually to cross over and breathe the same air as the natives at their goings-on in the park.

Still, that wasn't enough to make anybody really nervous. When we'd each given our drop for the morning I asked him what he was worrying about. "The future, Dom," he said indignantly. "My future. This is a fresh start I've got and I want to make something of it—only—only there doesn't seem to be much need for mortgage brokers in this Eden."

"Or for senators," I said. He wasn't listening.

"There's banking, I guess," he said, leading the way as we threaded through the stacks of furnishings in the Palm Court. "I didn't see anything like that listed, but it stands to reason—only this damn arithmetic drives me crazy." He was doing better than I was, at that; binary numbers scared me so much I hadn't even begun to try to understand them, as long as our comset was willing to translate into decimal for us uneducated ones.

I guess what I had said had slowly been percolating through his fog of concentration, because he blinked at me and said, "Oh, yeah. You too. Well, I don't know, Dom, what did you do before you were a senator?"

I laughed. "I was a lawyer."

"Aw," he said sympathetically. "They don't have much of that around here, either, do they?" He stopped and nodded to the foreman of our work detail. "Reporting in, Chuck," he said. "What have you got for us to do this morning?"

"Plenty," Chuck said tersely. He was a black man, still wearing the uniform with the lieutenant's bars on it. He had been a tank commander in the invasion army and thus my enemy, although that didn't seem to matter much any more. What made the difference for us was that he had arrived twenty-four hours before us, so he was a foreman and we were tote-and-carry labor. "There's seventy-five new ones coming in this afternoon, so the ninth floor needs to be cleaned out. Get on it, you two."

By then I wasn't surprised any more to be given orders by someone who was a Peety-Deepy, just like us. That was about all we saw. Even the woman who took the blood from our fingertips was a Cat—well, of course we were all Cats, because this planet had been empty of human beings entirely five years earlier. But there were Cats and there were Cats, and the original colonists stayed out of the quarantine hotels. Now and then we'd see one, complete with face mask and coveralls, coming in to pick up the blood samples or hand out orders. They didn't linger.

So what I knew about the original colonists was scanty, mostly from what we could glean from the comset. The original settlers didn't come from a single paratime. They were from a whole congeries of them, eighteen or twenty different worlds. The way in which they were most different from us was only in that they had learned of the existence of, and managed to establish communication with, each other nearly twenty-five years earlier.

It hadn't all been gravy for them. They'd had some terrible times with "ballistic recoil" before they learned how to minimize it, mostly by limiting their connections to communications channels, with only carefully measured and controlled portals allowing them to, for instance, start to colonize the empty worlds.

But what rewards there were! They had twenty worlds, not one, working to solve the problems of paratime. They had twenty times as many people doing research. And, besides, they had the great asset of being able to "peep" any number of other worlds.

They had, in short, a research and development complex that moved a hundred times faster than our own. They learned everything that anyone else knew.

Computer technology from one world, space satellites from another, nuclear fusion from a third, genetic engineering, wizardly chemistry, marvelous medicine—you name it. They had it.

I had plenty of time to think about all that, all the time Nicky and I were swamping out the ninth floor, because Nicky wasn't talkative. He was still fretting away at his private worries, whatever they were. It was only when we'd dumped the last drawerful of rotting shirts and collars into the last cracked and disintegrating pigskin valise and dragged them to the one working elevator that he seemed to come out of it. Out of nowhere, he said, "It isn't so bad here, Dom, is it?"

"That's what we don't know yet," I said, starting down the stairs to dinner.

He followed, shaking his head. "It's tough on us," he said, "because we didn't have anything to say about it. But the original colonists came here voluntarily, and I think they had the right idea. A whole new planet, Dom! Gosh, I kind of like the idea myself. I mean, we don't even have to explore it, or anything— we *know* where everything is."

I paused on the landing for him to catch up. "What do you mean, we know?"

"It's the same planet as our own, don't you see? All the resources have been mapped. If your people located an oilfield in Alaska, or the Brits of my time found it in Arabia—it's still there in this world! Every resource is waiting for us. And clean lakes, clean rivers, uncut forests, clean air—gee whiz, Dom, doesn't it excite you?"

"I'm more interested in what we're going to get for dinner," I said.

"Aw, Dom! You don't mean that."

I said patiently, "I sort of mean that, because I don't want to think too hard about the future, Nicky. I don't like the idea of being trapped here forever. I wish I could go home."

He looked thoughtful, but he didn't say anything more just then—neither of us did, because we still had six flights of stairs to descend. Only when we'd reached the ground floor and were standing in the line outside the restaurant, he turned around and looked at me. "Dom?" he asked. "Did you ever hear anyone say that we positively couldn't ever get home again?"

"Well, sure," I said, annoyed. "What do you think this is all about? Once they get us all settled they're closing the portal. That's the whole point, to seal us off so we can't mess things up with ballistic recoil. So we're stuck here, right? Or do you think that sooner or later we can build our own portals?"

He shook his head. "No, that's not going to happen. They'll be peeping us all the time. They wouldn't let us do that."

"Then don't talk silly," I snapped. No excuse. I was tired and irritable.

But so was Nicky. "Who the hell are you to tell me I'm silly, DeSota?" he flared. "Maybe you're a big man when you're home, but here you're just another darned Deepy!"

Of course, he was right. Bad habits persist. I had started out thinking of this other self of mine as a wimp. If I diagnosed my feelings toward Nicky carefully enough, they would turn out to be at best tolerance, more accurately contempt.

He didn't deserve that. The contempt didn't belong to him in the first place; what I found contemptible in him was a reflection of the worse side of me. The side I didn't like to think about. The side that kept Nyla Bowquist in a sneaky, sleazy affair because I didn't have the courage to make it right— and that kept its options open, too, so that the other Nylas looked really tempting to me. Because he *was* me, good parts and bad. Wearing the shorts and shirts of this new Eden, identical to my own, with that cheap, flashy sports suit now no more than ashes in some incinerator, he looked more like me than ever. And what was inside was the same.

"Nicky," I said when we were seated at a table, "I'm sorry."

He flashed a smile. "No harm done, Dom."

"It's just that what we're up against scares me," I apologized.

He said firmly, "What we're up against isn't a bunch of supermen, Dom. They're people exactly like ourselves. They *know* more, because they've swiped knowledge from all over, but they aren't *smarter*. It's August 1983 in this world the same as yours and mine. They aren't from the future. They're us."

I thought that over. "Well, you're right," I said. "Is that what you meant before? That all we have to do is catch up, and then we can do what we please, won't have to get their permission?"

His face fell. "Not exactly," he muttered. He didn't explain what he really did mean, and I didn't press the point.

As I learned later—much later—that was a mistake.

When I first got elected to the Senate I had to learn a whole new life in no time at all. There were a lot of privileges I had to learn how to use: the senatorial bell-ring that brought an elevator to me at once, no matter how many other people were waiting on some other floor; the right to the little subway that took us from our offices to the Capitol; franking mail; the facilities of the gym and sauna reserved for senators only. I also had to learn the less agreeable things, like never appearing in public again without a fresh shave, and responding to every greeting from a passerby, because you never knew who might be a constituent. With all that, for the first couple of weeks I hardly remembered at all that I'd had a life in Chicago before.

It was the same here—almost. I had so much to

learn that I almost forgot the world I had left behind. I forgot the farm bill. I forgot the war that had been raging when I was kidnapped. I forgot Marilyn, even—well, I'd had plenty of practice at forgetting my wife, for some time.

I didn't forget Nyla.

The more surely it seemed that I would never see her again, the more certain I was that I had lost something very important to me. All that Nicky said about this world was true. I could easily imagine that, once the transition period was over, I could build quite a good life for myself in this new Eden. Could do productive things, meet a handsome woman, marry her, have kids, be happy. . . . But whatever my life might be without Nyla, it would be only second best.

That feeling did not go away.

By the fourth day we were certified reasonably clean, which meant privileges. For one, both Nicky and I were reassigned to food-handling instead of shifting garbage—a big step upward. For another, we were allowed outside!

To be sure, we couldn't wander at random, and we had to take measures to avoid contaminating Eden's pure air with our still potentially disgusting breath. Nicky and I lined up for I.D. badges, coveralls, and micropore masks. He went one way. I went another.

What I had in mind was to look up some friends in one of the other hotels. The comset had told me that the Dom DeSota who was a physicist was located just cat-a-corner across the square, in another of the abandoned hotels that had become Cathouses.

It had rained hard the day before, while we were cooped up. The air was cooler and dryer, and the tall trees that stretched all up along the edge of the park were bending in the breeze. There were plenty of people in the streets, strolling or hurrying from one place to another. A few of them were faceless, like myself; the ones who were not gave us masked ones a wide berth. I didn't mind. Just being out of the hotel gave my spirits a lift. I wished that Nyla were there with me, walking hand in hand along the streets of this wondrous new place, but even without her I was cheerful. By the time I entered the lobby of the Pierre I was almost beaming, and the first face I saw was a familiar one. He was sitting on the counter of the old registration desk, talking irritably into an old two-piece telephone. "Which one are you?" I asked, peeling off my face mask. He gave me a scowl.

"I'm the one you got into this trouble in the first place, schmuck," he said bitterly. So he wasn't Lavrenti Djugashvili or the scientist; he was the con man from Time Tau.

"I'm not the one you think I am," I told him. "I'm the senator; Nicky's my roommate, in the Plaza."

"I hope he rots there," he said. Then he put down the phone and shrugged. "Hell, I guess I don't mean that. No sense hanging on to hard feelings, right? Want a cup of coffee?"

Well, he was trying to be nice. And he had coffee! There were advantages to knowing a con man, even here and now, I could see. So we sat and talked for a while. I told him what little there was to tell about Nicky and me. He told me more than I wanted to know about himself. He'd roomed the first night with Moe—the FBI man! He saw my look and shrugged. "Like I say, no use carrying a grudge any more, is there?" But Moe had found another Moe—another identical copy of himself, and the two of them had decided to room together. More than that, they'd found out there was still a third one, and they'd made plans to go off together when they left quarantine— maybe to sign up for construction on the new natural-gas pipeline that was going to go from Texas to somewhere in Southern California, maybe join an advance crew in one of the cities that hadn't been refurbished yet, maybe get into dam building down in

Alabama, the place they called Muscle Shoals. There were always plenty of jobs for big guys with brawn. And did I know that Nyla was in the hotel?

Sudden rush of hope and shock. But, of course, the Nyla he was talking about wasn't my Nyla. It was the FBI woman.

I drank the rest of the coffee without tasting it, listened to the rest of Larry Douglas's gossip without hearing it. What was on my mind was a moral question, and it filled my mind. The Nyla I loved was hopelessly out of reach.

Was I willing to settle for another Nyla?

I did not even consider the question of whether that other Nyla, that hard-bitten policewoman, would settle for me. That didn't really matter. The answer I was looking for was in my head, not hers. Who was it I loved? Was it the physical, corporeal female human being with whose body my body found so much pleasure? Was it the traits and graces of the Nyla who played so beautifully on the violin and behaved so warmly, kindly in all the intercourse of the world? Would I have loved Nyla Bowquist less if she had been less able to show me the difference between Brahms and Beethoven—or less used to the glamour and excitement of the elite world we both moved in? Would I have loved her, in short, if she hadn't been famous?

Or—getting rapidly down to basics, the kind of question that never has an answer that makes sense— what did I mean by "love," anyway?

When you get into that kind of navel-gazing soul-searching it isn't too easy to keep track of what is happening in the real world. It wasn't surprising when Larry Douglas's prattle slowed down, then stopped.

I came to. He was gazing at me disagreeably. "Sorry," I said. "I was thinking."

He sniffed. "Mind telling me what it was you came here for?" he asked.

"I was looking for Dominic DeSota—the other one, the scientist."

"Oh, *them*. There's a bunch of them that spend their time talking about paratime and all that stuff. There's a couple of me there too. You'll find them in the bar, probably."

I did. It was as he described. There were ten or eleven people in the bar, nursing beers and talking animatedly. Two of them were Larry Douglas, four were Stephen Hawking in one state of health or another, two were John Gribbin, of whom I had met two examples at Floyd Bennett Field. They didn't even look around when I came in. They were, as the con man had said, comparing notes.

I went behind the bar and picked out a can of beer for myself, half listening to them, mostly thinking about my own problems. It wasn't hard to think, because their conversation didn't disturb me a bit. I didn't understand a word of it. "We started with oltron fission," one of them would say, and another would cut in, "Hang on a minute. What's an oltron?" And the first would say something like, "Uh, it's charged, it's light, it has a point-five variance—" and the other would say, "Variance?" And then they would start drawing particle-reaction diagrams until one of them would say, "Oh, you mean a Neumann body! Right. And it splits into an aleph-A and a gimmel, sure." And they would be off again. I let it all wash over me until the Dominic DeSota turned around to reach for his beer and saw me there.

"Oh, hi, Dom," he said. "Back already? Listen, Gribbin here says they used vanadium targets in the accelerator and got nearly twice the brilliance. What do you think of that?"

I grinned at him. "Not much," I confessed. "I'm the one who's a senator when he's back home, Dom. The one you were with in Washington when we got snatched."

"Oh, that one," he said, amused. "Well, I'm not that Dom either. He's off checking up on his wife."

I winced. "Well, tell him I was looking for him," I said, turning away, wishing I'd been as lucky as he. If only they'd caught my Nyla up in the sweep, instead of the No-Thumbs woman . . . and then . . .

I stopped, swallowing hard.

"Hey," I said. "They didn't snatch his wife, did they? She was in her own time, and she wasn't working on paratime!"

"No, of course not," said the other Dom. He gave me a puzzled look. "He applied for her to join him, that's all. He just went to see when she's coming in."

"Applied . . . to join. . . . You mean . . ."

And he did mean just what I thought he meant. That was policy. The kidnappers weren't inhuman. They were willing to let us bring our families over, provided our families were willing to come.

All I had to do was apply.

Forty minutes later I was in the Biltmore Hotel, waiting my turn to—to, I guess the word is *propose*. I wasn't alone. There were fifty men in line with me on the same errand. We didn't talk much, because each one of us was busy rehearsing the speech we were about to make. When I felt a tap on my shoulder I flinched.

But it was only Nicky. "You, too, Dom?" he said, grinning. "I've just finished. Now if Greta will only say yes. . . ."

Suddenly we were the center of attention, as the men before and behind me in the line turned to hear what the man who had already done it had to say. "She didn't answer?" I asked.

"Answer? No! You don't talk to her directly," he explained. "They don't have enough channels for that, I guess. What you do, you go into a room and they sort of film you—I don't suppose it's really film—anyway, you say what you have to say. Then they locate your wife, or whatever, and transmit it to her.

What did you call those things? Holograms? It will be a sort of hologram image of you, and you can talk for one minute. Then it's up to her—"

Then it would be up to her.

What do you say to a woman to make her give up a world that loves her for the sake of chancy adventures in exile? All the time I was inching ahead in the line, all the time I was giving information about Nyla Bowquist to the attendant who would have to locate her, I invented reasons. Not reasons. Bribes. Airy-fairy promises of what our life would be like. . . . As if I knew any of that!

And when at last I was in front of the lens, with the bright lights glaring into my eyes, I abandoned the reasons and the bribes. All I could find to say was, "Nyla, my darling, I love you. Please come here and marry me."

By Saturday we were wholly germ-free and ready to start our new lives. By Saturday the woman at the Biltmore desk was already tired of seeing both Nicky and me. There were only a limited number of channels to other times, she explained, and very heavy demands on all of them. No, she didn't know whether Nyla had even received my message yet. Yes, Nyla would be told everything she needed to know about what this world was like and how to get here. No, she couldn't even guess how long it would take. Sometimes it was less than a day, but some people hadn't had a response even three weeks later. . . .

I didn't want to wait three weeks. I didn't want to be lonely that long . . . especially when it might happen that all I would get at the end of the three weeks was the knowledge that I would be lonely forever.

Meanwhile I had to fill my time one way or another. Nicky had the same problem, but he didn't seem to have the same trouble doing it. When he wasn't working he was exploring; when he wasn't exploring he has hunched over the data-machine terminal in our room, trying to learn as much as he could. About the third time I came to him to ask how many ooties went into a oddy-poot he said, "Really, Dom, how are you going to get along here if you can't even make change?"

"It's so confusing, Nicky. All those ones and zeroes."

"It's binary arithmetic," he corrected me. "One equals one. One-oh equals two. One-one equals three—" And he drew me a column of figures:

1	1
10	2
11	3
100	4
101	5

"Sure, Nicky, sure," I groused, "but what do you do when you get up to those ten or twelve digit numbers? How do you even say the suckers?"

He said seriously, "What you do, Dom, is learn the pronouncing codes."

"Why should I? No, no, I know," I said, to head him off, "the reason I should learn is that I'm stuck here, and when in Rome you learn to use Roman numbers, right? Only it's dumb! Maybe there's some little saving in time or something; but it must have cost them millions to switch over from decimal to binary."

He laughed. "You know what it cost them? Bear in mind, they've put all their data into electronic storage. So they pushed a button somewhere and the machines did a global search-and-replace. All at once. All over the world. All over all the worlds that were involved; and from then on it was standard."

I gazed at him. "That's computer talk," I said.

"You've learned a lot since you got out of your own time."

"I didn't have the choice, Dom," he said, "and sooner or later you're going to realize that neither do you. Here. I'll get you started." And he punched out some commands on the machine and got up. "Start by learning how to count," he ordered, and left me to it.

Of course, he was right.

So I got serious. I took my mind off me and my problems, I even took it off Nyla, and I tried to concentrate. What Nicky had called up for me was an old document called *On Binary Digits and Human Habits,* and it told me all I wanted to know about binary arithmetic and the way to write it and say it.

The writing conventions were easy enough. The custom was to write numbers in binary in groups of six digits, with a hyphen in the middle, 000-000. When there were more than six digits they used commas, just as we used to for thousands and millions: 000-000,000-000. I laboriously converted the present year into binary, and 1983 came out as:

$$1\text{-}111{,}011\text{-}111$$

It looked pretty dumb to me.

Then, reading on, I discovered that they pronounced each group of six according to some cockamamey rule that looked ridiculous at first, but got easy after I'd studied the table for a while. You pronounced each three-digit group slightly differently, according to whether it was before or after the hyphen, but that was only to make saying the words easier:

Binary quantity	Pronunciation in first group	Pronunciation alone or in second group
000	ohly	pohl
001	ooty	poot
010	ahtah	pahtah
011	oddy	pod

100	too	too
101	totter	tot
110	dye	dye
111	teeter	tee

So numbers like "ten"—i.e., 1-010—became "ooty-pahtah" and "fifty," or 110-010, became "dye-pahtah," and when Nicky came back into the room I was able to tell him, "Four months or so from now, on New Year's Eve, I am going to wish you a Happy New Ooty-tee, oddy-tee."

"Well done, Dom," he grinned, "but that's *this* year. *Next* year will be 1984, and that's ooty-tee, too-pohl."

I groaned. "Hellfire. I don't think I'll ever learn all this stuff."

He said cheerfully, "Sure you will, Dom. After all, as I said, you don't have any choice."

I couldn't spend all my time mooning over Nyla, or even learning. There were decisions to be made. Not just decisions; we had to go to work. We could not stay in the Plaza forever, because the quarantine quarters had to receive thousands of new cats, arriving every day. Nor could we go on halfheartedly working at chambermaid and busboy jobs, because there were no free rides in Eden. There couldn't be. Before the mass transfers there had been hardly fifty thousand venturesome pioneers on the whole planet, whether malcontents or heroes. Now nearly two hundred thousand cats had already been transported to strain the resources available, and the number would more than double before the transfers were complete. Every one of us needed food, housing, all the million little gadgets and services and conveniences that made up civilized life. Food most of all. I had never been even a backyard gardener, but my first job-hunting trip was up to the north end of the park, where crews were busy harvesting lumber, pulling stumps, plowing fields, sowing winter crops. My second was down to the Brooklyn Bridge, where there were engineers testing the strength of the cables and supports, and forty times as many people chipping rust and slapping on paint to get the old bridge ready for service again. My third and fourth and fifth were all over the city, where the jobs were repairing water mains and power lines, or checking out apartment buildings to see if any could be made livable for the winter, or collecting scrap that would (somehow) be transported to the steel mills that would (somehow) be put back in operation to create new plows, and cars, and I-beams out of the discards of the old times, pending the day when the Mesabi iron mines could (somehow) be started up again for ore. Oh, there were jobs, all right! There were more jobs than there were people. It was just that none of them seemed to be for a man whose basic skills were making speeches, running fund raisers, and conniving to trade a pilot-training program here for a slum-clearance project somewhere else.

"It'll be fine," Nicky encouraged. "Gosh! They need *everything*, Dom, and sooner or later they'll need government people too. You'll make out, and so will I. When Greta comes—" He clasped his hands with a seraphic smile. "A home! A wife! A family—a big house, with a half acre of ground, surrounded by tall hedges so we can go skinny-dipping any time—"

"I've got an interview," I said, and left him with his dreams. I wasn't lying. The "interview" was with the woman at the Biltmore, and she recognized me at once. "Dominic DeSota, right? Just a minute." And she huddled over her comset, studying the screen.

And then her expression clouded.

I could feel what was coming even before she found the words she was looking for. "I'm really, really sorry," she began, and didn't have to end.

I had a smile all ready, saved up for some time when I would need a smile a lot. When I put it on, wonders, it worked. "Those are the breaks of the game," I said, grinning at her. "Well, honey? You doing anything special tonight?"

The smile might have fooled her, but I could see that the tone of voice was a dead giveaway. She was a good person. She had probably already had to tell five hundred of us Peety-Deepies that their nearest and dearest couldn't really see their way clear to a new life in a new place. "A lot of people get really frightened about paratime travel," she said.

The smile was beginning to ache, but I held on to it and made an effort at conversation. "Who doesn't?" I asked, and managed a shrug. "Nyla's as brave as anybody, but this kind of thing is an awful lot to ask. I don't blame her. If the positions were reversed, I'd probably say no, thanks, too—anyway, I'd have to think it over pretty hard. . . ." I trailed off, because the woman was looking puzzled.

"What did you call her?"

"Nyla. Nyla Bowquist. Is something wrong?"

"Oh, *hell*," she said, busy with her keyboard again. "You're *that* Dominic DeSota. I just can't keep you straight—same room number and everything; it was a woman named Greta that said no. Yours—" She frowned at the screen, tapped out a command for a double check, and then looked up at me with a smile of heavenly gold. "Your request was for Nyla Christophe Bowquist, and she accepted. She's already at Floyd Bennett for preliminary disinfection. She should be here in the hotel by tomorrow morning."

Staff Sergeant Nyla Sambok wasn't a staff sergeant any more, because nobody was. The American Army had been disbanded, along with the Soviet, by the League of Nations' peacekeeping forces. She still wore her uniform, however, dirty and wrinkled though it was. She didn't have anything else. As she waited in the Indianapolis terminal for the train home, the ex-captain on the bench next to her was listening to a little radio. It was repeating the terms of the one and only message her world had received to explain what had happened. We have removed all of your temporally displaced persons and your researchers in paratime physics, as well as inducing radioactivity to make your research centers unusable. No further research in this area is permitted. *Nyla Sambok didn't need to hear it again. She only wished it had come earlier. The submarine-launched cruise missiles the Americans had not known the Soviets owned had been only marginally effective. Still, they had taken out Miami, Washington, Boston, San Francisco, and Seattle. The bomber-launched smart bombs the Russians had not known the Americans owned had done the same for Leningrad, Kiev, Tiflis, Odessa, and Bucharest. It was the prevailing opinion that the worst was over, since the exchanges appeared to be under the limit for a nuclear winter to follow. It would be months, though, before anyone* knew.

Yr 11–110 111–111, mo 1–010, da 1–100
Hr 1–000, mn 1–111
Nicky DeSota

Mary Wodczek, the pilot of the blimp, came back to wake me up when we were somewhere over Scranton, or anyway where Scranton used to be. "Wakey-wakey," she called through the door. "New York in about an hour."

I called out thanks and crawled out of the crew bunk, shivering. They kept the living spaces in the blimp at what was supposed to be a bearable temperature, but it wasn't anything like Palm Springs. While I was getting up enough courage for a shower Mary called again, to make sure I was awake, "You know we're going to be airborne again before sundown, don't you?"

"Go fly your blimp," I advised through the door. I heard her friendly laugh, and then she was gone. Before my nerve failed me I stumbled into the little shower. It wasn't as cold as I had feared. It was warmer than the air, anyway, but all the same I was glad to get out of it and into some clothes, so I could get started on this day.

It was a holiday for the collective, which was why I was able to take the time—that, and working a weekend or two to build up some reserve. We might call it the toddy-ott of ooty-pod, but we still celebrated the twelfth of October as Columbus Day—anyway, most of us did. You couldn't expect the displaced Arab and African date growers who farmed outside our crop areas to get all mellow about the discovery of

America. Columbus Day was just one more American eccentricity to them; the Ethiopian who ran our pumps had asked me when we put the tree up to decorate for the Columbus bunny.

Most of us were U.S.-born, though, and nearly all of us were cats. I mean the involuntary kind of cats. The farm community had been set up originally by the restless colonists from the twenty-era congeries, but they weren't that fond of farming. As we Peety-Deepies moved in, they moved out, to do what they considered more interesting things in this new world.

That suited me well enough. We were all equal in the Desert Agricultural Consort. That's not to say that any of them knew anything about Tau-America—*my* America. I hadn't found a single person who had ever heard of the Moral Might Movement. They didn't have rich Arabs buying up everything in sight—the only Arabs were part of the collective, just like me. They didn't have laws prohibiting drinking by those under thirty-five, or prohibition of abortion or contraception, and there wasn't any rule about how much of your skin you had to keep covered up. (Except the natural law, of course. No sane person wanted to expose too much skin to the California desert sun.)

What I had first called this new world to myself was Eden. The name was fair enough. And, although I wouldn't have guessed I'd like farming, it beat the dickens out of calculating mortgage rates in Chicago.

What made it even better, of course, was that my special skills kept me away from stoop labor, except now and then when a crop had to get in *right then*. Learning the binary arithmetic had been a bit of a strain, but once that was out of the way I took over all the financial problems for the collective. I was a solid asset to the consort, and they treated me that way. They were sorry to see me take off for New York.

Not many people had ever been sorry to see me leave before.

So, as the blimp swayed gently down toward the old New Jersey swamps and I counted over my crates of avocados and lettuce, I was actually looking forward to going back home. My real home. The one around Palm Springs.

It was very nearly what I had dreamed of as a kid. When I was young I was very religious—I didn't have much choice, did I? The Moral Might Movement was getting itself together, especially in the suburbs of Chicago. I wanted to be Good. Mostly what I wanted was to avoid getting crisped for eternity in the fiery flames of Hell, where (so Reverend Manicote assured me every Sunday) I was almost certainly going to go if I drank, missed Sunday school, or went skinny-dipping. He also mentioned Heaven now and then. That was sort of like Tahiti in my six-year-old mind; I knew it was there, but didn't see much chance of ever visiting it in person—at least, not without a really good lawyer to find a loophole in the rules. I mean, how could God possibly forgive my weighty six-year-old burden of sin? I'd told lies. I'd stolen nickels from my mother's purse. I'd shown disrespect to my elders. Oh, I was a bad one, all right! But I did daydream sometimes about what Heaven would be like if I ever found a way there. And what I dreamed was close enough to the Desert Agricultural Consort, even to the fact that, as Reverend Manicote had assured us, there was no marrying or giving in marriage in Heaven. That was true enough for me in California. There were women there—more than forty percent of the population was female—but they had mostly come to join husbands or lovers, and there wasn't much of a pool left over for single men like me.

But that was what I had wangled the New York trip to do something about.

We floated down to the Great Meadow, where winchmen were waiting to grab our cables, and I peered out the cabin window. New York City hadn't changed much. There was no real reason it should have—it was only about six weeks since I'd headed out for my new job in California, but, my goodness, it seemed a lot longer.

As soon as we were secure I stepped out into a rainy, chilly New York October day, and got my tennis shoes full of mud on the first step.

Herby Madigan was waiting for me on the pad, trying to peer past me to see what was in the cargo hold. He grabbed the manifest out of my hand before he even said hello and ran his eye down the list. "Tomatoes?" he asked indignantly. "What'd you bring us tomatoes for? We've still got plenty from Jersey and the Island."

"In a couple of weeks you won't have," I told him, "and then you'll be begging us. Anyway, there's dates and avocados"—his eyes lit up—"and I've put in some cases of oranges and coconuts, just to show."

"Oranges!" he said.

"We can't deliver much quantity, I'm afraid," I said, "because it'll be a while before the groves are really producing again. Can we get out of the rain while we talk?"

We didn't quite make it on the first try, because one of the air-traffic people stopped me to ask if I'd seen any signs of ballistic recoil on the way from California. He looked pleased when I told him I hadn't, less pleased when I explained that I'd been asleep about half the time and busy with paperwork most of the rest. Still, he was content to tell me that nobody had experienced much of it in the last month or so; evidently the resonances were damping down on schedule.

So then we were allowed to go into Herby's office, a brightly lit, messy cubicle in one of the bubble structures in the park. We haggled over prices for half an hour. I took my wet shoes off and let my socks dry while we talked. He had some real coffee and gave me a cup, and I wondered if we could grow the stuff. Decided against it. People from the consort had already gone exploring down into Baja and other parts of Mexico. Someday we might want to hive off a colony to grow coffee and maybe bananas and papaya there, but they were too far from Palm Springs to be good ideas right now. Anyway, I had plans enough for the next year. "We'll have fresh spinach and grapes for you in about a month," I told Herby, "and Crenshaw melons around Christmas. We're short of labor, though. Do you know if there are likely to be any real farm workers coming through?"

"Nobody's coming through any more," he said absently, thinking about Crenshaw melons for Christmas. "They've closed all the portals, except for a couple of signal-only peeping stations. You might pick up some workers anyway; there's still a few hundred physicists and soldiers and so on waiting for assignment in the hotels."

I sighed. Retraining physicists and soldiers already took a lot of time away from trying to revive old orchards and planting new crops. "If you've got twenty volunteers," I said, "we can take them back tonight. Families would be best. Or single women?"

He laughed. I expected him to; that was a joke. When we'd finished haggling over prices and contracts for future delivery, he poured another cup of coffee for us both and leaned back, gazing at me. "Dominic?" he said. "How would you like to come back and work for me in procuring?"

"No, thanks."

He persisted. "You'd have a hell of a lot better job. I'd match anything they pay, and you'd be in the city. We've got power and water in half the West Side now. It's going to be really nice here."

"After you get it cleaned up," I said, grinning.

"Sure! It's happening. Five years from now—"

"Five years from now," I told him, "we'll be cleaning up San Diego. Now, there's a pretty place for a city! Not to mention the climate."

He said thoughtfully, "You know, I wouldn't mind living in California sometime, after we get things straightened out around here. I've been thinking about Los Angeles—"

"Los Angeles! Who would want to revive Los Angeles?" I looked at my watch. "Nice talking to you, Herby, but my return flight's not going to wait for me and I've got some things I want to do here. Any chance of borrowing a pair of dry shoes somewhere? And maybe a raincoat?"

The lobby of the Plaza was cleaner than I'd left it, and emptier. Something like twenty-two thousand Peety-Deepies had come through the New York City relocation centers. Only about two hundred were left in the Plaza, and some of the other hotels had already been closed down, mothballed, pending some time in the future when they would be needed again for people who came in planes or cars instead of portals.

I didn't linger. My first business was with the transient desk, where they let me borrow a terminal long enough to type in a name and get an address. I asked the man at the counter how to get to Riverside Drive, found out I could pick up a taxi in front of the hotel, and only then realized I didn't have any money to pay a taxi fare. Or anything else. "Can I pay with my California money card?" I asked, and he tried not to laugh.

"You'll need cash," he told me. "Out in the lobby there's a cash dispenser. If you've got your card, it'll probably take care of you."

It did. It took the help of two bystanders for me to figure out how to make it work, but then it spat out twenty-four sixteen-dollar bills, *k-chew, k-chew, k-chew,* and I scuttled away. Hick in the big town! Some things didn't change.

In the taxi I turned the money over curiously. It was really a nuisance to use cards for little things, or even for such bigger things as dealing with the independent communities in Palo Alto and Santa Barbara or playing poker on Saturday nights. They were interesting colors: greeny-gold and black on one side, gold and scarlet on the other. The numbers were in binary, of course, and they weren't made out of the kind of banknote paper I'd seen all my life—all my *other* life—but of something that had a feel almost like silk, and, I discovered when I risked a corner of one, was distinctly harder than paper to tear. Altogether it was neat-looking money. The picture of Andrew Jackson on one side and the White House on the other weren't steel engravings but holograms. As I turned the bills in my hands the perspective shifted slightly, and halos of other colors appeared around the pictures, red, white, and blue behind Jackson, a full-spectrum rainbow over the White House. The name of the printer was on the notes, an outfit in Philadelphia—first I knew anything was going on in Philadelphia—and I made a note, as best I could while the taxi jolted up the potholes and cracked cement of Broadway. Next council meeting I would take up the question of whether we wanted to print some of these for ourselves.

Then we were at Riverside Drive; I paid off the taxi driver and looked around. The Hudson ran clear and sweet. There were big trees growing over on the cliffs at the Jersey side, and I couldn't see the George Washington Bridge—hadn't been built yet, I supposed, when all building stopped. But the apartment house I was going to was in good shape. There was glass in the windows. The hall floors were clean tile. And while I was climbing the stairs to the sixth floor I heard the whir of motors and realized that the climb wasn't necessary—they'd even got the elevators running. And when I got to apartment 6-C and knocked on the door it opened right away, only the person who looked out at me wasn't who I expected at all. It was the senator. "Nicky!" he cried. "Hey, Nyla! It's Nicky DeSota. Come and say hello!"

Then she appeared, looking pretty and happy and very much like the person I was looking for—as much as I looked like the senator—almost as much, because there was that very visible difference when she shook my hand. And nothing would do but that I come in, and have some more of that real coffee and talk for a while about what I was doing and what they were doing and how, really, we were pretty well off where we were, the worlds we'd left behind be darned.

It was a pity she was the wrong Nyla.

But they were able to tell me where the right one was, and twenty minutes later I was on my way. To the old Metropolitan Museum of Art. No more than two minutes from where I'd landed in the blimp in the first place.

The senator and his Nyla had been surprised to see me. The Nyla without thumbs was more than that. She was flabbergasted, and a little suspicious. "All that stuff back home," she said at once, "is over. If you're sore, you're sore, and I wouldn't blame you. But I'm not apologizing, either."

"I'm not sore," I said. "I just want to take you to dinner—maybe across the park, in that restaurant with the trees around it."

"I can't afford that!"

"I can," I said. "Mind if we walk? I'd like to keep an eye on how they're loading the blimp."

So we walked, and I showed her how they were loading tractor parts and case after case of data cards for our memory stores in exchange for the produce we sold. And she told me about her work at the museum. It wasn't skilled work, she said at once, a little belligerently, but it was *good* work. "Fortunately," she said, "they were building a new wing when the war wiped them out, so a lot of the best stuff was stored carefully and it's in pretty good shape. But the stuff that was on public view! Especially the paintings! I can't restore them, none of us can very well, but we're spraying them to kill the mold, and drying them, and trying to save all the little flakes of paint that fell off onto the floor. I think someday somebody will be able to put a lot of them together."

"I didn't know you were interested in art," I said, steering her into the restaurant. The smells were marvelous; of course, the restaurant was right there at the market, so they got their pick of the first and freshest stuff that came in.

"I guess," she said objectively, not meanly, "you didn't know much about me at all, did you? And maybe I wanted it that way. So you'd be more scared of me."

I let that pass. We got a table and ordered. We started with avocados stuffed with crabmeat; the crab came right out of the Hudson River, but the avocados were our own, no more than five hours in the city, and absolutely perfect.

"That is a good job," I said, "although I guess there isn't much of a need to get it all done right now, is there? I mean, the paintings, sure. But the other stuff—I saw that Cleopatra's needle thing as we came by. Nothing much is going to happen to it that hasn't happened already." The obelisk had been flat on the ground, and in several pieces, broken as it fell. It had lasted for thousands of years in Egypt, but a few decades of New York City's freeze-and-thaw had knocked it over.

She looked up from scraping the last of the meat out of the avocado shell. "So?" she asked.

"So I wondered if you might be interested in another job. Not in your specialty, of course—there's not much in the secret-police line around here. How would you like to conduct an orchestra?"

She put down her fork. "To con— An orch— Shit, Nicky, what the hell are you talking about?"

"Call me Dominic, all right?" I had forgotten she was such a potty-mouth. Probably she'd get over it, though; most of the people seemed to.

"Dominic, then. What do you mean? I've never conducted an orchestra!"

"Didn't you tell me you once wanted to play the violin?"

"I *did* play the violin!" But she put her hands on her lap instinctively.

"You can't now, right," I nodded. "I understand

that. That wouldn't stop you from leading other musicians, would it?"

"*What* other musicians?"

I grinned. "They call themselves the Palm Springs Philharmonic. Actually, they're amateurs. Not bad, though. It's part-time stuff for them; they all work on the collective."

"*What* collective?"

"I'm head financial officer for the Desert Agricultural Consort," I told her. "It's like a kibbutz, only we don't call it that because most of us aren't Jewish. We're going to have a good orchestra someday. Right now— Well, you'd have time for a couple of other jobs, at first."

"*What* couple of other jobs?"

"Well, one, teaching music to the kids. And any grown-ups who wanted to learn. We don't have a music teacher."

She pursed her lips. The rabbit stew had arrived and she sniffed it approvingly. "And?" she asked, dipping a spoon to taste.

"Well, the other thing isn't a job exactly. I mean, I thought you might like to marry me."

I don't think I had ever surprised her before. I'm not really sure I'd surprised very much of anybody very often before. Not even myself. She stared at me, while the rabbit stew got cold—hers did. Mine I dipped into. I was starving, and besides it was delicious.

"What about Greta What's-her-name? The stewardess?"

I shrugged. "I asked her, you know? Made my one-minute commercial? She said no." I began to grin, because it was kind of funny, when I thought about it in retrospect. "I got this Dear John holocard, you know?" And I'd taken it back to my room when the senator was out and played it, and there she was, pretty as ever. I didn't quite cry. But nearly. "She said, 'You're a sweet man, Nicky, but you're nothing but trouble. I don't *need* trouble. I just want to get on with my life.'"

Nyla laughed too. For the same reason. At the notion of me being too excitingly troublesome for anyone. "Well, you are a sweet man, Nicky," she acknowledged.

"Dominic."

"Dominic, then."

"So that's what about Greta. What about Moe?"

She gave me a startled, almost angry look. "That ape? What the fuck do you think I am, Ni—Dominic?" Then she tasted her stew and mellowed. "Anyway," she said, "he's gone gay. He and the other two Moes—they found each other, all three of them, and they'd never been gay before, but— I guess they couldn't resist having lovers who knew all about them. I mean, you know, knew exactly what everything would feel like." She hesitated, looking at me. "Do you know what I'm saying? I mean, knowing exactly how to do, well, everything, so that—"

"I know what you mean," I said firmly. "What about it?"

"You mean, what about getting married?" She ate industriously for a moment, frowning. She was frowning over the idea, not the stew, which was perfect—I thought I'd try to get the recipe to take back to our own cooks. She finished the last spoonful and looked around for coffee. I waved to the waiter to make it come.

"Well," she said doubtfully, "it's always nice to be asked."

"I did ask. Now what happens is, you answer."

"I know that, Dom," she said. "I'm trying. Only I'm not sure about— Well, what about me? I'm not exactly what you could call a virgin bride, you know, and no offense, uh, Dominic, but you always struck me as a pretty tight-ass type about that kind of thing."

I said, "Nyla, we've both got some kind of a past that doesn't do us a lot of credit. As you say, no offense. You were as mean as a snake. I was a wimp.

Past tense, Nyla. We didn't have to be that way—no, wait a minute," I said, as the waiter brought the coffee and the check, "I want to say this just right. Let me start over. In a way, we *did* have to be what we were, because of the world we lived in. 'Have to' might be too strong, because some of it was our fault—we took easy ways. There were better ways, even in our own time. But it wasn't all our fault, and we could have been a lot better. Look at our duplicates! The senator, and the scientist, and Nyla Bowquist. We could have been like them! And we still can be, honey."

I hadn't planned to use that word. I'd thought it, but it just slipped out without my intending it. She heard it. I could see her examining the taste of it in her mouth, a new flavor. It didn't seem to repel her. I hurried on: "The senator's running the administration of the whole west side of this city now. Nyla's pregnant. They had to change their lives. We can change ours."

She sipped the coffee, studying me over the rim of the cup. "That's what you're talking about, isn't it, Dom? Not just marriage but kids? A little house in the country, with roses growing over the veranda and hot coffee among the flowers every morning?"

I grinned. "I can't promise the coffee, because the consort isn't that rich yet. But the rest of it—yes. Even the roses, if you like roses."

She weakened. I could see her weakening. "Shit," she said, "I *love* roses."

"Does that mean yes or no?" I pressed.

"Well, there's no law says we can't *try* it," she said. She put down her cup and looked at me. "So, yes. Do you want to kiss your fiancée?"

"You bet I do," I said with a grin, and I did. It was the first time I had ever kissed her. She tasted of coffee, and rabbit stew, and herself, and it was a great combination. "So then," I said, settling back in my chair, "we'd better get a move on. You'll have to get your things, and tell the people at the museum that you quit. Say two hours for that. That gives us about another hour or two to maybe shop for anything you think you'll need in California before the blimp takes off. We can get the captain to marry us on the way."

She had picked up her coffee cup again, and she actually spilled some of it. "Jesus, Dom," she said, looking as though she were just finding out what she was getting herself into, "you do move a greased streak when you want to. Is that legal?"

"Honey," I said, on purpose this time, "it just might be that you've kind of missed the point of what's happening here. It's a *new life*. We don't have to worry about what's legal in stuff like this. There are too many different kinds of rules, back in all the places we all came from, so we just make it up as we go along. And that's exactly what's the best thing of all about it."

So a few hours later we were well and truly married, and we proved it to each other in the little crew bunks of the blimp, somewhere over New Jersey. And over Pennsylvania, and probably over Ohio, though we weren't checking geography at the time. We might have proved it again over somewhere around Indiana if Mary Wodczek, who had said the vows for us as soon as we took off the night before, hadn't decorously knocked at the door with coffee and orange juice and toast. "I thought you might like some breakfast," she said, smiling at the newlyweds. It was a kindly thought. Kindly she disappeared again at once.

And a while after that we were sitting propped up in the narrow bed, with our arms around each other and feeling pretty good in the gentle sway of the blimp, when Nyla said, "Dominic? You know, I'm not sure I'd really go back now even if somebody offered it to me."

"Me too," I said, nuzzling her neck.

She pressed her cheek against me absently. "That's funny, though. All the time I was working in the museum I was just praying for a miracle. I had all these fantasies about how great it would be if I could return for a heroine's welcome, or something— But it would really be the same place, wouldn't it? And this is all different and, honestly, I don't think I'd mind if we were stuck here forever."

"That's good," I said, kissing her warm, damp armpit, "although I don't guarantee that it's true. About being stuck here forever, I mean."

She pressed back, then sat up straight, looking down at me with an uncertain smile, as though she suspected there was a joke in there somewhere but hadn't located it yet. "What do you mean? They said they were closing all the portals permanently!"

"And so they have, hon," I conceded. "That might not matter. Listen, the shower here is pretty small, but I bet the two of us could fit in—"

"In a minute, boy! Tell me what you mean!"

I leaned over her to take a swig of cooling coffee from my cup. "I just mean that these big-time people are only human, hon. They aren't gods. I don't doubt they've closed all the portals, not counting some electronic peepholes, because they can't stand what would happen if ballistic recoil got out of hand."

"Well, then?"

I said, "It may not be up to them. See, they were the first to get the portal. They located maybe thirty or forty other times that either had it, or might get it pretty soon, but that's only twenty or thirty. How big a fraction is thirty divided by infinity, Nyla?"

"Don't pull mathematics on me, Dom!"

"It's not mathematics, it's just sense. It's October 1983, right? Not just here. For everybody. They're not *ahead* of us. They just got lucky fifty or a hundred years ago. But it's October 1983 for an *infinite number* of parallel times. Not just them. Not just us. All the times, and time is a-marching on in all of them. Maybe right this second, in some time nobody yet has ever even peeped, somebody like me, or you, is just making the breakthrough. And maybe there are four or five others that haven't got quite that far yet but they're on the trail. By Christmas there could be a dozen times with paratime capacity—and maybe twenty-five or thirty more in January . . . and in February . . . and next year, and the year after—"

"Oh, my God," said Nyla.

"And someday," I finished, "there's going to be so darn many of them that there'll be thousands or millions, all breaking through at once—and do you think anybody's going to be able to hold the lid on *that*?"

"Holy sweet jumping baby Jesus God," said Nyla.

"Exactly," I said.

"All that ballistic recoil," she said.

I nodded, letting it soak in.

She looked at me with what was either fright or respect—I hadn't known my bride long enough yet to know which. "Are you the only one who knows about this?" she demanded.

"Of course not. The people who snatched us are bound to know, but they're not around to ask about it. And I'm sure there are others. I've tried to bring it up a few times. Some people don't seem to get what I mean, like the senator. Most of them—well, they just don't want to talk about it. Scared, I guess."

She flared up. "Damn right, they're scared! Personally, I'm *panicked*."

"Well," I said, "considering how bad all this might turn out to be, you'd be crazy if you weren't. But look at the good side. You and I ought to be okay. We're going to be out in the desert, where it's not too likely anything really scary is going to be going on in any time. It'll be bizarre, all right, oh, boy, will it! But it won't be as physically dangerous as it would be in a city, say—where, I don't know, maybe a zeppelin could fly right into your bedroom or something."

Nyla gave me a really unbridely look. Not loving a bit. "What you're telling me," she said scathingly, "is that we'll survive and screw the rest of the human race, right? *Right*?" she yelled. "And you've been having the nerve to tell me *I* was a tough, selfish, hard-boiled—"

"Na, na," I said, gently putting my fingers across her lips, "I never said any of that. Exactly. And I do care about the human race. I care a lot."

"But—but then what are we going to do about it, Dom?"

I said, "Nothing, love. There's nothing we can do. It's just going to happen. . . . There's one good thing, though."

I waited for her to ask what the good thing was. When she started to scowl and her eyebrows knotted and she opened her mouth, I didn't think I was going to like the way she was going to ask me, so I said hastily, "That is, it will start small. I'm pretty sure of that. There'll be lots of warning before it gets really bad—time to evacuate the cities, maybe, or do whatever anybody can do. And—it can't be prevented, do you see? So we'll just have to do the best we can."

She hopped out of bed and stared down at the empty plains below. I let her think it over. Finally she turned to me. "Dom?" she said. "Are you sure we're doing the right thing? I mean, you were talking about having kids and, I don't know, sometimes I think maybe I'd like that myself. But isn't this a kind of scary world to bring kids up in?"

I got up and stood beside her, the two of us naked and touching, hip to shoulder, with my arm around her. "You bet it is," I said. "But was there ever one that wasn't?"

ABOUT THE AUTHOR

FREDERIK POHL has published more than 30 novels and short story collections: as an editor, he published the first series of anthologies of original stories in the field of science fiction, STAR SCIENCE FICTION. He was, for a number of years, the editor of two leading magazines, GALAXY and IF. His awards include five Hugos, two Nebulas, two International John W. Campbell Awards, the Prix Apollo, the Edward E. Smith Award and the American Book Award. His interests extend to politics, history (he's the *Encyclopedia Britannica's* authority on the Roman Emperor Tiberius), and almost the entire range of human affairs: in 1982, he was elected a fellow of the American Association for the Advancement of Science. Currently he makes his home in Palatine, Illinois, with his wife Elizabeth Anne Hull.